UP AGAI

ALSO BY LISA ELLIOT

Dancing It Out
The Light in You

Up Against Her

~

Lisa Elliot

Copyright © 2021 Lisa Elliot

The moral right of the author has been asserted.

All rights reserved.

Edited by Gia Darwin

Cover design by Eve A. Hard

ISBN: 9798462345722

This is a work of fiction. All characters and events in this publication, other than those clearly in the public domain, are fictitious and any resemblance to real persons, living or dead, is purely coincidental.

For Grace

~ 1 ~
Skye

Picturing my colleagues mingling and enjoying the BBQ on the roof, I desperately wanted to join them. Parties at Your View were legendary. I was probably the only one still at their desk. Both of my screens loomed over me as I sketched out the next steps for a new project I'd won. It had been a big win for the company, and for me. As I hurried to get things wrapped up before I could switch off and get upstairs, a new email came in from the client sent with high importance. I sighed and made the mistake of opening it. About half an hour later I finally shut down my computer and put my phone on silent. Even though I had to work late at times like this, I still loved the job. The thrill of winning a new contract and the excitement of starting a new project more often than not saw me through.

I finished the water I'd been meaning to drink all afternoon then left my office. A couple of stairs creaked as I made my way up to the party. The sound of talking and laughing rolled down to meet me. The entrance to the roof was through a window. The huge four-storey Georgian building was full of quirks like this. I squinted as my eyes took a few moments to adjust to the brightness. The rooftops of other buildings glinted in the sun. The slight breeze was lovely, and necessary.

"There you are!"

I smiled as Hayley came towards me through our colleagues. Her smiling face was framed with long wavy hair and thick dark glasses. She was my work bestie, a fellow department head and the loveliest person I'd ever been fortunate enough to work with.

"Where have you been, woman?"

"Just finishing up."

Hayley frowned. "You've got to stop the overworking, Skye. It'll catch up with you."

"I know. You're right. I just had to tie up a few things. Helen wants an update first thing on Monday on our implementation strategy for the new project."

Hayley nodded towards Helen sitting on a deck chair with her feet up, cocktail glass in hand, chatting to her husband.

"Doesn't look like she's too bothered about it right now."

"Right. It's time for a drink. And some food."

It was nice seeing my colleagues together like this. In relax mode. They deserved it. Some sat around tables or stood in groups holding drinks underneath the summer bunting that had been put up. Reggae music played from speakers in a corner giving the party a mellow vibe that went with the sunshine. We helped ourselves to the buffet, filling up our plates until they were stacked high with food. I'd missed the BBQ itself; the grill was now shut and cooling down. It took both my hands to take the plate back to a table. Hayley grabbed us a bottle of wine.

"Thanks for waiting for me before eating by the way. It's nice to have someone to eat with."

"This is my second plate."

I laughed. "Well thanks for keeping me company."

"Cheers." Hayley tilted her glass in a salute. "To the end of a stressful week."

I nodded in agreement, tipped my glass to hers and then took a drink. "How's Liam?"

Hayley frowned briefly, before putting on her smiley face again. "We're starting couples counselling next week."

"He agreed?"

"He did. If this doesn't fix us, I don't know what will."

"I hope it's helpful, Hayley. I really do."

"Thanks, Skye. I do too."

Lynn, the receptionist and office manager, ambled towards us through the crowd fanning herself with her hand. Lynn was the heart of the office and the person who knew everything that was going on at all times.

"This is some heatwave, ladies. Puts me in mind of Tenerife. Good to see you finally made it, Skye. I can't believe you had to work late during the summer party. That's terrible." There was real concern in Lynn's eyes. She reminded me of my mum, warm, cuddly, and maternal.

"It's all right." I wanted to change the subject. "The bunting is lovely, Lynn. I can't believe you made that."

She stood a bit taller. "Thank you. It's good to be useful for something."

"And I love your dress." Lynn had on a sundress, which she probably wore on her many holidays. "It makes me feel like we're on a beach in Spain."

"This old thing? Bought it five summers ago in Cyprus. Anyways, you two put your feet up and have fun. I'm off to see what the young 'uns are up to."

Lynn moved onto the next group. I missed my mum and decided to give her a ring soon.

"I love Lynn. She's so sweet," said Hayley.

"Heart and soul of this place."

At the moment I went to take a bite, Siobhan, one of the junior researchers, or kittens, as they were affectionately called, rocked up.

"Hi Skye, how's it going?"

"Good, thanks. How are you?"

"Grand. So, amazing job winning the pitch. I just wanted to say I'd be super excited to start working on the project and would love to be considered."

I put my fork back down on my plate. "Thanks for saying that, Siobhan. I'm glad that you're keen and I did see your report on—"

"Siobhan, you're a frontrunner for sure. But now's not the time to discuss shop. Skye has just got here, and she needs to switch off for a bit. Can it wait until Monday?" There was a finality to Hayley's tone making it not a question.

Siobhan took it like a pro. She brushed her bangs away from her eyes and raised her chin a bit higher. "Of course. It can wait. Sorry to bother you."

As she went away, I turned to Hayley and smiled gratefully. "Thank you."

"You're too nice to the kittens sometimes."

I shrugged. "I was like that at her age. She's just keen."

"Careful. If you feed a stray, it will follow you. I keep telling you you're going to have to start saying no to people more."

I did know this, but it was a lot harder to do in practice. Hayley had been mentioning it at least once a week lately. "I'll start saying no tomorrow. I promise."

Hayley looked sceptical then returned to her food. We ate in a comfortable silence. I people-watched and soaked up the August sunshine. The young ones were necking shots and throwing popcorn into empty cups.

"Aww. Look at the kittens." I tipped my glass towards the junior researchers in their twenties.

"They better watch they don't have a repeat of the Christmas party. Helen won't stand for it."

"They're just young. We're too hard on them."

"Tell that to Helen. She found a pair of knickers in her top drawer. I had to convince her not to sack them all."

"It wasn't their finest moment."

"Oh look," said Hayley. "Brianna's over there on her own. That's a shame."

I followed where she was looking. At the edge of the roof, Brianna Phillips was leaning on the wall, looking out towards the skyline as if lost in thought. She was wearing a sleeveless mustard blouse, navy-blue slim fitting suit trousers and heels. Her brown hair hung just below her shoulder blades.

"We should call her over," said Hayley.

I grimaced. "Let's not."

Hayley clocked my reluctance. "Why not? What's your problem with her, anyway?"

I thought about it. Something about Brianna just didn't sit right with me. It never had.

"I don't have a *problem* with her. I just find her a bit arrogant. Insensitive, even. I've noticed she doesn't make much of an effort with anyone, or how shall I say, that she seems to do no more than the bare minimum, and yet everyone thinks she's amazing. Have you seen how bland her birthday messages are when there's a card going around? 'With best wishes, Brianna'. Don't you think that's a bit," I searched for the right word, "unfeeling?"

"I talk to her now and again. I think she's nice. She likes cycling and cats."

When Brianna joined Your View earlier in the year as Head of Quantitative Research, she'd come in with loads of ideas, asked tons of clever questions and generally picked it all up super-fast. While she was calculating and a bit cold, I was more interested in getting on with everyone and creating a good atmosphere. She was a total shark. We were polar opposites and it grated on me. Thankfully, though, we headed up different departments and worked on different floors, so we hardly came across one another.

And that was fine with me.

"Well, we've barely said a word to each other since shortly after she joined. I tried to make small talk in the downstairs kitchen once, and she made some dismissive comment then strolled off. Then there was a time in a meeting when we clashed. I was fuming for days after it."

"So, you don't really know her then."

"I know what I see in meetings. Her cold logic gives me the chills. It's like she's just waiting to find flaws and holes in other people's ideas before swooping in to undermine them. And how she can spend all day looking at numbers and statistics is beyond me. It must be so boring."

"You know, she's very charismatic when she presents."

"I don't see that."

"Well, we see what we see."

I looked at Hayley in confusion. Brianna was one of my least favourite people at Your View. I thought Hayley knew this, though we'd never spoken much about it until now. I pressed my hands firmly to my cheeks. "Sorry. I'm being so judgy."

"It's not like you to get this riled up about someone."

"I know."

"You probably wouldn't be saying those things about a man."

"I know. I know. I'm a terrible feminist."

"Don't be so hard on yourself. But maybe you should give her the benefit of the doubt?"

"I'll build up to it."

Hayley hesitated. "You know she's also a lesbian, right?"

This I knew. I was painfully aware. "Yes. And you're telling me, why?"

Hayley laughed at me and rose to her feet. "Thought you might want to know."

I gave her a steely stare of disapproval. "So we're duty bound to be girlfriends?"

"You could be friends."

"Just because Brianna is a hot lesbian does not mean that I have to like her as a person."

Hayley grinned. "You think she's hot?"

I glared at her.

"You said it, not me."

"Forget it." I shook my head. "Do you want some dessert?"

"Great idea."

Back at the fast-diminishing buffet, we helped ourselves to some crisp white wine and sweet things. Everything looked appealing and I piled up a new plate. As did Hayley.

"I could eat this whole table," said Hayley, between mouthfuls.

"Me too. Here, have you tried these? There's whisky liqueur in them," I said, then necked about half of my wine. Letting off steam was feeling so good. I hadn't celebrated winning the contract yet, so this was my blowout.

As Hayley tried one her face softened in a sort of ecstasy. "That is so good. *So* good."

"Ah, girls. There you are. Glad to see you are enjoying yourselves. The caterers have exceeded expectations."

Helen was gliding towards us, all glamour and sophistication. She was tall, slim, blonde, and heavily made up. She was always heavily made up. I don't think I'd ever seen her looking anything less than celebrity-like styled. Also, we were not girls. My thirty-six years and Hayley's thirty-seven need not be likened to a sixteen-year-old girl. Still, it was good to see Helen outside of the building for once. Not many people knew, but she owned the whole building. Ignoring the comment, I put on my best professional face, as the wine made its way to my head.

"Are you having a good time?" said Hayley.

Helen put down her empty cocktail glass and poured herself a generous martini. She smelled of expensive perfume and old money.

"I'm having a magnificent time. All is well. Everyone is here. The kittens are behaving themselves. It's good to be alive."

Hayley and I caught each other's eyes. I don't think I'd ever heard Helen be so positive. Perhaps the cocktails were all it took.

"To you, Skye." Helen held up her martini. "You are a credit to this agency, and we are very lucky to have you."

I let the compliment hang in the air for a moment, bewildered at this very unusual showering of praise from Helen. It meant a lot.

"Thank you."

She turned to leave and then pivoted back to face us, a glint in her eye. "And one more thing, please can you come by my office on Monday, Skye? I have a proposition for you which I think you'll be very interested in."

I was nearly lost for words. This was it. This had to be it.

"Yes, of course. Absolutely."

"Excellent. Now I'll let you both get back to your food. It's good for the younger women to see you both enjoying your food like this. That's the kind of leadership I'm after."

Helen left. I turned to Hayley, with my mouth open.

"Oh my God, this is it. I bet this is it. She's going to offer me the promotion. Do you think it sounds like that? I think it sounds like that."

"It does sound like that. I'm so excited for you!"

"Why can't she just tell me now? I can't wait until Monday. The waiting is going to kill me."

"This is classic Helen. Building suspense. Asserting her authority. I guess you have to have some tricks up your sleeve to get where she's got to in life."

"I need this, Hayley. It's everything I've been working for. With David retiring soon, I want his job. I've been making him look good for ages. She better not even think about getting someone else in. That job is mine." What I didn't say was that I badly needed the extra money because I was financially supporting my mum after her divorce and had to pay for structural repairs to my house that were long overdue.

"It's the recognition you deserve. You're a rock star, Skye, and everyone knows it."

"Thanks. But you don't have to say that."

"It's true."

"Can I ask you a HR question?"

"Sure."

"Assuming that she's going to offer me the job, do you think I should negotiate the salary? I know how good a negotiator Helen is."

Although Hayley and I were close, I was conscious of the fact that my question was potentially putting her in an awkward position.

Hayley looked me squarely in the eyes. Her friendly, approachable face turned more serious. "Skye, you must. You've got to value yourself highly. If you don't, who will?" Hayley lowered her voice. "I probably shouldn't be saying this, but there are others in this company in senior positions who have had no qualms asking for more money. And some have been awarded it. I think Helen does it so we don't lose people. So, you're completely within your rights, especially since you are such a high-performer."

"I hadn't realised that was going on. We never hear about it."

"The gender pay gap is real. It's in this company. It's in others. That's all I can say on the matter."

"Of course."

"Skye, it's kind of odd you haven't asked for a pay rise already. Helen will be expecting it."

I took another sip of wine and tried to work out why I hadn't. Apart from me, Hayley, and Brianna, the rest of the senior managers and above were all male, except for Helen of course. This was still common in the market research industry, despite higher numbers of women working in the lower paid positions. Things were changing from when I first started out over a decade ago, but the rate of change was slow. I was working longer and harder than I ever had. Thank goodness it was all about to pay off.

I puffed out my cheeks. "It doesn't come naturally to me."

"Be direct. Don't hesitate when you say it. She said you were a credit to the agency and that we are lucky to have you, so use that. She practically handed you some bargaining power."

"I will."

I visualised the conversation going well on Monday. Of it going better than well.

"And go high. You're more than worth it."

I smiled. Hayley was going out on a wine-fuelled limb for me. "You can bank on it. Thanks for the advice. I appreciate it."

"Wine. We need more wine after that conversation," said Hayley.

I let Hayley lead me astray even though I wasn't planning on drinking too much. "Ah, all right. Go on then."

~ 2 ~
Brianna

Work parties are not my thing. It's the not having a choice about attending that bothers me most. You show a face and try to forget that it is essentially compulsory and no one is being their true authentic self. I had far better ways to spend my free time. At least now I was in a management position I could just focus on the job.

But tonight was different.

Compared to most of the stale or overly rowdy functions I'd attended in the name of my career in the past, this party was lovely. We were on the roof of the building, in the evening sun. I nursed my first glass of wine looking out over the rooftops towards the horizon taking in the fresh air and enjoying the slight breeze. The perfect antidote to my stressful day. I turned around and scanned the party while taking a sip.

It was time to go in.

I made small talk with my new colleagues and found myself genuinely laughing a few times. I listened as the IT guy regaled us of his time in the boy scouts and the mischief they got up to, and as Lynn the receptionist told me about a big drama with her neighbours. I had a long conversation about music with one of my young researchers and surprised him with my own music knowledge, which was oddly satisfying.

Across the rooftop, Skye McCulloch my counterpart in the qualitative team unscrewed a bottle of wine while talking to Hayley, Head of HR, and a couple of others. She had on a short-sleeved white linen shirt, olive chino shorts and white trainers. Very casual for the office. Her long blonde hair looked nice today. It was wavier than usual, and it suited her. She looked freer. She normally wore it straight, and dressed smarter. She held the bottle up and Hayley laughed at something she said. Skye shrugged, then held her arms out wide gripping the bottle by its neck. She seemed unconcerned about the fact that she was getting pissed with her co-workers. Skye looked perfectly at home among these people as she poured into various colleagues' glasses. People she managed, people whose careers she'd nurtured. Laughing, relaxed, popular. This was how she was around here. Always smiling and always chatting to people. Quite lovely, in fact.

Just not to me.

If anything, she'd been faintly hostile towards me since I'd joined earlier in the year. I didn't know what her problem was, and in truth, I didn't care. I turned my attention back to my young colleagues, who didn't seem to notice I wasn't completely involved in the conversation. A young woman called Siobhan was talking about a musician she adored or knew, I couldn't be sure. I struggled to focus on what they were saying. My attention drifted to the view over the city more than once. Since it was such a delightful party, I decided to prolong my stay and have one last wine before heading home.

Empty glasses and wine bottles peppered the drinks table. I didn't fancy touching any of it. I settled on a box of wine by the edge of the table. As I guided the last of the wine into my glass, I sensed someone waiting behind me. I kept my attention on the small lever as the liquid came out at a glacial pace. When I turned around Skye was there. I flinched, then tensed up.

"Sorry, I didn't mean to startle you," said Skye. "I think that box is the last of the wine and I've had my eye on it. I just opened a bottle and managed not to leave any for myself."

"You didn't startle me."

"Okay," said Skye, stepping around me towards the box. "How're you enjoying the party?"

"It's not bad." I hesitated, unsure if this was a conversation or just a passing few words.

"Nice views, right?" Skye held her glass below the wine tap and tilted the box, half-looking over her shoulder at me, half-watching it pour.

"Yeah, they're good."

"This is the fifth year in a row we've had our summer party up here. Every year I say I don't know if the roof can take any more and all we seem to do is add more people the year after."

"Well, clearly it can hold."

She straightened the box and flicked off the lever, frowning slightly. "So, are you working on anything interesting at the moment?"

I gripped my glass harder. "Yeah, you?"

She faced me. Her cheeks were flushed. Her blue eyes were confident. I liked that about them. This felt like the first proper chat we'd ever had.

"Yes, actually. I just won a pitch. It's a multi-year ethnographic study into the transition from school into further or higher education. The government's big on employability right now. They're going to have to learn about the mental health crisis of our teenagers if they seriously want to do anything about jobs, though, and I'm going to make sure their stories get told. I can't wait to get it up and running."

Skye's eyes sparkled. It was good she was so passionate about her project. I also got the distinct impression she was trying to impress me.

"That sounds great." I meant it.

"Thanks."

"What's the deal with David? Is he retiring yet?"

Skye shifted from one foot to the other. "Soon, probably." She looked back towards Hayley, who glanced our way.

Our conversation ran out of steam. While I appreciated her making an effort, I could think of nothing else to say to her. We both stepped away from each other at about the same time. The conversation ended with a polite smile and a brief nod that belied our previous, and ongoing, ill-feeling.

After the chat with Skye, I was in a bad mood. If she thought I was going to fawn all over her because she asked me a few questions and gave me the time of day for once, she had another thing coming. I found my spot by the edge again and watched the sun set behind some buildings in the distance.

There was a tap on my shoulder. I turned around to find Helen. She smelled faintly of gin.

"Not bad for an office party, is it? Owning the building has its perks."

"It must be a huge privilege."

"Six months in, aren't you? How do you like the job?"

I hadn't passed my probation yet because my boss Simon was too busy to meet with me, so the question felt like an imposition. As I considered my response, I realised the wine had gone to my head a little, too. This was not the best time to be discussing my position, but I was willing to go with it. There was a hint of glamour to it all that I liked. I cleared my throat.

"Things are going great, Helen. I'm enjoying my role here and I feel like I have settled in well. I'm very excited about the—"

"That's excellent. I suspected as much."

Her interruption pissed me off. I held her eye contact and tried not to be too dominant with the owner of the company. I'd never been fond of people evaluating my abilities or performance. That was the role I preferred.

"Can you come to my office on Monday? I'd like to talk to you about some things regarding your position. Don't worry. All good. All very, very good."

"Of course." This was exciting. Intriguing. "I'd be more than happy to." Helen smiled as I cringed inside. When did I get so good at sucking up? When had it come so naturally to me?

Helen seemed to approve of our interaction. At this, she left, with a parting note for me to make the most of the weekend. She had game, this woman. I could learn a lot from her. It was a strange time to pick to tell me important things about the job. Almost all activity was done within the floors below us, save the odd big client meeting at their offices or the occasional dinner.

I decided it was time to call it quits and get on with my weekend. I'd almost forgot this was a work thing before chatting with Skye and Helen had brought me back to reality. This was exactly why I wasn't fond of these social activities. You let your guard down for a second, and there's someone there letting you know you are being watched, covertly, and that someone is factoring your behaviour at the party into their overall impression of who you are and how capable you are at your job. One in five people felt pressurised to socialise with their work colleagues, according to a recent study. Right now, I so identified with that fifth. Yes, now was definitely the right time to leave.

***

"I have a question for you," said Liv, my date. I looked at her pale complexion and wondered where this sudden burst of interest had come from. She'd looked as bored as I'd felt for most of the thirty minutes and half a drink we'd shared in each other's company so far.

"What's that?" I replied, without feeling.

"Are you not into this either?"

I knew from the moment I'd sat down that I wasn't into her. She looked the same as her profile picture and it wasn't that she wasn't attractive, but there was something … off. An inexplicable lack of chemistry that there was no coming back from. At least I'd had the decency to hide my lack of interest in her romantically and tried to make conversation like a normal human being, which was especially tiresome given how much I disliked small talk. She'd given barely more than one-word answers and only seemed to want to talk about her job.

"No, I'm not feeling it. I think we'd be better as friends." I couldn't see that happening. It was just the sort of thing you said in these situations. Why did I have to waste my Saturday nights like this? I was too busy for this. It was incredibly inefficient.

"I'm sorry I've been so rude," said Liv.

I took a drink and nodded, stopping short of trying to make her feel better about it. If she wasn't going to pretend any more, neither was I.

"I just couldn't carry on like that, you know, as if this date was going somewhere," said Liv, with colour in her face now and an interest in what she was saying. It was an improvement.

"No. I agree. And I appreciate your candour. I'm glad you were upfront." If anything, we were too alike. Maybe that was why there was no spark.

"I'm just disappointed. I've been dating for a while and not finding the right person." She took a large drink of wine and was quiet for a few moments. "The truth is, I'm lonely. And I hate that I'm lonely."

Yes, we were definitely alike. "I know what you mean." I sat back, feeling increasingly despondent, and also relieved somehow. The two emotions clashed inside me. All I could do was look into my drink and try to make sense of them.

"But it doesn't have to be a serious thing. We don't have to think about finding The One tonight."

I raised an eyebrow. What was she getting at?

"I have an idea."

I sat forward.

"Why don't we go back to mine and just have sex. No talking for hours about our childhoods and our life stories. No more pretending we care about each other's jobs. No stretching out the night out of politeness. We keep it simple and help each other out. What do you say?"

She was attractive. Maybe I could overlook the lack of chemistry. "Where do you live?"

Up Against Her

***

The church bells did nothing to ease the slight headache I had as I walked up the steps. It had been a late one last night and had turned out not too bad, all things considered. I wouldn't see Liv again, but it had been a fun way to spend my Saturday night in the end.

This morning I was accompanying my mother to her local church. She asked me to go because my father couldn't make it. She was there because she wanted to meet someone who was important to a new policy she was working on. She was a politician through and through.

"What are you wearing?" she'd asked me in the car park, where we met.

I was wearing a navy-blue blouse and my favourite light blue jeans. I even had heels on.

"My Sunday best?"

"It's not appropriate for church." She sighed. "But it'll have to do."

That hurt.

She had on a conservative black and white dress and matching clutch bag. She looked like she was going to a funeral.

Inside the church now, sitting on a pew while my mother talked to someone else she knew, I realised that I hadn't been to church in a long time. The high arched ceilings and thick stone walls were imposing. The only things that appealed were the ornate and beautiful stained-glass windows. My mother pointed at me while talking to a man and woman in the aisle. I gave a half-hearted wave and I saw the disapproval in my mother's eyes.

After a long service we were back out on the steps, having just spoken to the priest. Parts of the service were quite lovely, but other parts made me want to fall asleep. My mother's neck was on full swivel duty, and when she spotted her target person, she grabbed my arm, uncharacteristically.

"There he is." I went to go with her but she stopped me. "Stay here. I'll point you out."

Right. Great.

I hovered by a planter filled with flowers trying to work out why she'd asked me to join her this morning if not to actually introduce me. I crossed my arms over my chest and held my chin. This was typical of her. Everything for show. Not actually wanting to see me to catch up. Always too busy with work. Putting other people first. My headache came back.

Maybe I should leave.

I didn't though. I just stayed there, waiting for her to see me.

~ 3 ~
Skye

The office was quiet this Monday morning. There was no trace of Friday's party. Helen's warning had been heeded, which was a relief. Hayley and I had stayed late, but we weren't the last to leave.

I put my lunch in the fridge and made myself a filter coffee. The place was starting to fill up as I walked through to my office. The big meeting with Helen was foremost on my mind, as it had been all weekend. I clicked on my calendar for the day hoping to see my promotion meeting with Helen, but it wasn't there.

How odd.

When it reached four in the afternoon and I still hadn't been told anything about when the meeting was, my nerves were on edge. As I was half-considering storming up the stairs to her office, Jacinda, Helen's assistant, came gliding onto the second floor. She was young, Australian, and not to be messed with.

"Skye. Helen will see you now,' said Jacinda.

My breath caught in my throat. Hayley's pep talk popped into my head, and I remembered my positive visualisations. This was my meeting. This was my time to get what was rightfully mine – David's job, Director of Qualitative Research. I had been promoted through the ranks and had grafted my way to head of department. I'd dreamed of being the youngest ever female director at

Your View. It had a certain ring to it. That is what I wanted. And that is what I deserved.

I picked up my notepad and pen, and put them down again, not sure if I'd need them. I decided that this was a power talk. A 'have you got five minutes' type conversation. Not a project meeting. I straightened out my clothes, turned my phone upside down on my desk and left the notepad where it was. With one last look at my comfortable little office, I headed upstairs to claim victory.

At the doors to the stairwell, I bumped into Barry the IT guy. We both stumbled. He had pushed through as I'd reached out.

"Sorry!" I said.

Barry steadied himself. "What're you sorry for? It was me who bumped into you." His deep voice boomed.

I bounded up the stairs to Helen's office at the top of the building.

What was she doing here?

Brianna was sitting at the meeting table. She barely acknowledged my presence as I took a seat next to her opposite Helen. She was facing Helen and her chin was angled just high enough to be annoying. She held a heavy-looking black pen, poised over a brown moleskin notebook.

Typical.

Helen wore a royal blue suit jacket with neat shoulder pads. Her eyes were bright and sharp. "I apologise for keeping you both waiting today. I had hoped to speak to you before now but I've been on the phone to the press all day about our report on social mobility in Britain that was published over the weekend." She looked between us, gauging something. So she kept Brianna waiting today as well? I did not have a good feeling about this. "Well, I'll get right to it. As you may know, David is retiring. He'll be stepping down immediately. For the next couple of months he'll be winding down and taking some outstanding leave but no longer in charge. He confirmed last week that he is fine with that. What you may not know is that Simon has parted ways with us as well. There will be an announcement to the rest of Your View on Thursday."

I was speechless.

My pulse raced. David was the director of my department and Simon was the director of Brianna's. David was my friend and trusted mentor, although in recent times I felt as if I'd been carrying him. Simon was less nice, but he was a big name in our industry. This was so much change, and all at once. It was hard to take in.

Brianna looked as stunned as I felt. "Why did Simon leave? Has he already gone?"

"He isn't on board with the direction I want to take Your View now that David is retiring. He's currently on holiday in the Caribbean not answering his phone. Honestly, I've forgotten about him already."

I shifted in my seat. "What direction do you want to take us in?"

Helen stood up and walked over to the window. She looked out for a few moments then turned back to face us, as if we were about to get a lecture.

"This is one of the leading market and social research consultancies in the UK. If we're not running the opinion polls for government elections and referendums, we're providing the kind of customer insight that makes our clients a lot of money. We're effectively shaping government policy as well. We're a household name and

I'm proud of what we've achieved here." She grimaced and looked down at the table for a moment. "But we're falling behind. And if it's not addressed soon, we'll decline into obscurity."

I stared straight at Helen as I gripped the armrest. What on earth was she talking about? Where had my promotion gone? What about all that new business I'd just brought in?

Things were fine.

"So here's the deal. I'm merging your departments. And I want the pair of you to work together to make it happen. This will be phase one of the merger: restructure and integration. Then in two months, interviews will be held for a research director position. There will be one director in charge of a single research department. When they take the role, we will begin phase two: consolidation. The new director will have final say on any jobs still undecided at that point. By the time the new director is ready to start, they'll come into one department, structure fixed, and a clear remit. I don't want to hand over the reins before I've addressed the fundamental flaws in Your View. I don't want them thinking they can come in and do what they want and take us in God knows what direction. So, for two months you two will be joint heads of a sole research department. You will assess what needs to be done, then put forward a strategy to me and the board of trustees on how to merge and restructure the teams. Then you will lead the merger and ensure the two teams fully integrate. Finally, we'll need a report at the end of the two months with your overall assessment and recommendations. You are both very welcome to apply for the director role, and I can assure you that your performances over the next two months won't go unnoticed. The experience will give you an advantage over the external applicants, but you didn't hear me say that."

This could not be happening. How could this be happening? A hot rush of adrenaline and anger coursed through my veins. My cheeks burned and I didn't care. Brianna's pen had been put down. Helen re-took her seat, but everything had changed. She leant forward, clasping her hands on the smooth and expensive table.

"I need you to put your heads together to determine the best possible structure of this new integrated research department in preparation for the new director taking us forward with phase two. We will re-brand the whole business around it. It's the biggest transformation this company will have seen in well over a decade."

Helen paused. I had no idea what she was going to say next. I hung on her words as if they were life or death itself, which they felt like.

"I'll level with you both. You are already my two leaders. You are doing a great job with what you have. You are at the top of your games in your respective fields, and I want to keep you both. But that lack of synergy is hurting this company. I want to be very clear about this, the issues we have as a company are not your fault. Quantitative and qualitative have been operating like two separate companies for too long now. One deals in numbers and statistics and the other deals in words and feelings. I need them both. The fault lies with Simon and David, they've never particularly worked well together, and ultimately, with myself for not addressing things sooner." Helen sat back in her chair, crossed her legs, and took a deep breath. "Things are changing out there. And fast. New methodologies. New technology.

New ways of doing things. Big data. Real-time research. Our competitors are innovating and giving clients more value and to a very high standard. So we need out-of-the-box thinking. We need mixed methodologies and cutting-edge research techniques. I want you to work closer with Digital, who won't be affected by the research merger. And I want you to pitch as one team on the new health segmentation for the Department of Health. I need you to come up with new ideas, new joined up methodologies, to innovate. It's a wonder we've lasted this long with our dated approach."

Helen loved being dramatic. I didn't care for it.

"Think of this as a two-month job interview slash trial run. I will be watching you. The board will be watching you. In the meantime, I want you to do everything in your power to make this work, and to work as a team. Now, do you have any questions?"

I bit my tongue. I didn't trust what I might say.

"Will the new director have full control over the new department once they are appointed?"

My head snapped around to look at Brianna. She looked composed given the situation.

"Yes. Their title will be Director of Research."

Brianna sat forward. "Will there be budget to grow the team?"

Helen bristled. Clearly, she wasn't used to being asked such a direct question. "I can't answer that. It will depend on the new structure. However, I won't be surprised if the team expands. The important thing right now is to focus on the merger."

"Will there be a need to move where everyone sits?" I said, instantly regretting how stupid and un-strategic a question that was, and how fine about the merger it sounded.

I was not fine about the merger.

"Yes. I've had a word with the board and we think that by switching your department with IT on Brianna's floor that will allow for a straight swap."

Great. My team had to be the ones moving and not Brianna's. Why should my whole department suffer because her team was failing?

"Remember, I want to be very clear about the message: this is a long overdue merger and restructure. Jobs will be changing. Some people will be reassigned, some people will have to apply for their new roles, and some people may be offered redundancy. If people don't like it, well, I'm sure we can write them a nice reference. I can't make any guarantees to anyone." Helen emphasised this last sentence, as if to suggest she wasn't going to make us any guarantees either.

I forced myself to take a deep breath as my brain scrambled in a million different directions. I was close to my team; the prospect of any of them losing their jobs felt awful. Helen's behaviour was bordering on a betrayal. I'd worked so hard for this company for so long. And for what? My chest tightened.

"Who has final say during the next two months if Brianna and I are sharing the role?" I blurted this out before thinking. My comment could have been a lot worse, in fairness.

"You both do. You both have to agree on things, or it can't happen. I want you to learn from each other and use this as an opportunity to really move the needle and shake things up. The research director will necessitate governance in both of your specialisms, so I recommend you learn what you need to know from one another about your respective areas so you can demonstrate that you will be capable of handling everything when you do your interview. It's going to take collaboration and creativity. Having said that, ultimately, I will have final sign off on the new structure and the major changes. You'll have to convince me." Helen smiled. "I'm quite excited to see what you two come up with. And I want it to come from you both, as you know the current market inside and out. Please take the night to sleep on this. I'd like you to confirm with me first thing tomorrow whether you are up for this challenge or not."

"I understand," said Brianna.

I scoffed. She looked at me then, probably for the first time during the meeting. Her dark eyes looked through me. It was unnerving. She turned back to Helen as if she'd owned the situation between us already. "We will make this work. I promise you that. I don't need to sleep on it. I'm in."

I bit the inside of my cheek. I wasn't getting my promotion today. Instead, I was now being thrown together with Brianna Phillips of all people to deliver a merger in a ridiculously short timeframe to fight for a job that was rightfully mine. Throw an experimental joint pitch into the equation and I was fucked.

My heart pounded. On the one hand, this was an opportunity for an even bigger promotion. But on the other hand, Brianna and I didn't get along, so how could we possibly work together on something as big as this? So many questions raced through my mind. How could I show Helen I was worthy of the director position when I already knew I couldn't work with Brianna and her arrogance?

I was totally fucked.

"Excellent," Helen paused, looking at me expectantly. I continued to keep a straight face. No way was she getting an answer out of me on the spot. This was a shitshow of epic proportions.

I had to process.

"Skye, I'll hope to hear from you in the morning. I've had Jacinda clear your schedules tomorrow so we can all sit down together and go through the details. You'll get started on the assessment and strategy for the restructure right away and help me communicate it to the organisation. I will hold an all staff meeting on Thursday where I will announce it. We'll need to be ready with details on the process for everyone and be ready to communicate how people's roles will be changing and what team they will be in. I have some ideas, but I'll need your help." Helen paused, and in that pause I felt totally manipulated. "And one more thing. I want you to know I have every confidence in you both. You are both capable of delivering this restructure and I do strongly encourage you both to apply for the director role."

Helen thanked us for our time and Brianna and I headed for the door. My legs carried me out, quite disconnected from the rest of my body. I shut the door behind us as Brianna hovered in the corridor beside me.

"Can you believe what just happened in there?" Brianna said as we walked away.

"I don't know what the fuck that was." We stood by the lift, neither of us pushing the button.

"What an opportunity though. I can't believe she's giving us a shot like this."

I took an aggressively sharp breath. Ten minutes ago my career path was about to solidify. I was about to climb another rung on the ladder. Now it wasn't so clear. I might lose everything I'd worked for. What I had instead was a two-month competitive job interview. A fight to the death, under the guise of 'working collaboratively'. This was not *The Apprentice* but it was going to be a blood bath. I gritted my teeth, frustrated at the situation and the woman standing in front of me. My rival.

"Of course you see it that way. Nice going, by the way, giving her an answer on the spot like that."

Brianna fixed me with an icy stare, as though her eyes were sizing me up, assessing the level of threat I posed to her. I held my own. Her eyes were a deep brown. Mesmerising, even. I swallowed, feeling a mixture of dislike and something else.

"I was being decisive and enthusiastic. I'm sorry if that didn't meet your approval."

That was not an apology. I hesitated, reminding myself to be professional. Brianna was still looking at me, waiting for an answer, and still not pressing the button for the lift. "Look. I get that you're keen. This whole thing has thrown me. I wasn't expecting this. Helen's plan is crazy."

"I don't think that it is."

"How does that not surprise me."

"We do need to innovate. And our teams don't collaborate on projects. It's a weakness. Plus, Simon and David are the old guard. Things do need to change."

"So she puts our jobs on the line?"

"She's trying to motivate us. I think she's made a smart move."

I shook my head and made for the stairs instead. I had to get away from her. "I'd better go. I have a lot to think about."

"Are you in or are you not?"

I stopped at the top of the stairs, took a deep breath, and gave her my best poker face. "Of course I'm in."

***

As I left the office for the day and joined the busy street full of commuters, I got my wireless headphones out of my bag and placed the neat little buds in my ears. There was only one person I wanted to talk to right now. I tapped 'Mum' on my phone and listened to it ring.

"Hello, Skye."

"Hi, Mum."

"Did you hear about the promotion?" Her voice was hopeful.

I paused, not knowing where to begin. I felt tears form but pushed them away.

"What's wrong?"

I filled her in on the situation.

"Oh Skye, I'm so sorry. That's a lot. I know how much you wanted it. And now you have to climb another mountain. How are you feeling?"

All I wanted to do was get home, have a cup of tea, and go for a bath. "Exhausted. Angry. I can't believe it."

"Is it legal? Can they change your job description like that?"

"I don't know. Basically, this company is a dictatorship so she can do anything she wants."

"There are laws against this kind of thing. Don't you have a HR department?"

"We do. My friend Hayley runs it."

"Can you see what she says? See what she thinks of it?"

"I can."

"Skye, is it still possible for you to get the promotion?"

"Yes."

There was silence on the line.

"Do you still want to go for it?" she finally asked.

"Helen wants an answer first thing tomorrow. I've already said I would to Brianna. I feel so pissed off about the whole thing. Helen's thrown this on me and wants me to jump up like a stupid little kitten to this new crazy idea of hers."

"I thought your young employees were the kittens?"

"Mum, that's not the point."

"Oh, sorry."

"I have no choice, do I?"

"Skye, we always have a choice. You don't have to do anything you don't want to."

"I don't see why she couldn't have promoted us both to Associate Director or Interim Director at least, since she's basically making us both do the job of a director."

"You could always ask for it? If you don't ask, you don't get, you know."

"Mum, how on earth am I supposed to just ask for something like that? That's not how it works in these kinds of workplaces."

"Oh right, sorry."

My mum had been a housewife for twenty-five years and then worked in retail for a while. She had a knack for making complicated things sound simple. And she was often right. She could see the common-sense solution at times when I couldn't. "I'm sorry, Mum. It is an option. I'll think about it."

"Who's this other head of department? You've never mentioned her before."

I exhaled roughly down the phone as I walked. The train station was coming into view. "She's a bit difficult. And she's quite new. She's only been here for like five minutes."

My mum went quiet. I knew what was coming. "Maybe you should go easy on her, Skye. It must be hard for her too."

I bit the inside of my cheek. "Mum, I am a nice person; I would do that but she's a total shark."

"Be that as it may, you've got to hold yourself to a higher standard. Especially if you are going to be a director of a company soon."

I smiled. She believed in me so much. Always had. "You're right. I'll see what I can do."

~ 4 ~
Brianna

The streets were busy this morning, as were the cycle lanes. It being a sunny summer's day, more people commuted to work by bike. I did this commute come rain, hail, or sunshine, but days like this made me feel happy to be alive. It was only two kilometres, so I wasn't sweaty by the time I got to work. My legs felt strong and powerful today as I spun through the city centre.

I locked my bike to one of the cycle racks at the back of the building. Since I was usually one of the first in, I had no problem finding somewhere to park. Sometimes, when I left in the evening, there were oily and muddy bikes stacked everywhere and not a single space left. I had to climb over handlebars and in between pedals to get to my lock. Every now and again, I'd get thick black grease from a chain on a tailored suit. Still, it was a small price to pay for not adding to the pollution on the roads. Plus, the fresh air and exercise set me up well for the day.

Lynn was on reception already. I thought I'd be the first one in. She looked up at me and smiled warmly. "Good morning, Brianna. How are you today?"

"I'm good, thanks. How are you?"

"This is my first cup of coffee and it's doing the trick," she held her mug up in a sort of reverence. "Oh, and you just missed Skye. She arrived a few minutes ago. You're both very early. Big day ahead?"

I nodded.

"Well, good luck."

I signed my name on the sign-in sheet on the reception desk. Skye was indeed the first one in, in at seven twenty-five. Her handwriting was large, sprawling, and difficult to read. My handwriting was small, neat, and legible. Wasn't that the point?

I walked up the three flights of stairs to my office with my pannier bag hanging off my shoulder. By the time I got to the top, I started to notice the weight of it. I usually took my laptop home with me at night, so that weighed a little, as well as the litre bottle of water I carted around with me. Making my way past the IT desks, I was disappointed they were going to be moving off the floor. I'd got used to them and enjoyed their banter. But change was good. Hopefully, Skye and her team would be as good company.

I put my bag and helmet on the floor by my chair and sat down, letting my head fall back onto the headrest. Skye would need to loosen up around me if this was going to work. Yesterday in the corridor was not a good sign. Her resentment towards me had been clear. She seemed bothered in a way that was quite unprofessional. Possibly toxic. I was going to have to watch out for that.

There was an email from Jacinda about a three-hour meeting starting at nine in Helen's office. Skye must have confirmed last night then. I accepted the invite. I admired Helen's speed at getting on this. After that, I answered a few emails that couldn't wait, and then spent the rest of the time preparing for the all-important first meeting and jotted down some points.

By the time I made it up to the fourth floor, I was raring to go. Skye was already in the office. She didn't smile as I came in. In fact, her demeanour was so defensive I chose not to look at her again this morning unless I had to. Helen was typing quickly on her laptop. A cup of coffee sat beside her, steaming. When she was done, she shut the laptop lid and regarded us carefully.

"I'm glad you've both accepted. Now that you've both had some time to think about it, are there any further questions this morning?"

A heavy silence hung in the air. I would have liked more money, since I was going to be doing the job of a director seeing through a merger, albeit jointly. I decided to wait. The situation still felt precarious. And Skye over there was not shaping up as an ideal partner to merge a department with.

"Okay. I'll take that as a no. Let's get to it then."

Over the next three hours, Helen laid down the law and outlined her blueprint for how this was going to go. She used her whole office, and we had to follow her around at times. At one point the Smart Board got fired up, and she took us through an enormous Prezi presentation. Another time, we were looking at multiple screens attached to her computer. She had diagrams printed out and strewn all over the meeting table. Surprisingly, Skye worked well with Helen and listened intently. Some of Skye's points were not at all what I thought was most important or logical, but her questions were open enough to allow Helen to decide. And when the controversial topic of the desk moves – which she clearly wasn't keen on – came up, she kept it professional. I was glad to see she was able to do this, given the few interactions we'd had always seemed to end up in some sort of conflict. We didn't have to speak to each other much during the meeting, as everything went through Helen.

I hoped this wasn't all a fake front.

Helen faced us both directly. "I hope all that is clear and makes sense. Is this sounding like what you expected?"

We replied that it did make sense and was more or less what we expected.

"And you know what you have to do next?"

If I hadn't known this was a step up, potentially, I'd have taken this as a massive step backward given the level of micromanaging that was going on from Helen so far. Even so, I knew it was her company and I had to respect that. If it were my company, I'd have paid as much attention to detail as she had.

"Yes," I said.

"Now. We should do a toast to this," Helen said, getting a bottle of whisky out of her cabinet.

"I'm okay, actually, thank you," said Skye.

"Don't be silly. Here," she poured the yellow-brown liquid into three glasses and handed one to each of us. The glass was heavy. "Have a drink."

Skye accepted the glass without further protest. We held our glasses up to match Helen, as if parodying a film with a bunch of old men in suits.

"To Your View, and its future."

"Your View," we repeated, taking a sip.

"You two should go for lunch today. Get to know each other better."

We looked at each other briefly.

"I can't today," Skye said.

"Neither can I." I could think of nothing worse at this point than having lunch with Skye. I finished the rest of my whisky.

"Sometime soon then. I'd recommend it. Working with people is always so much easier when you know who you're working with, when you get on with each other."

We avoided each other's eyes, and I would have preferred we talked about anything else. I was not contracted to make friends with the people I worked with, and I wasn't going to start now. Especially not with someone who was so obviously rude to me and used words and phrases like 'this feels right' or 'I feel that we should do this' instead of 'I think we should do this because' and then back it up with reasoning. I had little confidence in her style of management or technical approach to research problems. Plus, I felt mentally drained after this meeting of listening to Helen drone on and on for hours. Good ideas they may have been, but it was still tiring to follow along to. I wanted to disappear to my own office, shut the door, and have a sandwich in peace.

"We'll do it another day," said Skye, clearly to Helen, and not for my benefit.

"Another day." I repeated, feeling the burning effect of the whisky on my empty stomach.

When Helen dismissed us, and Skye and I stepped out of the office together again, our familiar frostiness returned.

Skye sighed. "What time do you want to meet after lunch?" Her voice was hard and cold. It didn't suit her and seemed to put a terrible strain on her to speak like that.

"Why don't you come up to my office, since that's where you'll be working from now on."

She glared at me.

"I mean, on the third floor."

"Right. Well, I don't feel like coming up to the third floor so could you come down to the second floor?"

"It really doesn't matter."

"No, it doesn't."

"It's just that we need to start thinking about the practicalities of the move too, among many things, and I think it's better we do this while being able to see the floor itself."

She rolled her eyes. "Fine. I'll come up."

"Great. At two? Would let us catch up on emails."

"I won't be doing emails over lunch. Two's fine," Skye stabbed the button of the lift. "I'm going out for some air."

I spun on my heels towards the stairs this time. "Fine," I called out as I walked away.

***

Skye was nowhere to be seen by quarter past two. I'd also emailed her and received no response. Sitting in my chair, I clicked my pen constantly as thoughts about everything we had to do raced through my mind. Being an independent agency meant that these types of things were handled in-house, instead of outsourcing the problem. This was one of the reasons I took the job here, so that I could be more hands on with my research projects and my team. My last place involved cutting up every aspect of the job so that no one had any ownership or incentive to do things to a high standard, yet it all fell on my shoulders to make sure it went well. Part of me was relishing the chance to rip everything up and start again. I wanted the merger to go well, and I wanted the top job. Helen had shown confidence in me, and I wasn't going to let her down. I thought of my parents and how proud they'd be if I got the job. A director job. At my age.

The only problem was Skye and her attitude.

We had so much to do. There simply was no time for stunts like this. I scowled at my empty office before putting my pen down and snatching up the handset of my desk phone to call her. When no answer came, I slammed the handset back just as there was a knock on my door.

"Yes," I snapped.

Skye came in. "Sorry I'm late. A call ran over."

"You're here now. Let's get started, shall we?"

"It's very neat and tidy in here," she said, taking a seat at my small meeting table. It didn't seem like a compliment. "How long have you been with us now?"

"About six months."

She nodded but didn't say anything else on the matter.

We looked at each other for a moment. Her 'us' comment was still ringing in my ears. She had consistently been the most unfriendly person to me in this whole company and now she wasn't even trying to hide it.

"Helen is being a dictator," Skye said, running her hands through her hair, sighing. "I still feel like I've got whiplash from this bombshell. She's taking the piss."

I waved her away. "We had that conversation yesterday. You've already agreed to Helen's terms. We need to get on with it now."

She glared at me for several seconds. "Yeah, well I'm not happy about it."

"You don't have to like it. You just have to do it."

"See," Skye sighed, "that's where we differ. If I'm not enjoying my work, I change it."

"How privileged."

"You don't know anything about me."

"We don't have time for this chit-chat."

Skye stood up.

"Where are you going?"

"I need to take a breather."

I watched as the door closed behind her. As if I didn't have more important things to do than watch this drama unfold. I stood up, knocking my chair flat out behind me. I knelt down to pick it up, cursing the fact that I was going to have to be around this level of unprofessionalism. This was not what I'd signed up for. I was no one's babysitter. I had interns and junior researchers to worry about, not other heads of department.

I found myself trampling up to Helen's office. My shirt felt tight around my neck. I loosened the top two buttons as I marched. By the time I got there, Skye was standing over Helen's desk with her hands on her hips. I arrived as the words 'difficult person' came tumbling out of Skye's mouth.

I locked eyes with Helen as Skye finished what must have been a full-on rant, most likely about me. Skye frowned when she turned around and realised it was me. It hurt a little, which made no sense. I couldn't be that bad, could I? What right did she have to pigeon-hole me as anything when she knew nothing about me? She had been mollycoddled at this agency and this was probably the worst thing that had ever happened to her.

Helen stood up. She was eerily quiet. The kind of quiet where you knew you were really in trouble. She walked around her desk and perched on the front, looking between the two of us, frowning, before her eyes settled on me.

"And why are you here?"

She said this as if we were two children who'd both gone to the headteacher's office to tell on the other. Which is exactly why I'd come up here. I was kind of disappointed I wasn't going to be able to let rip about how ineffective this arrangement was proving to be. That if it were up to me, I would do things differently. My way. But there was no way I was going to say that.

I could get the upper hand here.

"I came to let you know that Skye had walked out of my office. I was concerned about the merger and wanted to let you know."

A glance told me that Skye was scowling at me. I probably shouldn't have gone that far, but then, why not? She'd clearly been running me down. So what if I was resorting to acting like a ten-year-old?

Helen bowed her head and clasped her hands in her lap. Was it disgust? Or defeat? I couldn't tell. Whatever it was, it didn't look good.

She raised her head slowly, which seemed deeply ominous. Her face was hard, and the lines around her mouth were more visible.

"I suspected this might happen. Not right away, mind you. This behaviour is simply unacceptable. It's unacceptable. You have been given a job to do and you are both letting yourselves down. I see no enthusiasm. I see no co-operation. No real interest here. I know that it must have come as quite a shock but that's business.

Things change. You have to keep up or you'll be left behind." She looked between us a few times. "I need you to put aside whatever differences you may have and make this work. I know you can put your heads together and turn this company around. But if this is the way you're going to go about it, you'll make a mockery of us all and I won't have that level of mediocrity in my organisation. And this is my organisation. I am the boss. I give the orders. If you don't like it you can leave. But if you stay, I expect you to do exactly as I ask you to do. Have you got that, the pair of you?"

I nodded. I'd never come this close to getting fired before and it scared me. To my side, Skye nodded too.

"Now sort it out and get it done. If you want to become a director, you've got to show me that you can handle doing hard things. That you can be professional enough to carry a whole team through a period of change. Can you do that?"

"I can do that," said Skye.

"I can do it too."

We shuffled away. I hoped I didn't look as sheepish as Skye did post telling off.

"And ..." Helen had put on her glasses and was typing; she hit enter and gave us her full attention. "And don't fuck it up."

I nodded again and got the hell out of there. Skye was right behind me. My blood was pumping. "Look, if you have a problem with me, you come to me, don't go telling our boss."

I couldn't even be bothered with the look of outrage that appeared on Skye's face. She'd accused me of being difficult to Helen, so I felt justified in having a go. I turned away, wanting to walk away, but deep down I knew that wasn't the solution and that it wasn't professional. None of this was professional, and it bothered me. This had to be dealt with head on. My feet stayed glued to the ground. Skye looked close to tears. Perhaps I'd been too harsh. A quick glance into one of the meeting rooms showed it was free. "Why don't we go in there and talk?"

Skye followed me into the room with her head down and a defeated look about her. By the looks of it, she'd never come that close to losing her job before either. The room was small, square, with nothing in it except a round table, four chairs, and a telephone.

Skye sat down on the edge of a chair, like she wasn't quite committing to it. "I wasn't saying I wasn't going to work with you. I just needed a minute. I thought Helen might be able to help."

"I shouldn't have said that to Helen."

"And I'm not privileged. But I do love this job. I love this place. I do want to improve things. I just didn't think they were that bad before."

"I get that now."

Skye roughly ran her hands through her hair and sighed. "I don't know why Helen thinks we can drop everything else to work on this. I can literally feel myself falling behind on my other work. On everything. Not even Jacinda has the power to fix that."

"Now *that* we can agree on."

We shared a look of mutual recognition then. Recognition of how unwanted this situation was, to a greater or lesser extent, for both of us.

Skye put her hands on the table. "I'm sorry I've been so negative about all this. I thought I was getting promoted yesterday. I'm just disappointed. I still haven't got my head around it."

"You've been here awhile, haven't you?"

She looked at me sceptically again. "It's not favouritism. I've worked hard to get where I am. Really hard."

"I wasn't suggesting it was."

Everyone was allowed to have a work persona. Especially in corporate workplaces. There was no reason to believe that Skye wasn't just doing what she could to get by and be successful at work, albeit, in a way that contrasted to mine. We both knew that we had very different styles and probably wouldn't talk to each other outside of work. I didn't have to like everything about someone in order to work with them. I don't know why she did. It wasn't even about me. She said herself she was just disappointed. I could understand that.

Skye sat properly on her chair and leaned on the table. She held my eye for several seconds as if gauging something. "Okay."

"We're both professionals. I don't see why we can't make this work," I said.

"You're right."

I let out a huge breath. "I have some ideas already. I thought we could—"

Skye held up her hands. "Could we make a start properly tomorrow morning. Would that be okay?"

Despite my better judgement, I relented. "Okay. Whatever you need."

She relaxed her shoulders. "Thanks."

We shared a small, polite smile, before getting up, and walking back down the stairs together, side by side. We said goodbye on the landing by the entrance to my floor.

In that small amount of time Skye had perked up and left me with an actual smile. I found myself returning it and it didn't feel completely forced. Maybe this wasn't going to be a complete disaster after all.

~ 5 ~
Skye

I went to my mum's house after getting a telling off from Helen. Although I'd never lived there, it still felt like home because it was hers, and there was nowhere else I'd rather be when I was upset. My mum and I were sitting at the small dining table beside the back door.

She looked at me gravely. "Do you think you could just get on with it now?"

Arlo, my mum's black labrador, lay sprawled out at my feet, enjoying the cool tiles.

"I'll do it. I'll see it through over the next two months. But I won't like it. Not until I get the job."

"It'll make your life easier if you can accept and embrace it for what it is, and you'll be more likely to get the job that you've been wanting for so long."

I thought about this for a few moments. She knew I was angry about the situation because I'd ranted non-stop since getting there.

"It is a chance to revolutionise the organisation."

"That's good."

"And I guess I'll get to work with some new people."

"See? That's the spirit."

I shrugged. This was the task at hand, and there was no getting away from the fact I'd need to work closely with Brianna in order to get what I wanted. There was nothing else to be done but get on with it. The job could be mine, if I got a grip of myself.

Mum was right, again.

"The money would be nice too. Directors at my company earn a fortune."

"Skye, honey. You won't need to support me for much longer. I'll be getting a job soon. I'll be out of your hair."

I felt responsible for her now. She was getting older and hadn't had a job in a couple of years due to all the stress around the divorce. "You should just enjoy yourself, Mum. You've got your pensions coming soon."

"I want to do things, Skye. I've got plans. I've wasted enough of my life with your father. Now is my time. And you, dear, trust me, don't want to throw everything away because you're upset about the merger. You're better than that."

"I know, Mum. I know."

"Helen is testing you so try not to show any more signs that you're anything less than a true professional about it."

"I don't think I can put another foot wrong after today."

"You were rattled."

"I might not have any job at the end of all this."

"That won't happen, honey. Not after everything you've done for them. Not with your million degrees, Dr McCulloch, believe you me. They'd be mad to let you go. You're a star."

"Thanks, Mum."

"You might want to explore exactly what it is about this Brianna that sets you off so much. Find some common ground if you can."

I puffed out my cheeks. She waited. Arlo stuck his head up, momentarily considering whether it was worth his while to get up and check what was going on, but he rested his head back on the tiles again.

"It's just a feeling I get. She's got this emotionless, untouchable streak to her. On the one hand she's this clever person who is very good at her job, but on the other hand I think she'd step on people to get ahead. She probably already has." The truth was Brianna had got under my skin even before all this. I just couldn't work out why.

"That's quite the assumption."

"Do you mind if we talk about something else? It'd be nice to switch off from the world."

"Of course."

"What's for dinner?"

She turned to look at me and a big smile broke out across her face. "Macaroni and cheese, your favourite."

"And chips?"

"Of course. I prepared the potatoes earlier. They're in the fridge ready to go in the oven."

"Do you need any help?"

"No dear, you go and relax. Why don't you sit in the garden with Arlo. He'd like that."

"Mum, you're the best. I don't know what I'd do without you."

I took my wine out into the garden. Arlo followed me without request, implicitly knowing his duty was to accompany anyone out into his garden. He found some shade under the elder tree and sprawled out on his side. I went back inside the house for my book, a lesbian romance I'd started at the weekend, before everything had kicked off at work. I read for about an hour before my mum called me in for dinner.

"Sorry I haven't been around lately."

"It's okay. I know you're busy. And you'll be getting a lot busier, by the sounds of it."

That reminded me. Anxiety gripped my stomach. For a while I'd forgotten about work. "Yeah, I probably will be. But I'll try to come around more."

When we'd finished eating, I cleared the plates away and tidied the kitchen. Mum said I should leave them but I wanted her to put her feet up and feel looked after for a moment.

"Thank you, sweetheart."

I poured myself a glass of water and turned around and rested against the counter. My mum spoke to Arlo in her baby voice for him. Although not meant for me, I found it so comforting. I made her tea and left her watching a home improvement show while I went upstairs to the guest bedroom, which I'd claimed as my own, for a lie down. Then I took a bath in the tiny bathroom. My mum tapped on the door outside and asked why I was having a bath when it was so hot.

"I don't know. It relaxes me."

"Make sure the window is open, I've just re-grouted the tiles."

I said it was. My mum's new lease of life and recent passion for fixing things around the house was wonderful to see after so many years of being passive and waiting on my dad to do these types of things. And while it was comforting to escape from it all at my mum's, comments like that reminded me of why I liked my own place. Even if I got lonely sometimes.

I wanted to get in early tomorrow, so I went to bed not long after my bath. I made a mental list of things I needed to do and came up with some ideas to discuss with Brianna. Realising that I wanted her to be impressed with my ideas was a bit of a surprise. Since when did I care what Brianna Phillips thought?

***

Hayley poured coffee into my cup for me without asking. We were totally in sync when it came to our coffee breaks. We were a well-oiled machine to maximise the short amount of time we had. I dealt with the milk and then we were done. The kitchen was oddly quiet this morning.

"Still no news about your promotion?"

I wished I didn't have to lie to her. "No. No news." I sipped some coffee.

She eyed me suspiciously. "That's strange. I think I've seen you go up to Helen's office a few times this week. I've even seen it in your diary. Meetings."

I sipped my coffee and avoided her eyes. How was I going to handle this? "Are you stalking me now?" Her face was still full of unanswered questions. I cracked. "I can't say."

She gasped. "I knew it. I knew something was going on. I've also seen Brianna head up there, too. Something's afoot."

I kept a neutral face, inwardly impressed at her skills of deduction.

"But you can't tell me. I understand. Well, I hope it's a good thing for you. Whatever it is. You sure do deserve it."

"Thank you."

Brianna appeared in the kitchen then, assessing the space like she was a surveyor or architect without a hardhat. It was rare to see her on this floor. She wore a loose, dark-grey power suit with the sleeves rolled up to her elbows. She was lean and looked like she went to the gym. I let my eyes roam over her body before I realised what I was doing and that Hayley had seen. She raised an eyebrow at me in question; I ignored it and took another sip of coffee.

Brianna was about to leave when Hayley spoke to her. "Hey, how are you doing? Are you looking for something?"

Brianna's eyes settled on her. Her dark hair was tied back at the base of her head. She was hot. I wondered how aware she was of her looks.

"No. I've got everything I need, thanks. Just making some calculations."

When she turned her attention to me, her eyes were observant, and cool. I felt them penetrate me.

"See you in five minutes, Skye," she said, before leaving.

Hayley's mouth fell open. "What was *that*?"

"What? What was what?"

"Uh, the furtive glances, the tension?"

"I don't know what you're talking about."

She eyed me suspiciously and took a few sips of her coffee. "What's the meeting about? This is new."

I grimaced and shook my head.

"Ah. Same thing. I see. Well, I'll be looking forward to knowing what's going on at some point."

"I'll tell you as soon as I can. It's big. That's all I can say for now."

Hayley's squeal made me laugh. We left the kitchen and went back to our desks. I closed the door behind me and looked around my office, thinking about how it would come across to Brianna. We'd agreed to meet in my office, or rather, Brianna suggested we do. Maybe she was worried I'd flake again and was trying to control the situation. It irritated me a little, but I was also glad to be on my own turf for our first proper meeting. I frantically dashed about straightening things up and clearing papers off my desk. By the time I was ready, Brianna knocked once and then came straight in. Didn't she know that was rude? I gritted my teeth and forced myself to smile.

"Come in," I said.

~ 6 ~
Brianna

"It's nine thirty, you are ready, right?"

"Of course. Take a seat."

I walked across the compact office and took a seat across from her. Skye was looking at her computer screen and giving off those frosty vibes again. Her hair was tied up in a messy bun. I liked the way her glasses set off her face. She didn't normally wear them to meetings, so I think this was the first time I'd seen her with them on. They suited her.

Hardly any surface of her desk was clear. How could she work in such a cluttered space? I needed everything to be tidy around me and in its proper place. I'd never agreed with the saying, 'messy desk, creative brain' or whatever it was. For me, messy desk equated to messy brain. Overwhelm. No, a clear space helped facilitate clear thinking. What did this chaotic room suggest about Skye? Hopefully not chaos. I don't do chaos.

The windows were open bringing in the sounds of cars and buses from the street. Road works were taking place and the drilling was coming straight up into the room. Trophies and certificates lined the wall behind Skye like badges of honour, 'Winner: Best Research Project 2018' and 'Market Research Ambassador Award: Distinction'. Not bad, I had to admit. I'd never won an award.

"What do you want to tackle first? Team restructure or the Department of Health pitch?" Skye faced me and crossed her legs.

"The team."

She nodded a few times in approval but didn't smile. "Good. I was hoping you'd say that."

Was she testing me? I got the distinct feeling that I was being assessed or even interviewed.

"It all starts there. Happy team, happy customers," I said, hoping she'd agree.

This time she smiled, but thinly. "That's true. I didn't think that would be top of your list. You don't seem overly close to your team. Sometimes you refer to them as," she paused and made an air quote, "'resources'."

"Aren't they though? Management theory is no longer rule by fear. It's incredibly inefficient and unproductive. People take more sick days and they end up leaving, then you have to train someone else up. I make sure my team are okay, and I do care to a certain extent, but you're still getting them to work for you at the end of the day. That's resources in my book."

Skye rolled her eyes. "I like to think of the people I work with and manage as human beings first and foremost." Her unimpressed face was back. She clearly did not share my way of thinking. Her style was different to mine. Softer. Open to abuse from lazy employees.

This was going to be interesting.

"I don't think being logical about what we're all doing here takes away anyone's humanity. If anything, it protects people from the mistaken idea that we're all one big happy family. We need people to perform in their jobs, that's all. And restructures are notorious for causing bad atmospheres, negative work environments, and staff to leave."

"Not if they're handled well. If we put people's feelings at the centre of how we approach this, we can make sure that doesn't happen."

Feelings. Ugh. She was one of those. Maybe we would make a good team being so different.

"You're right. We should do this sensitively. We should also have a clear rationale for the changes we make to people's jobs and stick to it no matter what. This isn't a negotiation with staff." We held each other's eyes, neither of us looking away. I felt my pulse quicken the longer it went on. I knew I was right, and I wanted her to submit to my opinion.

"I agree," she finally said.

"Great."

"So how are we going to structure this new all singing all dancing research department?" Skye touched her face.

"The pressure is on us to come up with something big. Something she can shout about to the outside world. Or else, we're toast."

Skye scratched her head. "Yep, the pressure is on. You don't have to remind me. Regardless of whether you're quant or qual, the research process is exactly the same. The methods are different, but the stages are distinct, and they are shared. We could keep the existing structures of both teams and have one massive research team? Strength in numbers, and we keep doing what we do best."

"No. I don't think that would work. That's basically just a merger. There would be too many people going after the same contracts with no clear speciality."

Skye shot me a look. I could see I'd annoyed her with this but it was also true. She crossed her arms and touched her face again. Her face softened as if she'd come to a realisation.

"Okay. That was the basic option. It'd be easier for people to get their heads around as it would involve less change, but you're right, it's not big enough for Helen. It's not a restructure. A free-for-all won't do."

I liked how she was able to critically assess things and come to a good decision.

"Right, so that leaves us with the complicated option. I've got some ideas if you want to hear them?"

"Please."

"Just a second." Skye stood up and shut the window. I sighed in relief. The noises from the street had been so distracting. Now it was calm. The room seemed smaller, and I felt as if we were sitting too close together. My office was a similar size but felt bigger because I didn't have it stacked full of things. For starters, I'd have a meeting table instead of a couch. How did she get that signed off? Next time we'd meet in my office.

She sat down again and moved her chair backwards. "Well, based on the type of clients out there, and the type of contracts we already get, I think we should take a leaf out of the industry playbook and organise around that. We could have four teams: Brand and Communications, Advertising and Marketing, Consumer Insights, and Research with Children and Young People. We'd keep our biggest clients happy and hopefully diversify into new ones. What do you think?"

"I like it. I was thinking along similar lines. However instead of Children and Young People I'd go with Emerging Markets or Emerging Trends. We could be the voice of the next generation. Truly ahead of the curve. And I think Helen would go for that. It's what she's hinting at."

"That's an interesting idea," Skye lips parted. "It's got more scope. It would allow for four heads of department, one under each specialism. That way if neither of us gets the director job we might be able to side-step into one of these."

"Good point."

"So do we have our new structure then?"

"We do." I was pleasantly surprised at how easy that was. "Shall we assign people to these new teams?"

Skye took a sip of coffee. "Yep."

"How do you want to do it?"

She put her cup down and stood up again. "I printed out everyone's profile picture and prepared some sheets for us to pin them to. I want to see it all mapped out."

I was surprised and impressed by her level of preparation and organisation. When had she done this?

"You might need to come around here so we can work at my desk. That's another thing, I need a meeting table in my room."

"Yeah, the couch was a strange choice."

She looked at me a bit funny then. "Not fitting for a future director, is it?"

And there it was. We were both going for the same job, and she believed it was hers, as I believed it was mine.

"On second thought, do you mind if we lay them out on the floor? There's not enough space here," said Skye.

We took our chairs to the middle of the room, squeezing past boxes and leaned over the A1 papers on the floor. As we went through everyone who worked for us, we discussed who would fit best where. We earmarked people who would be considered for promotion soon. Not normally the type of knowledge I'd give away, but I had to learn to trust Skye or this would never work. When we agreed on a position, one of us bent forward and stuck a profile picture to the drawn-on hierarchy. I noted her attention to detail and good judge of character.

We couldn't agree on one person, however. I didn't think this candidate had the necessary skills for a particular team, but Skye did. Granted, this person wasn't in my team and I didn't know much about them, but I'd seen them present and I was not impressed. Having impact and gravitas with clients was a huge part of the job. I thought they would be better suited to more of an analyst role.

"I'm telling you, she has a brilliant mind. She's exactly right for Brand and Comms," Skye said.

"So you keep saying."

"You haven't worked with her, so I don't know why you think you know so much about her. What are you basing it on?"

I told her about the time I'd watched her present.

"That was her on an off day. We all have those."

I relented.

Skye fist pumped the air. It was cute.

"You praise everyone a lot. Your team must appreciate that."

Skye smiled at me, and a warmth spread through my chest. She had a lovely shaped mouth and perfect, soft-looking lips. Her skin looked so smooth. I shook my head. What was I doing?

"I'm glad you noticed. It's a big part of how I try to motivate people. I know how much I like to be praised and that it motivates me, so I try to do the same to those I manage."

"If it's deserved, you mean."

"Even when it's not. You can give people constructive criticism and still praise them for what they did well. How do you do it?"

"I tell it to them straight."

"Nice. How's that working for you?"

I frowned. "I don't know."

"Like you said, fear doesn't motivate people. I'm sure you're not as harsh as you think you are if you're keen to keep people happy."

"I wouldn't say it was my top priority. I try to be firm and fair." I sighed, knowing that my direct style didn't sit well with some people. "I could probably be a little softer in my approach."

I could not believe I said that. I never showed weakness like that. Not to anyone.

Skye watched me. She didn't jump in and take advantage of my show of vulnerability. "It's a skill, like anything else. I'm sure you could develop it more."

I appreciated her kindness. I bet she was a good boss after all.

"So, I think we're done with the team stuff for now. Is there anything else on the structure we should cover?" Skye said.

We'd been at it for hours, and it was lunchtime. "No, I think that's it for now. We know what we want it to look like and who we want in which team."

"Okay, so what are our next steps?" said Skye.

"Since Helen is announcing this tomorrow afternoon, and we're due to meet with her tomorrow morning to take her through it all, I say we focus on changes to job descriptions. HR will need to review them soon. Then we start on drafting the new strategy document."

"Oh the joys."

"And after that, we should start on the pitch."

"Yep, I agree."

I wheeled my chair back around to its place. Skye watched me move but didn't say anything.

"Can you believe she's given us all this responsibility?" Skye said.

"And zero time to think it all through?"

"I know, right?"

"She's a real powerhouse. Even if she is a bit scary."

Skye laughed. "You know this means we're probably going to be here all night."

We held each other's gaze then for a few seconds. There was something in the way she was looking at me. A curiosity? Kindness? I wasn't sure, but I liked it. This had gone better than expected. I nodded. Her telephone rang, startling us both.

"I'd better take this."

"Sure, I'll see you after lunch," I said on my way out.

***

I went back to my desk and checked my emails and messages. As I quickly dealt with various things now piling up because my week had been hijacked, I decided to have my lunch outside. I headed out after collecting my lunch from the fridge. Lynn asked me how my day was going, and we shared a few words. Small talk was not my forte, but I'd accepted it as an essential requirement when working in business. There wasn't the same pressure on my male colleagues to engage to the same extent. They could be grumpy some days and allowed to be so. But not me. Women were held to a higher standard in the workplace, no doubt about it. In the end, I chose to fit in. It would hurt my career otherwise. Besides, I'd got used to it in some ways. And it wasn't so bad when you were talking to someone as pleasant as Lynn.

"You have a good lunch. It's a beautiful day for it," she said. "I had mine a little while ago on one of the benches in the park. It was absolutely perfect."

"Thanks, I will."

I got a takeaway coffee from my favourite stand around the corner. The guy working there greeted me with, 'espresso today?' every time I showed up. This worked well for me. I couldn't spend long on my lunch, so I walked briskly up to the little park nestled amongst the bustling city and found a spot on the grass. The park was full of office workers having picnics. There weren't many spots left. I took my blazer off and folded it neatly.

I concentrated on my sandwich. Having lunch on my own felt like a necessity. Like a pressure release valve. I needed it. I was constantly talking, listening and making decisions during the day. If I had lunch with others, I didn't feel like I'd even had a break at all. Even if the conversations were pleasant. Part of me couldn't understand people who did that every day. I often wondered what it must be like to be able to be around people all the time and not become exhausted.

Not far to my left were three of my younger colleagues having lunch together. I caught eyes with one of them and smiled back. They didn't know that their jobs were going to change. Hopefully they'd still want to stay at Your View. This morning had gone well. Way better than I thought it would after Skye's antics the past couple of days. She was a mystery to me. I hadn't expected her to be *so* intelligent. So well-reasoned. I thought about where my opinion of Skye as a colleague came from. I settled on the fact that it must be to do with the fact that she did a different type of research to me. I didn't particularly rate qualitative or social research. Talking to people is so subjective. Even by engaging with the research participants, you alter their answers in some way. It's never a *true* test, like my studies were. There were too many factors that couldn't be controlled.

A pigeon walked by, side-eying my space for crumbs. It waddled away moving onto the next person. I finished my sandwich and sipped on my coffee. The only problem I had with her approach this morning was her unwavering attempt to try and keep everyone happy. There was no way we could go about this restructure and not piss someone off. I was okay with that, but she was desperately trying to avoid it. Commendable in a way, but naïve. How had she got this far in her career behaving that way? I had had to muscle my way into every promotion I got. Compete against the blatant favouritism bestowed on my male colleagues. I guess going the other way and being a people-pleaser had payoffs too. After lunch I'd explain to Skye that whilst we could try to do our best for everyone, ultimately some people weren't going to like the changes and there was nothing we could do about that. Helen hadn't said much about job losses, but I didn't believe that there weren't going to be any. As soon as we hit a brick wall, Helen would claim she had no other choice but to offer redundancies. It'll be Helen's decision about everything.

I angled my face up towards the sun to get some much-needed vitamin D and closed my eyes. Skye was warming to me, which was good. Obviously, she was just being professional, but it was an improvement to the cold-shoulder she used to give me. As she was one of the most popular people in the organisation, it had hurt more than I realised until now.

~ 7 ~
Brianna

The window of Skye's office was open again, though it was quieter outside now the working day was over. It was the type of humid evening where any clothes felt restrictive. I undid the top few buttons of my blouse, feeling oddly self-conscious as I did so. Skye had changed into a thin black vest top hours ago.

We clashed over a further three people and how they fit into the new structure. In the end, we agreed to put it to Helen tomorrow, which is exactly what I'd expected.

Heads were about to roll.

Skye hung up her phone. "Pizza shouldn't be too long."

I'd stopped thinking clearly as I was so hungry. The blue light from my laptop felt like it was burning through my eyes. We still had more to do on the pitch. I thought about Helen and how she was most likely dining out in some elegant Michelin-starred restaurant right now.

"Are you okay?" said Skye, looking up from her computer screen on the other side of the desk from me. Her eyes were getting a little bloodshot. I wondered if mine looked the same.

"Yes. Just a little tired. The pizza will help."

Her eyes softened. "I feel the same. We've been at this all day and we're not done yet. This is so crazy."

"It is pretty intense."

Skye sat back and her shoulders relaxed. She looked great despite the long day. We looked away from each other then back again, before our eyes settled on one another. We held eye contact and my pulse quickened. Skye was attractive. I'd always thought so, but after spending the day with her in this tiny office, getting to know one another, I was kind of in awe of her now … and she really did look great in that vest top.

A knock at the door startled us. "You girls still here?" It was David. He'd literally popped his head around the door while still standing outside. "She's cracking the whip at you two, isn't she?" He pushed the door open further and stood just inside it. He was always so well put together. Today he had on a salmon shirt and blue chinos. His grey hair was styled carefully but you could tell it was the end of the day.

"David!" Skye sounded happy to see him. "Look what your retiring has done to us!"

He looked over his shoulder as he shut the door behind him. "If I knew she was going to go this crazy I'd have stayed," he said in a hushed tone.

Skye and I glanced at each other but I couldn't read her expression.

"In my day, this would have been unheard of. Still, I bet one of you will be running this place soon. That's got to be a huge carrot for you both. Breaking the glass ceiling and all that, girls, am I right?"

"Yeah, it's a great opportunity," Skye said, in a clipped tone. "And what about you, retiring? David, you said you'd never let that happen. What on earth are we going to do without you?"

He laughed politely while shaking his head but he obviously loved this sort of chat with Skye. I was reminded again of why she was so popular.

"I know, I know. It had to happen one day. The wife wants us to travel. She makes all the decisions. I've no choice in the matter really."

"Travelling will be amazing, David. You've been saying for years how much you want to see more of the world. You deserve it."

He beamed at this and scratched his head. "I hope so, Skye, I hope so." He looked between us and at our papers, sticky notes and the two whiteboards.

"Make sure she looks after you both, if you know what I'm saying. Don't let her play you."

His words hung in the air. I respected him for saying that. He was right. She was playing us. I knew this, but after today, I really felt it.

"Thanks, David. We're on it," Skye said.

"I know, I know. And I don't want to disturb you since you're here so late for a reason and not to talk to me." He backed away out of the door. "We should talk tomorrow; I'd like to know what the plans are. See if I can help at all."

"Thanks, David," I said. "That'd be great."

David hesitated. "You know, I've heard on the grapevine that they want an internal person to become the Director of Research. Just sayin'. I think you two girls have an excellent chance."

Skye and I caught each other's eyes briefly. I squirmed in my seat. This couldn't get any more uncomfortable.

"Good to know, thanks, David." Skye held out an arm. "Oh, before you go, David. When's your leaving party?"

"The ninth of October. And you're all invited," he chuckled, offering us both a smile.

"So I'm finally going to see those dance moves you've been bigging up for years then, am I?"

"You certainly will. If you can't dance off forty years of blood, sweat, and tears during your retirement party, when can you?"

"Quite."

We said our goodbyes and his parting shot was that we shouldn't work too late.

Skye had perked up and was smiling to herself about something. She had such a beautiful smile and I found myself staring at her again. I liked how good she'd made David feel. Making people feel special wasn't something that came naturally to me.

"That's the pizza." Skye sprang up. "I'll go down and get them."

She left in a flash and I felt glued to my chair. To my astonishment, I was happy to stay. Although, I didn't have much energy left for work. It was foolish to think we'd get much more quality work done this late.

Skye came back without any pizza. "We've been stuck in here all day. Would you like to have it in the canteen? It might be nicer than in here."

"Fine."

She looked at me uncertainly, smiled a little then headed out. I scolded myself for sounding so abrupt. I followed her, a few steps behind. There was something slightly awkward about this. About consciously going somewhere to eat together. In the canteen the pizza boxes had been laid out on a table for two, with napkins already placed.

"So, I'm thinking a beer would be quite nice right now. Don't judge me," Skye laughed. She must have got them from the fridge meant for entertaining clients upstairs in the boardroom or downstairs in the viewing room. They were normally off limits to staff. "Want one?"

"I see we're already assuming absolute power over this place. I'll take one, thanks."

She laughed. It warmed me to hear it. I opened the massive box and was hit by the addictively delicious aromas. Skye placed our bottles of beer on the table. We ate in silence for a while, both enjoying the food and the beer. I could feel my face go red as I ate, from relief or the gluten, I was never sure. I hoped she didn't think I was blushing.

"It's good, right?"

"Hits the spot perfectly," I replied.

She watched me for a bit then, which was kind of unnerving. And I didn't get unnerved by people very often. The canteen and the office were completely silent. I decided now was a good time to share my idea.

"So, I think we should ask for a temporary change in job title, given what's being asked of us. I think we should push for it since she's extending us so much responsibility, even if it's only temporary. What do you think?"

"It's a brilliant idea. It'll look great on our CVs."

"It makes sense."

"I thought you were all, 'yes, sergeant, how high would you like me to jump, sergeant?'." Skye's eyes sparkled. She was being cute, and a little bit flirty.

"Yeah, sorry about that. Sometimes I get very left-brain, command and control about things. I've been told this can come across a bit," I mimicked her and used air quotes for effect too, "'harsh'."

She laughed. "Never."

I shrugged and had some more beer. Somehow, her gentle tease about my personality didn't annoy me at all. I was enjoying her company. I'd been enjoying her company all day.

I had not expected this.

"Thanks for suggesting we ask for the change in job title. It would be nice if both of us came away with something. I'm glad you feel we can ask for this jointly."

"From today, yes." That came out wrong.

She grimaced.

"I mean, today's the first time we've actually worked together."

She nodded a few times. "That's true. How would you know anything about me?"

"I know that you kick ass at what you do. The youth transitions contract was pretty impressive."

"Thank you."

She smiled now. I was relieved to see it. I ate some more, pleased that she liked my idea and I was able to make her smile. A few moments passed.

"Do you think Helen will go for it?" Skye started another slice.

"I don't know. But if you don't ask, you don't get, right? She's showed her hand, so we know we have leverage."

"Asking for what I want has never been one of my strong points." Skye looked away after saying that. A hint of regret passed over her face. Did she think I'd use this against her? I was not that sort of person.

"You seem to have no problem asking clients for what you want."

Skye shrugged. "That's just business." She took a sip of beer. "So how should we put it to Helen? I'm not sure how an ultimatum would go down."

"I think we just state that we are both in agreement that what's being asked of us is not appropriate to our job descriptions and salaries, and that we would appreciate it if she reconsidered her proposition. We sell it to her as a win-win, because we'll both be more motivated in the short term."

"I'm in. Fuck it."

I dabbed my mouth with a napkin, and then smiled in agreement. "Perfect. That's another thing we agree on, who would've thought?"

"I know, right?"

Still smiling at each other, we held eye contact for a crazy amount of time again. I took a deep breath and noticed my pulse had quickened a little. This had been a very long, and very strange day.

"Shall we go back in? Squeeze out a few more ideas on the pitch?" said Skye.

After such a huge amount of food, I was fading a little, but didn't want to let her down.

"Sure."

We went back to her office and worked steadily, and made good progress. It was dark outside. Skye said she thought we'd done enough for the day and should call it a night. By this point, the overhead light had gone off and we were illuminated only by one desk lamp and our screens. I said I agreed and got up to leave, packing away my things.

"Hey, you know, I thought we worked quite well together today," Skye said. "We got through a ton of work and we didn't bite each other's heads off too much."

I laughed and looked up at her. "Yeah, you're right. Once or twice isn't bad for us."

In one day my impression of Skye had completely changed. She wasn't nearly as annoying as I'd pegged her to be. Yes, she still talked a lot and we were very different but she was kind and she was logical in her own way.

"It keeps things interesting," Skye said.

"True."

"I'll see you tomorrow then. Bright and early." Skye beamed at me.

"Yes, I'll see you tomorrow."

All the lights were off as I walked back to my office. Sensors picked up my movement and turned on the lights as I walked, freaking me out a little. It was weird being here so late. And also a little creepy. I grabbed my jacket and bag, and made my way out. I found Skye at the front door, waiting beside the alarm system.

"We need to lock up and I didn't know if you were in the building still or not. I could have emailed you from my work phone but it's probably better if I have your mobile in case anything like this happens again."

"You want to swap numbers?"

"Yeah," she tucked some hair behind her ear. "If there's an emergency or something. Or if something urgent comes up, you know, I break a leg before a big meeting or something. Or you do. You know what I mean."

"Emergencies."

"That's it."

I gave her my number, speaking the numbers slowly, feeling self-conscious as I did so. Skye's stance was rigid, and she avoided my eyes. She gave my phone a quick call and then hung up.

"Always good to check."

She turned away from me and attended to the security alarm. I waited with her for some reason. It would have been rude to just leave her there. Once she'd finished, we fell into step beside each other and ended up walking up the street together.

"Where do you live, anyway?" Skye said.

"Near the centre, around the corner from the High Street. I usually cycle to work but I got a flat tyre last night and haven't had time to fix it."

"What a great location. And near the train station. That's where I'm headed. Also, that sucks about your tyre."

"And you, where do you live?"

"Oh I live out in the sticks in a cottage in the country. Twenty-eight minutes on the train."

"That sounds lovely."

"It's okay. The commute can suck sometimes but I do get lots of reading done on the train. It helps me ease out of the working day into the evening."

We chatted easily as we walked. Talking to Skye didn't seem to drain me at all. It energised me. We approached the neon lights of the newly refurbished train station.

Skye stopped. "This is me."

I stopped with her and dug my hands into my coat pockets. There was an announcement in the foyer of the station but I couldn't make out the words. Her expression turned more serious.

"Brianna. I want to apologise for the way I spoke to you yesterday. I was thrown by Helen's plan but it's no excuse. I think I took it out on you. It was rude and uncalled for, and I totally understand that you were concerned enough to go speak to Helen."

I hadn't expected an apology. I looked at the ground then back up at her. Her face was sincere.

She continued. "I understand that this was all a huge shock to you on Monday too. I'm sorry I didn't make it easy."

Was she over-apologising now? It's not as if I was an angel, the way I spoke to her yesterday.

"Hey. It's all in the past. Shall we start fresh, here and now?"

She smiled and her face lit up. I was smiling too. It felt nice to clear the air.

"I'd like that, Brianna."

We held eye contact and the world melted away. We did that thing where neither of us looked away. I felt almost giddy. Another announcement came from inside the station.

"Fingers crossed about tomorrow." Skye looked towards the departure board, then back at me.

"Yeah, let's go get this semi-promotion of ours. Don't want to be the stereotypical women in the workplace not getting paid what we're worth, now do we?"

"No, ma'am. Female boss or no female boss."

"Helen's not going to know what's hit her. Hopefully she'll recognise what's at stake here and give us what we want. We deserve to get something out of this experience besides doing the grunt work for her and then a shot at an interview."

Skye leaned towards me and lowered her voice as if telling me a secret. "It's all kind of exciting, though, isn't it?"

"Strangely, yes."

We said our goodbyes and I floated the rest of the way home in a sort of hazy high. My tired body carried me despite myself. I think I was pretty excited about it all too.

~ 8 ~
Skye

Standing at the head of the boardroom table, Helen loomed over us as we sat either side of her, anxiously waiting for her response. Like a talent contest, she made us wait for a ridiculously long time before she spoke.

"This is exactly what I was looking for. I love it."

I could hardly believe my ears. She was always so hard to please. We'd worked so late last night I wasn't sure if any mistakes had crept in, so this was a huge relief.

"You've responded to my brief admirably. This will make waves out there in the industry."

She sat down and turned her attention back towards the monitor we had been presenting on.

"Show me more."

Brianna and I took her through the rest, each taking it in turn to present. We worked well together, instinctively picking up on each other's cues. This synchronicity was a little strange, since we'd only briefly practised the slides. It came naturally to us. Brianna was a good speaker, Hayley was right. She put me at ease with her calm tone and reassuring voice. I could have listened to her for hours.

I sat back, enjoying the opportunity to really look at Brianna. No distractions. Her long brown hair was shiny and straight. Her shirt was open at the top, making visible her long neckline and collarbone. My eyes roamed over the exposed skin and then upwards to her facial features, noting how perfectly symmetrical they were, before I settled on her lips.

"Not only will we be more responsive to market demands, we will pool our resources better to take a more strategic approach to client briefs," said Brianna.

I finished her point. "It'll involve a whole new way of doing things. We've already lined up new processes with clear guidance for managers."

"Perfect. This is shaping up well. We will accelerate redundancies for the three people you haven't been able to fit into the new structure."

I clenched my jaw.

"We thought you might be forced to consider that," Brianna said, "so we prepared an alternative solution where we added in the expected additional revenue from being able to secure higher value projects." She tapped her iPad and it brought up a new slide. "Brand and Comms is where all the money is, apart from Polling obviously, so if we win one of the tenders on the horizon, it will be more than enough to cover the cost of an expanded team. If all goes well, we might be able to employ more people."

Brianna gave me a quick glance when she finished. I had no idea she'd done this, or when she'd added this in. It was good that she had, but I didn't like the lack of communication and that she would make decisions without talking to me first. Helen was quiet for a few moments. She clearly liked making us squirm. I clenched my jaw even harder.

"You should have pitched the expanded team to me first and included it within the overall proposition so that I wouldn't have noticed. If you are to step up to director level, you'll need to learn to negotiate better than this."

I caught Brianna's eyes for a second. They looked as enraged as I felt.

"But, since it all checks out, I'm willing to trial it first as an expanded team in Brand and Comms and see how we go. If we do well, and win some big projects, we can keep them and see how we're placed to grow the team. But if we don't, then we'll be looking at redundancies. And not in just those three roles."

No one spoke for a few moments.

"Thank you for going through this in so much detail. This puts us in a good position to move quickly on this. Well done."

Brianna spoke assertively. "Thank you. I'm glad that you think so. Can you confirm when we'll be announcing this to the organisation? If it is today, then we will need to get things organised quite urgently."

"No, no. I've changed my mind. Let's call an all-staff meeting at ten on Monday."

Ah Helen. How she loved to move goalposts and make you work late for nothing. I shook my head at the absurdity of her asks. I also didn't think it was right that she hadn't invited David to this meeting. He was leaving, yes, but he was still here and deserved to know what was going on. I would tell him before Monday, either way.

There was no sense of wrongdoing from Helen. I acted like I approved, but I very much did not approve of Helen's way of doing things.

"Okay, in that case, we'll have enough time to prepare for Monday. Brianna, can you pass me the iPad please?"

As she passed me the iPad, I felt a sense of solidarity with her that I hadn't anticipated I would when this all began. The dynamic wasn't perfect, but it was definitely a lot less painful than what I thought it was going to be. If we'd stayed at each other's throats, I don't know what I would have done.

"Take it away," said Helen.

I launched into our proposal for the health segmentation and spoke passionately about our ideas. I was excited about this project, and I think it came through. I believed we could do a great job and that it would make a difference to people's lives, in the end.

"We'll follow up the extensive qual with nationally representative surveys to validate the findings on a bigger scale. Brianna's team can cross-tabulate the data and generate bite-size statistics for each segment. By combining our efforts, we will make some really impactful findings."

"We know we can do it." Brianna backed me up.

"Ladies this is just excellent."

Brianna kept her eyes on Helen, but I could tell she thought I'd done a good job. It was one of my strengths, so I knew when it had gone well.

"How soon can you have this proposal ready?"

"It's already done," said Brianna.

"We worked on it together yesterday," I said, thinking back to how tired I was last night when we stayed late to finish it. I still felt tired.

"Impressive." She looked away from the screen and at us directly. "Splendid. I can tell this partnership of yours is going to be successful now."

We glanced at each other, now was the time to ask for what we wanted. My mouth was firmly shut. Speaking suddenly seemed beyond me.

"Helen, there was something else we'd like to discuss with you," said Brianna. She sat forward, looking every bit the professional. This was normally the only side to her I saw.

She looked between us with eyes that weren't used to being surprised like this. "With all that we have proposed to you this morning, we believe we have demonstrated the impact Skye and I can have. You yourself have made clear that we are valuable assets. Your suggested approach has its advantages for Your View, and we would very much like to implement all that we have presented to you this morning. However, you can appreciate that these responsibilities are those of a higher grade than we are currently receiving. We both feel," she glanced at me, "that the more appropriate thing to do would be to give us a new temporary job title to reflect the nature of the work we'll be doing."

Brianna sat back, crossed her legs, and casually rested her hands in her lap. She held Helen's eyes in a stand-off, totally holding her own. She was a bit like Helen in some ways. Her composure, self-confidence, and poker face were something to be seen. I gulped, forgetting that I was part of things for a second.

Helen looked at me. We both knew that I deserved it, and that I would never have asked like this.

"Well, thank you very much for the request. I will take it into consideration."

Both our mouths fell open, Brianna momentarily giving away her cool. How could she pass us off like this? I tried hard not to frown and failed. Brianna was scowling.

"Thanks for your time, Helen," I said.

We left the boardroom. As I shut the door behind me, Helen was already back on her laptop. I followed Brianna back to her office, fuming. Brianna had sprung the Brand and Comms stuff on me, which wasn't cool. And Helen was being downright unreasonable. Why on earth had she made us work so fast if she wasn't planning to announce it until Monday? And was she really going to consider our request? I felt like kicking one of the chairs in Brianna's office. Instead, I clasped my hands behind my back and bit my tongue.

Brianna leant against her desk, arms folded. "So, how do you think that went?"

I unclasped my hands and felt my mouth opening in anger. "When did you decide to work up those numbers on the three additional roles?" My tone was hard, and I couldn't help it.

"First thing this morning. It was only a backup in case she started talking about redundancies, which she did."

"You should have told me."

"I didn't have time to tell you."

"Of course you did."

"Didn't it save those people? I thought you'd be pleased."

"I am pleased about that but I'm not happy about you making decisions without me and then presenting them to Helen. If we are going to be a team we have to communicate about these things. You got away with it today, but if you do something like that in front of clients, we won't always be able to cover up the fact that we're not on the same page. It looks bad, and it pisses me off. I want to be able to trust you, but if you're going to pull stunts like that I don't know if I can."

"Geez. I didn't know it would be such a big deal. Like I said it was only a backup plan at the last minute."

My pulse quickened and I had started to sweat. This was stressing me out. I took a deep breath and sat down on the chair that hadn't met my foot. "If we are going to run a department together, we need to run everything by each other first. To talk about everything. There is no other way through this."

Brianna sighed and unfolded her arms. "Okay. I take your point. I should have mentioned it, and I'll run everything past you from now on."

"Great, thank you."

Brianna took off her blazer and hung it up on a hanger. She tied her hair up roughly in a ponytail. It was hotter today, and still humid. I remembered I usually got more irritable in the heat, even if things weren't as tough as they were right now.

"Anyway, can you believe the way she responded after you asked for the change in job title?"

"She's just playing hardball. She heard us."

"Sorry I didn't chip in more."

"It's okay. It got the message across. Without the ultimatum, it lacks a punch, but if she wants to keep us both happy, she'd better take it seriously."

"You did a good job in there," I said, momentarily forgetting that I was annoyed.

Brianna looked at me with a straight face, and then her expression softened and we stood there nodding at each other.

"Thanks," she said, still nodding. "So did you." Brianna put a hand in her pocket. "Do you think she'll go for it? Everything that we put forward? You know her better than I do."

"I think she seemed impressed. She's never impressed about anything."

"I guess all we can do is wait."

"True. And do more prep for Monday. Shit's going to hit the fan and we should be ready. These are people's jobs we're talking about here."

A more serious expression returned to Brianna's face. I liked that she got the magnitude of the situation. We spent the next hour dividing up more tasks for the afternoon and the next day. It was a relief, after all, that Helen had changed the announcement to Monday; we wouldn't have been ready for this afternoon. It looked like Brianna and I didn't need to meet in person until Monday and could do the rest via email. Part of me was a little disappointed I wouldn't be seeing her again for a few days.

What was that about?

She wished me a good evening when I left, and said to get lots of rest, we were going to need it. That was nice. Kind. In so many ways she was proving to be quite different to my initial impression of her.

"Take care, Brianna." I left with a smile on my face.

~ 9 ~
Skye

I took my seat in the front row of the boardroom, which was set up in theatre style, beside Brianna and Hayley. Helen postured at the front next to Jacinda. I clutched my cup of coffee, my third of the day already. Despite the constant chatter, there was an ominous feeling in the room. I turned around to the row behind me to see how everyone was getting on. I was met with polite one-word answers and forced smiles. I gave up and watched Helen, now stalking the room behind the podium.

Brianna and I had spent all weekend working on the plan, albeit separately. Helen wasn't joking when she said the department would be ours to run. She expected us to turn the merger around in a matter of days. If I wasn't so tired I would have been more angry.

Helen addressed the room and it immediately went quiet. "Thank you all for being here." She told them about David's retirement and Simon's departure. The room held its breath. "I hope you will all join me in congratulating David at this time, and at his upcoming retirement party."

A polite applause filled the room. David looked both thrilled about the attention and a little sad. Helen continued. "This has prompted me to assess what is required for us to stay competitive in this market and ensure we are fit for purpose moving forward."

Hopefully David wouldn't take that personally.

"There will be some changes to our two research departments." Helen paused. The room was still eerily silent. "Polling will stay the same. As the country's leading election pollsters, there is no need to change anything there." Hector, Director of Polling, was nowhere to be seen, as usual. Helen continued. "Digital will also continue as normal. Neither will there be any changes to our support functions: Fieldwork, HR, Finance and IT."

An audible sigh of relief could be heard from around the boardroom. Peter, Head of Polling, looked smugger than ever at the news that it wouldn't affect him. They had steady income from the political parties, civil service, and think tanks. Hector was best friends with people in high places. Of course their jobs were safe.

"Research colleagues, Quant and Qual will be merging. You have each been assigned to new roles and new teams within this new structure. There will now be four teams and one research department." Helen then continued with more or less the same speech she gave me and Brianna a week ago. She went on and on about why we needed to make this change, and what she expected from everyone. By the time she'd finished, shock had swept the faces of the actual researchers in the place. Helen filled everyone in on the rest of the details about the changes and the phases and what this meant for jobs. She hadn't addressed me or Brianna yet. When was she going to announce the strange situation she'd flung us into?

"I've asked Skye and Brianna to lead on the merger and deliver the restructure in the first instance. They will jointly be leading the new research department during this interim period before we appoint a permanent director of research. They have already been instrumental in orchestrating this restructure."

Despite the enormity of the meeting and what Helen was saying, I found myself continually stealing glances at Brianna sitting next to me. I was very aware of her movements, too, like when she crossed her legs or clasped her hands in her lap. Her smartwatch flashed up at me at an angle. A heart was clearly displayed, next to a steady fifty-eight heart rate. Damn that was low. Was she not affected by the stress of this at all?

"And to reflect the more senior nature of their roles now, their job titles will temporarily change to Interim Research Director, as they will provide steady leadership as we transition to this new way of working."

Helen glanced down at us, giving nothing away, then asked if there were any questions from the audience. I could hardly believe what I'd just heard. My body felt rigid, and my head felt light. She'd announced it before telling us, ambushing us.

Brianna turned her head towards me. We shared a glance, but I caught enough of her smile to jolt me into believing what I heard was real. I smiled back, and we caught eyes again.

"Well done you two," said Barry popping his head through the row, smiling. "Thoroughly deserved."

We both thanked him as Helen took a question from one of the managers on the other side of the front row. Helen answered but managed to say nothing at all. Management guff. I tried to avoid that type of non-answer as much as possible, but sometimes I'd found myself doing it. Realising this was exactly the type of role I'd be taking on, I listened to her responses. She made it seem so natural. Was I cut out for this level of seniority?

"Skye, Brianna, would one or both of you like to say anything before we close?"

My pulse quickened and my insides twisted. This didn't normally happen any more. I recovered quickly enough to take the opportunity before Brianna did.

"Yes, of course," I said, standing up.

Brianna joined me as Helen stepped back. I really was going to have to share this job with her. Brianna was looking at me with the same icy stare she always used to have.

"Thanks, Helen. Brianna and I are delighted to be given this opportunity. This is a first-rate research consultancy and I'm very proud to be able to lead you through this period of change. I can assure you there will be an abundance of new work we are more likely to win now because of this. It goes without saying that this is a hugely exciting moment for this company." I paused, noting the concern on my colleagues' faces. "I know that today will come as a bit of a shock for our research colleagues, and that it has implications for all of you. Like with any change, it will take some time to adjust to. We aren't making this change for the sake of it, we really do believe it will make Your View better. I urge you to bear with us as we take the research team through this period of transformation. Please know that my door is always open should you have any concerns. That's what we're here for." I felt a sigh of relief go around my team. Satisfied, I ended it there. "Brianna, would you like to say anything?"

Brianna nodded at me. "Yes, thank you, Skye." We swapped positions so that Brianna was now centre stage. She stood tall, with her shoulders back and head held high. "Since joining, I've really enjoyed working with you all and I'm delighted to be staying and taking on the role of Interim Research Director. I'm certain that with this new structure we will improve our way of working." She paused, glancing at me, then back at the audience. "Thank you very much."

"So just how, exactly, are you going to share the same job?" Peter stood up to ask his question, which wasn't necessary. "I hope you don't mind me saying, but this is a fairly unusual set up. Whilst it doesn't affect my department directly, I'm sure I can speak for those involved when I ask about what the plans are for a permanent research director to be appointed? Surely, he will want to come in and make the department his own."

He sat down, as if he'd burst some invisible bubble in the room and was proud of it. Helen glared at him but it was Brianna who spoke first.

"Good question, Peter. I think Helen has quite clearly laid out a process here over the next two months. No one knows these departments better than Skye and I do. And you better believe that we will both be throwing our hats in the ring for the job. But in the meantime, it's our shared department and we are determined to see this period of change through smoothly and as successfully as possible. If you have any more questions on the matter, I suggest you take them up with Helen, directly."

It was understood that no one took matters up with Helen directly. Brianna continued to stand tall, and she held Peter's gaze. She was magnificent. I took great satisfaction in seeing him deal with a strong counter punch. I particularly liked how she made it seem like we were a team. As if the rocky start had never existed. From her display of unity, no one would guess how patchy a coming together we had just gone through. And was that the nicest thing she'd ever said about me? About me knowing my team better than anyone. I liked that too.

One of the managers asked about existing projects and commitments, and if they were going to be involved in the restructure or delivered under the old structure. Helen passed that one onto Brianna and me, and as I was about to speak Brianna got there first. I closed my mouth and checked myself from frowning as I was still standing in front of a lot of people.

"All prior contracts will be honoured in terms of the methodology. The restructure will go ahead regardless of what stage different people are at with current workload."

There was a groan from the audience and a lot of shaking heads in disapproval. Apparently, this was not the answer they wanted to hear. It was the same answer I was going to give, but coming from Brianna, they took it a little worse than I thought they would have had it come from me. It was the way she delivered it. Far too abrupt. I would have wrapped it up in sugar and sold it as a win to all concerned. Perhaps I was better at the hot-air management speak than I realised.

Helen closed out the meeting and thanked everyone for their time and attention. I watched as my colleagues dispersed from the meeting. It was hard to gauge the overall reaction. Some weren't fussed as it didn't affect them at all. They glided out of the room like it was already forgotten. Those who were affected seemed shocked. I knew how that felt, and I wanted to comfort them somehow. I guess I would find out soon enough whether there was going to be a mass exodus or mutiny, or both.

I thanked Helen and nodded at Brianna, then loosened my neck with a gentle stretch. I had a new job title. I found myself smiling and I couldn't help but direct more of my attention to Brianna who had been brave enough to ask for it. Gratitude didn't do it justice.

I owed her big time for this.

Helen addressed us both once everyone had gone. "Well done, you two. Good start. I'm handing this over to you now. I have board meetings and financial matters to deal with all week. Keep me posted on how the merger progresses."

And with that, she left me and Brianna in the huge boardroom alone. Perhaps it wasn't a good sign that everyone had practically fled from the meeting.

Brianna hovered beside me. She didn't strike me as a person who ever hovered anywhere, so I was intrigued.

"Nice job up there," I said. "And thank you for making sure we got that promotion, even if it's just temporary. I'm extremely grateful."

"No problem. I'm glad Helen came around."

"Me too. Onwards and upwards, right?" I smiled. Brianna didn't return it straight away, but I got a small smile out of her after a few moments. I think she liked my positivity, deep down.

"Did you see those looks? You'd have thought we'd just sacked them all," said Brianna.

"They'll come around. Give them time."

"Yeah but not too much time," said Brianna. "We have a lot to do."

I frowned. Knowing that Brianna wasn't as concerned that her team were upset grated on me a little. But since I'd got to know her better I was willing to see past it.

"Well, let's get on with the plan then. They should be getting their emails about now."

"Shall we set up camp in our respective offices? Wait for the return fire?"

"Aye, sir. Or co-sir, right?"

Brianna smiled. I liked seeing her face relax like that. She had an alluring smile; I wanted to see it more.

"Wish me luck with my team," said Brianna, walking towards the door. "I think I'm going to need it."

***

By seven later that day I was exhausted and ready for home. I'd been at Your View for years and this day had been the hardest. Everyone had something to say about the restructure. On the whole, most people in my old team were positive about it. While many had to re-apply for their job, we would create new jobs in the long run. Work was going to come flooding to us. They'd be silly to go elsewhere at a time like this. I fundamentally believed in the merger now and had repeated as much countless times today.

I stayed late to catch up on things now that the office was empty. There was a gentle knock on my door. Brianna came in after my reply. I wasn't expecting a visit. She looked tired. I felt the same. It helped knowing there was someone else going through this.

"Hi. How did it go today with your people?" Brianna sat down on the couch. I checked out the curve of her hips in her tight-fitting suit trousers. She caught me glancing and I casually looked away as if nothing had happened, but inside I felt caught red-handed. I saved the document I was working on then returned my attention to her.

"Exhausting, actually. Don't think I stopped talking all day. It was like I was running an open surgery with back-to-back patients." I sighed. "I think I've smoothed over most people's concerns, but there's a couple of people who are openly criticising the direction. I've allowed them to make tweaks to their job descriptions and I've said I will, we will, take into consideration some of their ideas."

Brianna grimaced. "I've got a situation too. At least three people are not happy about how their jobs are changing. They're demanding more money or threatening to leave. I don't negotiate with terrorists. You shouldn't either."

"No, you don't strike me as the type. And I'm not."

"You're letting them call some of the shots. Helen explicitly said we weren't to do that."

"I know but they're good people and I don't want to lose them."

"Think of the precedent you're setting. It's not something I'd want to let loose. I've specifically not allowed the team to pull us in different directions at this point. It's not going to work if you have. They'll all be looking for it soon, when word gets out. Then we'll be nowhere and Helen will be pissed. You need to nip this in the bud."

I was too tired for this conversation and I was not particularly used to being spoken to this way. To being challenged like this. David usually let me do things my way. Brianna did have a point, so that was infinitely more annoying as I could see I was in the wrong.

"You might have a point. I hope I've not screwed up on the first day."

"Don't worry. Would you like me to help?" said Brianna.

"I'll deal with it," I snapped back.

"Sure. Okay. I'll leave you to it."

Perhaps that was a bit rude. Guilt compelled me to erase my outburst. "Sorry. It's just been a long day. It's been tough on everyone. I didn't mean to be so blunt."

She shrugged, her shoulders never leaving the back of the couch, so her blazer ended up riding up her neck. "You weren't. We got through today, that's what matters. And we got promoted, I almost forgot."

"Me too. Which is so weird. We should be celebrating right now, but all I really want to do is crawl home, put a candle on and have a bath."

"That sounds pretty good actually."

We were quiet for a few moments. I had the urge to walk over and straighten out her jacket.

She looked at me, puffed out her cheeks, and sighed. "Can you believe this is only Monday? I don't know if I've got the energy to come in tomorrow, let alone do all the things."

"I feel exactly the same. We can't both pull sickies tomorrow, can we?"

She laughed. It might have been the first time I'd really heard her laugh and it was wonderful. I wanted to hear her laugh again but had nothing to follow up with.

"That'd be one heck of a mic drop," said Brianna. She sat up and squared her shoulders, then fixed her blazer. She looked smaller tonight, or maybe just a little less guarded. She glanced up at me. Had I been staring?

We said our goodbyes and she slipped out of the door. I stared at the door she'd just gone through. I liked this more relaxed side of Brianna. And I liked that she'd come in to say hello. I shouldn't have snapped at her like that. I felt guilty and wanted to apologise again but didn't want to make things weird. We were getting along well now, and I wanted it to stay that way. It was strangely comforting having her go through this with me. She was confident, and she listened well. I'd been thinking about Brianna a lot lately, hadn't I?

That was normal, right?

My house was cold when I got home that evening. The thick stone walls of my cottage had been in the shade since late afternoon. I prayed my roof was still intact. It needed to be fixed, and soon. I picked up my phone and called my mum. I don't know why I waited so long before talking to her about the temporary promotion, but when I heard her voice I knew I should have told her straight away. "Good things are happening," she said, with happiness and warmth in her voice. "I'm so proud of you, Skye."

She was less thrilled about Helen and her way of doing things, but thankfully she didn't press me on it. She updated me on Arlo's walks, and how he'd nearly caught a squirrel in the woods.

While in the bath I'd so longed for, I continued to think about Brianna. The steam-filled bathroom was quiet, apart from a few drips of the hot tap. I used my big toe to turn the tap off fully. I found it hugely interesting that Brianna and I had reached a new level of communication over the past week. That we were finding this new common ground. Sharing the stress and the increase in responsibility with her had given me this up close and personal understanding of who she was. And she was a good person. She still frustrated me at times, but I think I could see where some of that was coming from now and it didn't bother me as much. From assertiveness and her no-nonsense approach to management, I could no doubt learn some things from Brianna through all this, and that would be no bad thing. I loved learning and I was the first to admit when I was wrong or didn't understand something. If there was a better way to do something I would be on board. I wouldn't dream of letting her know any of this though. I picked up the book I was reading and let the details of my job fall blissfully from my mind, except for the face of one person who still occupied it.

Brianna.

~ 10 ~
Brianna

Not much work was getting done on the floor since the movers had been in over the weekend and had shaken everything up. It was a strange Monday morning, a full week after Helen told everyone about the merger. Friday had been all about packing and goodbyes. Skye had sweetened the deal for everyone by ordering in loads of doughnuts. She and her team had now moved onto my floor in place of my buddies in IT. The weekly senior management meeting had been cancelled, so we could finish the move. It was a mess, with half-unpacked boxes, wires everywhere and desktop monitors not yet in their new homes. There were people all over the place setting things up and moving things around to where they wanted them. For an old building, the floor space was generous, and it allowed for a relatively large open plan office. We'd changed the layout to squeeze a few more desks in, including some much-demanded sit-stand desks. A few of my old team huddled behind their screens shooting grumpy looks at the newbies and the disruption they were creating. I would have to have a word with them about that later.

Admirably, Skye had been good about having to move out of her little den of an office. She was moving into the old IT storeroom, as my office was the only other permanent sectioned off office on the third floor. Barry was technically the most senior IT person but he didn't have a separate office. He spent most of his time in the storeroom, anyway. Simon and David's nearly vacant offices were on the fourth floor beside Helen. The movers had brought up the bulk of Skye's things. I'd checked as soon as I got in this morning. With the door open to my office, I could see straight across to Skye's new abode. She was in there, moving around, with her door open too. We'd agreed to keep our doors open most of last week to invite people in if they needed to talk about the merger confidentially. It had worked well. I'd try to keep it open more often, unless I had a meeting. Apparently, Skye was doing the same.

A loud crash came from her office. I jumped up and strode across the floor to see what it was. I found her crouched down, picking up shattered glass with her back to me.

"What happened?"

She looked over her shoulder. "One of my awards fell. I knocked it with the projector screen thingy."

"Oh no. That's terrible. Here, let me help." I crouched beside her, noting the large chunks of glass stuck onto the tough dark blue carpet and Skye picking at them. Together, we found piece after piece and placed the glass in a small cardboard box.

"I've been in here less than an hour. I hope that wasn't a bad omen."

She was superstitious, which figured. I was not. I didn't believe in things like that. "Maybe you can get them to re-issue it?"

Skye considered this for a few seconds then shrugged. "I've got more important things to do. I'll just have to let it go. Look forward instead of back and all that."

"You have so many awards. It's impressive."

Skye shook her head. "They're no big deal."

We carried on picking up the small bits of glass. Our shoulders brushed as we reached for one of the last pieces. It sent a wave of excitement through me, which I did my best to ignore.

"Thanks for helping me out. That was kind."

"You're welcome. I'm just trying to make a good impression with the new neighbours. I would have brought a pie or something, but it's like ten am."

She laughed at my awful joke. "I feel very welcomed nonetheless, thank you."

"Can I help you unpack for a bit? I'm not particularly doing anything at the moment what with the chaos out there right now." I gestured with my head over to the main floor.

She handed me a box of books. "Sure, be my guest. Want to put these on the bookshelf?"

"Yeah, go on then." I took the box from her and got to work. She had book after book about psychology, management, sociology, social research methods and a whole series of Market Research Society journals. Skye unpacked another cardboard box as I loaded the shelves and flicked through some of her books. She glanced over at me on more than one occasion. I pretended I didn't notice.

"I had them move the bookcase up. There was no way I was leaving that for Barry."

"I hear you. It wouldn't be an office without books, right?"

"Very true."

I got started on the rest of the boxes of books and journals, as Skye turned away and hung up her awards on the wall behind her desk. She hadn't been here long, but it was starting to look like hers again, save the pile of cables in the corner the movers had forgotten to take.

"Nice. You've sorted them by topic." Skye appeared at my side with her hands on her hips looking lovingly at her bookcase.

"Hope that's okay."

"I love it. I used to have them scattered in there at random. I should have known you'd identify a system and do it logically." She stepped back a foot, still scanning. "It's wonderful. I'll think of you and your manual labour every time I look at it now."

I laughed, then bit my lip, wanting to quip back but not take it too far. "I hope you do."

***

By the end of the week, I was dying for the weekend to begin. I'd had enough; although, it had been a good week. Skye popped into my office just after lunchtime again. She'd been popping into my office a lot since she'd moved up to my floor. Despite the strain everyone in the office was feeling in general, Skye and I were buzzing. And we laughed, which was very unusual in my experience in the workplace.

I wasn't expecting anyone this afternoon and my desk was a mess. I did not particularly like spontaneous interruptions. But when Skye approached my desk my irritation fell away and I was glad she was there.

"Hey, you doing okay? You look a bit stressed?"

I took a deep breath. She was right. I did feel stressed. I'd been pushing hard at things for hours. "Is it the weekend yet? It's been a good week, but I think I've just had enough."

She raised an eyebrow. "That's not something I ever thought I'd hear you say. I thought you were a workaholic machine who lives and breathes this stuff."

"No, I do actually have a life."

"Oh sorry, I didn't mean to suggest anything by—"

"Don't worry about it. I like your honesty."

"You should come out for a drink after work tonight. Hayley and I usually go for one or two on Fridays. We can low-key celebrate our new job titles?"

Damn it, I wanted to go. What was becoming of me?

"I'd love to."

"Perfect, we're heading out around five thirty. Meet us in reception?"

"Will do. Hey, what did you pop in for?"

"I was just passing and wondered how you were getting on in here all locked away for so long." Skye glanced at the lunch packaging on my desk.

"I'm fine."

She held my eyes, with an amused look on her face.

"What?" I asked.

"This is your Brianna cave, isn't it?" Her eyes were sparkling. "I'm going to make it my mission to lure you out of here."

"Good luck with that."

Skye smiled kindly and turned to leave.

"Skye," I called out. She turned back to me. "Thanks for inviting me tonight."

She closed the door softly behind her. The next few hours didn't seem so arduous knowing the day was going to end in something fun.

***

At five thirty I found Skye and Hayley waiting in reception. When Skye saw me she smiled with her eyes and gestured for me to join them. This gave me a warm feeling inside. We found our way across the road to the pub. I read the craft beer menu above the bar and ordered a pint of IPA I'd never tried before from a guy with a sizeable and manicured beard. At the bar, squashed in beside loads of people, Skye and I stood close. I had my hand on the bar and she was kind of wedged into my side, facing me. Skye watched me order but didn't say anything. Her face was angled towards mine. Her skin was flawless, and her blue eyes were framed with beautifully shaped eyebrows that gave her a certain sexiness. Up close, I had to admit, she was even hotter than I'd first thought.

She ordered a large glass of merlot and I noticed how her profile was perfectly proportioned. I probably should have offered to buy her a drink but wasn't sure it was the done thing with this crowd. My pint was placed in front of me, and I tapped my card to pay before turning around and leaving the wall of people waiting at the bar. Everywhere I looked, there were people from work. David, pint in hand, stood chatting to the junior researchers; and, for a second, I could picture him as their age, as if no time stood between them at all.

We found somewhere to stand, beside yet more colleagues, and I got that same feeling about hanging out with people from work again. I realised I only agreed to go to spend some more time with Skye and Hayley. Skye had grown on me a lot over the past couple of weeks. I found myself wanting to get to know her better. And Hayley had always been lovely to me.

I loved the hoppy fresh taste of my IPA and drank it like water at first, before a woozy feeling struck me. There was an awkward silence as Skye and I stood drinking our drinks, looking away from each other. I couldn't think of a single thing to say and it looked like Skye couldn't either. Strange, as she was always chatting quite easily to people. Skye was lovely that way, although I sometimes wondered if she tried too much with people and if she was over-compensating for something. Or maybe she was just a nice person and I was an asshole? I couldn't rule out the latter.

Hayley appeared and immediately made a toast to us 'smashing the glass ceiling and all that jazz'. The conversation turned to a discussion on why there were so few women in upper management yet so many at the lower levels.

"It's usually because some women take time out of their career to have children. And some of them don't want more senior positions. Also, men are still seen as more natural leaders, which is bollocks," Hayley said.

"And of the women in higher positions, don't most of them have to sacrifice their femininity to be seen as an effective leader. Take Helen, for example," Skye said. "Workplaces are still hotbeds of patriarchy. Sometimes it sucks having to live in my masculine energy all the time at work."

"It's true," said Hayley. "I feel the same." She took a big drink and kept nodding at Skye.

I nodded, half-heartedly. Workplaces were meant to be professional. Softness and feelings and nurturing didn't have a place at work. Why was it such a big deal to keep them separate?

Skye was quiet after that. She was clearly still thinking about it. She addressed me, intently. "Do you sacrifice your feminine side as a boss, Brianna?"

I thought about her question. Her eyes remained fixed on me. The truth was that of course I did. But I was okay with it. "I don't find it too much of a strain to be business-like and professional at work, I mean, that's work, right?" I paused, shrugging. "But yes. I probably do."

Skye gave nothing away. Hayley nodded non-committedly, her attention somewhere else in the pub now.

"Maybe we can change that," said Skye. "Bring in a more empathetic style of leadership. Start challenging the everyday sexism and calling out the mansplaining. Change has to start from somewhere, right? And why does professionalism and business-like have to mean less empathetic, for example? If it doesn't come from us who will it come from?"

"I totally agree. It's a hard thing to change though," I said.

David walked over to us at that moment and immediately interrupted to ask if we were having a good night. Hayley's eyes darted between Skye and me then she spoke, quickly filling the silence with mundane chatter and great enthusiasm. I half listened and wished I could be more like that. More positive and enthusiastic.

"How do you feel about Skye and Brianna taking over your department?" said Hayley.

"I think it's utterly fantastic," David said. "The future is female. It has to be. No question about it. Us men have messed everything up."

Skye was still quiet, resting against the pillar with her arms folded, listening.

He continued. "And they're a damn sight more attractive than I am so what's not to like?"

"We aim to please, David, what can we say," I said, with a sarcastic tone delivered in a way that only alcohol could produce.

"You girls enjoy yourselves tonight. God knows you're going to be busy these next few months, so take it while you can."

We politely replied to David when he parted, returning his well wishes. His exemplifying behaviour based on what we were just saying before he joined was so stark, it was almost embarrassing. I jiggled my empty glass and thought about getting a round of drinks in.

"You seriously don't think we can do better than that?" said Skye.

Had she been thinking about it this whole time? I quite liked that she had. It was tenacious. Thoughtful.

"I just meant that the capitalist patriarchy doesn't look like it's going anytime soon, but yeah you're right, if we don't keep fighting for change it won't happen. Anything is possible, right?" I said, holding her eyes. I could have stayed just looking into her eyes all day. There was a depth to Skye that I was craving. I wanted to know more about her thoughts and feelings like this, her likes and dislikes.

"What do you guys think makes a good leader?" said Hayley.

Skye broke our crazy long eye contact, slowly, and replied to Hayley. "I'd say that being a good leader is about being able to be uncomfortable. It's got to be, because progress and change come from getting out of your comfort zone."

I nodded, trying to formulate the words to what I'd say was the answer and cursed the strong IPA I'd just downed. "Good leaders listen to their teams, but even better ones listen and then take decisive action. They consult, but ultimately, they know when to make the call, and more often than not it's a good one."

"Yeah, I think you're both right. Is that how you plan to captain the ship? Decisive and uncomfortable?" Hayley said.

"I also think that leadership is about how willing you are to be vulnerable," said Skye, not quite answering Hayley's question, and looking at me. "How else can you be creative?"

"Now that would be uncomfortable," I said.

"I think that you have to look after yourself first and foremost. So many senior managers burn themselves out and then their health starts to struggle, and that's not good for anyone, right?" said Hayley.

"Totally agree," said Skye. "I still want to have a life, and to be healthy."

"The other day, I overheard Peter talking to one of the managers about whether or not I was ready for such a huge promotion, and whether I deserved it, having only been at Your View for a few months," I said. "So I think leaders also have to learn to shut out the critics. You have to accept that they're there, but don't take their criticism to heart."

A look flashed across Skye's face that I couldn't quite place, and then it disappeared. "Well said. And that sucks, by the way, I'm sorry to hear that. He's a bit of a knob, Peter."

I laughed. Hayley said she hadn't been very impressed with Peter lately and could off-the-record confirm she'd had some complaints about his management style. I wondered if she should have been telling us that but decided to give her the benefit of the doubt.

I went to get more drinks for us, leaving Skye and Hayley by the pillar. I waded through the after-work crowd to get to the bar and returned not too long later with the fresh drinks. I found a spot next to Skye and Hayley again and had no intention of finding someone else to chat to. Skye made space for me by her side. I just wanted to be around her. I could hardly take my eyes off her. Realising that while listening to her speak with Hayley was kind of strange. I never knew what she was going to say, and I liked that.

"Right, that's Barry calling me over. I'm gonna go talk to him. You two play nice, all right," said Hayley.

We looked at each other awkwardly as it became just the two of us. I couldn't think of anything to say again that wasn't work related, but I wanted to.

"What are your plans for the weekend, Brianna? Doing anything nice?" Skye asked this question and for a split second I pictured the two of us spending all weekend together in my bed.

Where the hell had that come from?

"Um, I'm meeting up with my brothers tomorrow. It's my mother's sixtieth birthday party soon. We're throwing her a party. It's supposed to be a surprise and we're trying to keep it that way, but we know she's onto us. It's ambitious to think we can keep it from her, but we'll try."

Skye laughed at that and her eyes lit up. "Are you close to your mum?" She leaned in, listening to me intently.

I thought about the question for a few moments. I wasn't. My mother was closer to her politician friends than she was to me. My family was far from functional, and I didn't want to get into it. "We get on well. On the whole. My mother and I are quite similar in some ways."

"I would love to meet her. I'd love to compare the resemblance."

"I don't just mean in appearance, we have similar personalities, although she's much louder and more outgoing than me."

"Then I have got to meet her."

Was she inviting herself to my mother's sixtieth?

"So you have brothers?" Skye said, as if confirming something in her head.

"Yes, two. Why?"

"I don't know," she shrugged her shoulders but in a playful way. "Figures."

"What? How does it figure?"

"Are they older or younger."

"Older."

"Of course. Did you climb trees, play football and be just as good as they were? Then grow up to have crushes on all their girlfriends?"

Wow. She was also spot on. I was speechless. I took a drink of my pint, wondering what specific lesbian stereotype she thought I was. "Something like that." I smiled, and she met it with her own.

I tried not to focus too much on the fact that she was also an out lesbian, but it was sometimes difficult not to. I didn't know what her life had been like, but we shared the experience of what it was to be different from the heteronormative majority at work.

"I knew it."

"I'll also be fixing up my new mountain bike tomorrow. I'm assembling it myself from parts I bought. There won't be a bike like it on the planet."

"No way! So cool."

"Yeah, that's me. I also like fixing up bikes."

Skye chuckled softly. "That's quite the hobby."

"Do you have any hobbies?" I felt like a fresher at university asking that question, but I wanted to know more about her.

"Apart from socialising, I like to read."

"Fiction? Non-fiction? Twitter?"

She grinned. "Fiction, mostly. Or biographies." She hesitated. "Loads of stuff."

"That's a great way to relax. I'm reading a few books at the moment. I say that, but mostly I end up scrolling on social media before bed rather than picking one of them up."

"That can't help you sleep well."

"No, I don't think it does."

"So, you're like a greased up, spanner wielding, fixer upper lesbian, eh?"

"Huh?"

Skye laughed. "Sorry, it's just that I'm totally seeing it now. I bet it suits you, black oil on your hands, a toolbelt. I bet you like taking things apart just to see how they work." She nodded, looking pleased with her powers of perception.

"It is satisfying." Why was I encouraging her? "I don't think 'greased up, spanner wielding, fixer upper lesbian' is a thing."

"Course it is!"

"I think I'd describe myself as a versatile lesbian. Or with no labels. I can feel comfortable in a dress and in a suit, or in my bike shorts. To be honest, I'm most comfortable in my bike shorts."

"That's 'cause they're just more comfortable."

"So now I'm feeling the need to say what type of lesbian I think you are."

"Oh really?"

"Yes. I think you're the well-read intellectual lesbian who in her youth was quite emo."

"Wrong. I was never emo. You are correct about intellectual. Bookish, more like."

"What did you study for your degree?"

"I have three degrees."

My mouth fell open. "Wow. I guessed right then; you are an intellectual."

"I like the sound of that. But no, I just worked hard. I did my first degree in sociology and politics, my master's in social research methods, and my PhD in the sociology of health inequalities."

"That's so impressive." I was blown away by this and wanted to know more.

Skye scratched her head. "So when are you going to try out your new one-of-a-kind bike?"

"Sunday. I'm going mountain biking with some friends."

"Cool. Where do you go?"

"Loads of places. As long as there's hills and good off-road singletrack, we're good."

"Do you do jumps and stuff? Like go down the side of mountains?"

"I wouldn't call them mountains. But yeah, I do ride downhill pretty fast. It's like summer skiing but on a bike and there's no snow."

"How high do the jumps get?"

"Depends on the descent. They can get pretty high."

"In metres?"

"Oh, only about one to one and a half. Maybe two metres sometimes, if I'm really going for it."

"No way! That's insane."

I nodded.

"Didn't know you were such a thrill-seeker." She regarded me closely. "But I can see it in you now. It suits you."

"Yeah, it gets classed as an extreme sport. I've never understood why."

"Because if you fall, you die?"

"Now that's an extreme interpretation. I prefer thinking of it as a calculated risk."

"What do you like about it?"

"Well like I said, I love bikes. Always have. There's something so freeing about going out into the outdoors, cycling for miles and miles. When I'm on my bike, I guess I'm not thinking about much else. And hanging out with friends is pretty good too. It's a great way to spend the day together and catch up."

"That sounds amazing, actually."

"You should try it."

"Oh no, I'd be way too scared to ride a bike over obstacles and downhill."

"You get used to it. Like anything."

She shook her head and took another sip of wine. I watched her lips touch the glass and the wine tip into her mouth. There was a warmth about Skye that put me at ease. I'd almost forgotten we were in a busy pub and there were other people with us. I just wanted to keep talking to Skye and for us not to be interrupted. I finished my IPA.

"And what are your plans for the weekend?" I asked.

"Oh nothing much. Just chilling. Finishing a book I've been reading. Participating in my one nameable hobby."

Skye darted her eyes everywhere else but at me. Was she nervous talking to me all of a sudden?

"It has been hectic at work recently. Having a weekend to recharge sounds pretty good right now."

"Yeah but it's good to do things too. You feel better for it."

"Well you should come biking with us. That is, if you don't make a start on a new book."

"Seriously?"

"Yes, seriously. I'll pick you up and drive us there. I have a bike I can lend you. I can't promise it won't end up raining and be muddy, but I can promise it'll be fun. Come, it'll be good for you. And I always like to convert people to the sport, so I have a vested interest."

She looked at me for a moment, as if gauging something carefully.

"Okay, I'd love to. I won't be any good, of course, but why knock something until you've tried it, right?"

"Great. And exactly."

Why I had just spontaneously invited her to hang out with me and my friends was a mystery to me. I hadn't planned on doing it, it just felt right. I guess I thought Skye would enjoy it and it sounded like she had the time. I also wanted to see her more outside of work like this.

"I won't hold your group up will I though? I imagine they're all hardcore like you."

I laughed. "You won't. Sunday is just an easy ride."

"Says you who cycles into work every day. You're probably all machines. I'll be a wobbly mess."

"I find that hard to believe. You do know how to ride a bike, though, don't you?"

She narrowed her eyes at me in mock indignation. "Apparently you never forget, so yes."

Our conversation felt a like it was turning a bit flirty. It wasn't an unpleasant feeling.

"You'll be fine then. I can teach you the basics of taking corners and using your weight to your advantage. We won't be doing anything too technical. It's mostly about the fresh air anyway, getting out into the countryside, having a laugh and just enjoying yourself."

"Nothing too technical you say? This should be interesting."

She smiled at me again. How had I gone from being mildly to hugely irritated by this person to now wanting to spend my free time with her? Was I so obsessed with my job I now invited work colleagues into my actual life? I shrugged off these thoughts quite easily and found myself looking forward to it.

***

The next day I found myself in another pub with my brothers. Three pints of beer were placed before us, and three hands reached out to pick them up as the waiter departed.

"Okay, so the most important thing about a party is the music. Do you think she'll want a band or a DJ?"

said James, who was one year older than me but acted ten years younger.

Ollie, our eldest brother and father of two frowned. "A band, dumb-arse."

"I just think if it was me and I was turning sixty I'd want a party atmosphere and DJs bring that. Bands are expensive and boring."

Ollie held his drink up. "Here's to another example of your shit taste in music," he swung his drink in the air then put it straight down. "Look, Mum's probably gonna want it to be Joe's band. They were half decent at Uncle William's wedding. Brianna, what do you think?"

I looked between them, amazed they'd started with the music. "It needs to be a band. Joe's band is ideal."

Ollie nodded, once. James shrugged.

"Great. Now we've got that decided, we need to pick a venue and think about getting invites out asap. Seven weeks is not a lot of time. In fact, it's pretty much last minute. I'm happy to sort these both out, if one of you can speak to Joe," I said.

"I'll contact him."

"Thanks, Ollie. That helps. I was thinking of booking a catering company for the buffet. I can give them a call on Monday," I said, hoping that they would let me organise everything and not get in the way.

"And what will I do?" said James.

I considered this for a few moments. James was unreliable and had no experience in this type of thing as far as I was aware. I didn't want him jeopardising Mum's big event.

"Can you get her some flowers? Go to Pollinate's website and order some of the luxury seasonal bouquets.

Some for arrival and some for inside. How does that sound?"

"Yep, I can do that," he said.

"There you go again bossing your big brothers about," said Ollie, shaking his head and smiling softly. It was true, I was weirdly the leader. "Just like Mum."

"This is the next most important gift we can give her aside from graduations, weddings, and grandchildren."

"It would be good if you could chill a bit, Bri," said James.

I sat back and shrugged. "Okay."

James looked at me sceptically. "You serious?"

I laughed and chucked a coaster at him. "No. You're both getting itemised action plans with week by week to do lists."

They both groaned.

I took a sip of beer. "I'm thinking an exclusive country venue, depending on what is available at this point." I could tell from their expressions they were glad I was arranging the venue. I just hoped Mum would be as grateful.

"Ollie, could you get some decorations, balloons, stuff like that?"

"Sure. I'm a pro at that for the kids' birthdays."

I continued. "And I'll find some pictures of her from her life. I'll get them professionally printed and we can plaster them all over the venue."

"I'll get the cake!" said James.

"No way," Ollie and I said at the same time.

"Why don't we both do it," Ollie said this to James. "Two heads are better than one."

"I guess," said James.

"FaceTime me when you're looking at them. I want in on it as well, ideally final say."

"What a dictator," said James.

"Guys. We need to get cracking on this as soon as possible. Earlier the better."

We talked for a bit longer and fell into the easy rhythm of us. Ollie bought fries for the table and we had another beer. James, who was single, evaded my questions about who he was seeing or not seeing, so I knew there must be something going on. I could tell when he was lying just by the muscles in his face. I teased him because it amused me then Ollie told me off.

"You're no fun, Ollie," I said.

"And you're both a pain in my arse. But I love you anyway." A sombre look came over Ollie as he spun his near empty glass on its coaster. "You know Mum and Dad haven't been getting on very well lately."

This, I knew. It had been going on for years though. I disagreed with the 'lately'. "I know. It's no surprise Dad isn't helping to organise the party."

"It's not right that he isn't," said Ollie. "Every time I bring it up he changes the subject."

"He can't be arsed. It's his way," said James. "It doesn't have to mean anything."

"Like when he couldn't be arsed to show up for either of my graduations." My brothers knew I still held a grudge about this.

"At least he's paying for the damn thing," said James.

"How's it going at work, Bri?" said Ollie.

I filled him in on the merger and my hopes to become a director soon.

"You're so going to get it, Brianna. You're the shit."

I gulped, feeling my eyes glaze over. I looked away and got it under control. "Thanks, Ollie. That means a lot."

He took a sip of beer. "Wouldn't have said it if it weren't true."

"Yep, that's our overachieving, competitive, bossy-as-fuck little sister," said James.

I kicked him under the table. "Hey, I heard that."

"You were meant to."

Ollie laughed. It felt like old times. I'd missed this. Our attention turned to another round, which I was grateful for. We left the bar just after eight with a lightness about us and a string of bad jokes.

We hovered outside the heavy double doors next to some smokers.

"How long has it been since we've caught up like this?" said Ollie. "Just the three of us."

"I can't remember the last time," replied James, a little unsteady on his feet.

"Well let's not leave it that long again, okay you two?" Ollie was looking more and more like Dad as he got older. I found it immensely comforting. If only Dad could be as warm and as loving as Ollie.

I play punched his shoulder. "Couldn't if we wanted to. Got Mum's party to plan."

We walked back towards my flat. We left Ollie at the train station to go back to his family in the suburbs. James was going to meet up with some friends, so he walked me home then headed off to the next pub. I let myself in and immediately went to the kitchen and downed a pint of water. I'd had a great time with my brothers. All was well.

Yet it wasn't.

What Ollie said played on my mind. Yes, I'd achieved. Was still achieving. But was it ever enough for Mum and Dad? I was mid-thirties and single. No children. It had been so easy for Ollie. Everything just seemed to work out for him. He was the golden child in Mum and Dad's eyes. He hadn't had to sacrifice his relationships for his career. Hadn't had to battle his way to the top. I loved my brother and wanted the best for him, but my parents had this knack of trying to make me jealous of him. Sometimes, they succeeded. And with James, he was free and happy to live his life. He could do anything he liked and still be praised for it. New girlfriend every Christmas? Fine. Slap on the wrist from the police for possession of some cannabis? Fine. Whereas I had to deal with this immense pressure from them to be the best, be perfect, make them look good, settle down and conform to their traditional stereotypes, find a wife, have children. Thank God they weren't homophobic. At least I didn't have that to worry about.

I washed my hands and felt the cold tiles of the bathroom floor underfoot. My skin was oily and most of my make-up had sweated off. I splashed cold water over my face and for some reason Skye popped into my head. Our conversations in the pub last night replayed themselves over and over in my mind. Something about it felt illicit, like if she knew I was thinking about her on a Saturday night she would laugh at me, or think it was creepy. We were working closely together these days, so I was bound to think about her a little, wasn't I?

~ 11 ~
Skye

Brianna was picking me up at nine. I'd decided to wait outside for her and sit on my garden wall as she could easily miss the turning. The street sign wasn't easy to see from the road because my neighbour's hedge blocked it. I don't know why I accepted the invitation to spend my Sunday with Brianna. 'Curious' was the word that kept coming to me since Friday night. I was becoming more curious by the day to find out who Brianna was behind those icy stares. The past week at work had gone by in a blur, and for some reason, looking forward to spending the day with Brianna away from the office had dominated my mind all of yesterday.

The stone wall was cold, despite the warmth of the day. I had shorts on but I wasn't sure if I should have worn leggings in case I fell off the bike. I was glad of my vest top though. It was perhaps a little too revealing but I was feeling good about myself today. And why not, right?

My tummy was doing cartwheels, however, much to my dismay. I had no idea how to cycle up a mountain, let alone down one. I was also nervous about spending the day with Brianna socially. Or was it excitement? It was hard to tell. I landed on nerves about the extreme sport, as the other thing was more unsettling.

A black Prius went past then came to a stop just out of sight. I nearly missed it. The boot of the car, with two bikes strapped to it and reverse lights on, crept into view as the near silent car returned. An arm rested on the passenger headrest, as Brianna looked over her shoulder guiding the car backwards. I did a little wave then stopped abruptly. I didn't want to seem too keen. Brianna manoeuvred the car parallel alongside the pavement.

When it came to a stop beside me, her door opened and she got out. The person that appeared from behind the car was not at all like the Brianna I knew from work. She was wearing a black muscle tank, loose fitting camo shorts and worn-looking trainers. I don't think I'd ever seen so much of her skin before or maybe it was the casual yet butch edge to her clothes that did it for me. The contrast to her corporate work look couldn't have been starker.

"Hi."

"Hi."

She checked out what I was wearing too. I'd never noticed her doing that before. This must have been as weird for her as it was for me, but hopefully in a good way, as I was a major fan of this version of Brianna. Major.

"Are you ready to go?"

"What?" I was still in a sort of daze at seeing her like this. "Yes. Raring."

"Great." She looked over my shoulder. "Is that your house?"

"Yep." I held my breath. My little nineteenth-century cottage was looking quite delightful in the sun's good graces. Thank God she couldn't see the side of the house with the garden waste I'd yet to clear. Why did I care so much about what she thought?

She continued to survey the front of my house and my garden. Her features were still as she looked closely at everything. I waited for the verdict.

"It's beautiful," she smiled, softly. "Totally you."

My breath caught in my throat. I think I actually stopped breathing for a beat, then forced myself to breathe out.

"Thank you."

"And it's so quiet out here. The city feels a million miles away. And it's not far at all, really."

"It is amazing to come home here at the end of the day. It's my sanctuary. I'm very lucky."

The mention of work jolted me back to reality. I didn't want to think about it. Today was different, and I was going to enjoy it.

"Who's this?" Brianna beamed as the neighbour's cat came stalking towards us along the garden wall.

"This is Malcolm. Next door's little tiger."

Brianna held out her hand and made some kissing sounds. I watched as her lips puckered.

"Hey there, Malcolm," she said.

Malcolm pressed his cheek onto the back of Brianna's hand a few times then sashayed away from her. We both watched him go.

"So cute," said Brianna.

"He's quite territorial. I hear him out here during the night screaming at foxes."

"I didn't know you were such a country bumpkin. Are you into cottagecore, too?" Brianna's eyes sparkled, seemingly enjoying her question.

"I keep it quiet." I picked up my rucksack, and then put my hand on one of the bikes. The metal frame was hot. "Which one did you build?" I ran my finger along the top frame.

"The one you're touching."

"It looks very professional. Such thick tyres. Like a motorbike, almost. And what are these?" I rested my hand on what looked like a huge trophy on the front wheel.

"That's the suspension. They cushion the impact when cycle over bumps and land from jumps."

"That's useful."

"The Specialized is for you. It's a good ride. Smooth, comfortable."

I scrunched up my face unsure of what she meant until I saw the massive writing on the frame. "Ah. The white one. It looks brand new. Thank you. It's so kind of you to invite me out and go to all this effort."

"It's nothing. Don't worry about it."

"Although I'm not sure why I'm thanking you for encouraging me to throw myself down a mountain on wheels."

Brianna smiled. "It'll be fine. I'll show you."

"I can't wait."

She caught my eye for a second then headed to her side of the car. I opened the passenger door and got in. Her car was as spotless on the inside as it was on the outside. She flashed me a gorgeous smile, put her seatbelt on and drove off. Her arm muscles were visible, and I could hardly take my eyes off how strong and lean they were. Her muscly forearms were nothing short of distracting, as were her hands and their steady grip on the wheel.

"You're awfully quiet, should I be worried?"

"Sorry. I think I'm just a little nervous. About the biking."

She glanced over at me. Her brown eyes were both calming and exciting at the same time. She knew what was about to happen, I did not. She was in control, I was not. I could tell she liked that, and I liked it too in some weird way. This was not at all like our usual work dynamic.

"You're going to love this, Skye, trust me."

In her soft but reassuring tone I knew immediately that I could.

"Have you always lived in the country?"

"Yes. I grew up not far from here."

"And do your parents still live here?"

"My parents got divorced a couple of years ago. My dad moved to the city. He likes being near the pubs. I don't see much of him any more."

"I see." Brianna simply nodded, rarely taking her eyes off the road. It gave me time to watch her drive. She had one hand on the steering wheel and an elbow on the armrest in between them, looking very cool.

"How are plans for your mum's birthday party?"

She glanced over at me then, a little hesitant. "They're coming along. I've given my brothers tasks and said no to a few bad ideas. A heavy-duty rave being the worst."

I let out a small laugh, not meaning to.

She noticed but kept going. "We should be on track to put on a great evening for her. In fairness, as long as there's alcohol and lots of it, she'll be happy."

I laughed again.

"What's so funny?"

"Oh, nothing."

She insisted.

"Just that it sounds familiar to how you are at work, but with family who probably aren't keen on taking orders from you. I bet they tease you about it."

"Ha," she exhaled. "You're spot on. Again."

I thought about her comment on her mum and alcohol. It sounded similar to my dad. His drinking had got a lot worse since the divorce. I didn't let that subdued thought linger and instead focused on being here with Brianna. It felt totally different today. There was a lightness to the atmosphere that wasn't there when we were at work.

The rest of the journey passed quickly yet we'd been driving for over half an hour. The mountain flanked car park was busy, with walkers and cyclists of all ages milling around. Brianna parked next to a silver van with stickers on the back doors. Three guys in their early thirties, hovered by the side. Two younger women straddled their bikes talking to each other. There were bikes everywhere. I'd never seen so many bikes scattered around.

"There she is!"

A group of women looked up. Two of the women had short hair and a butch quality. They looked so cool with their bikes and their gear. Brianna gave me a reassuring smile before she got out. It was a kind gesture and I appreciated it. Meeting new people was always a little daunting.

We did the usual introductions, and everyone was welcoming and friendly to me. Brianna's whole demeanour was different. There was an openness to her that didn't show up at work. She looked so relaxed. Like a different person, even. I'd seen glimpses over the past couple of weeks but the difference in her today was lovely. I felt privileged to see it.

I also enjoyed how hot she looked in her biking gear. Not wanting to be caught staring, I turned my attention to the mountains around us and wondered again what I'd got myself into.

"Is this your first time here?" One of the women, Lucy, approached me. She hadn't said as much as the others.

I said that it was. I found out that they were all friends from university, the mountain biking club.

"How often do you guys cycle up mountains together?" I asked, interested.

Another woman, Nicola, answered. "We go riding about once a month, don't we?" She nodded to the others for backup. "Used to be more often but these days it's hard to get everyone together."

"Your fault, mostly," Brianna replied. "You've always got something on."

"Ha, true. We probably go out drinking more than anything now," said Nicola.

"My kind of gang!" I replied.

Brianna turned coy when asked by the quieter woman, Lucy, how we knew each other. 'We work together' was all she said. Somehow I wanted more than that, to be more than that to Brianna, but there was no more. This was the first thing we'd ever done together outside of work, and we'd only begun speaking at work recently because we'd been forced together. We weren't even friends, were we? Didn't I use to dislike this woman? From our conversations since working together, I'd begun to see another side to Brianna, one that I really liked. Lucy nodded again, taking us both in as if she was placing us somehow.

Brianna stepped away and started undoing the straps securing the bikes to the car. I went to help but she said there was no need. She lifted the bikes off together, making it look effortless, and leaned mine towards me, balancing it with one hand. Her toned arms were almost sexual.

"Want to climb on?"

I looked at her. The thought of straddling her crashed into my brain. It shocked me. I should not be having thoughts like that about Brianna Phillips. I stepped forward as she went to grip the handlebars. We did this at the same time and nearly bumped into one another. I leaned into the space we shared, enjoying how easy it felt. So natural.

"The brakes are very sensitive to touch," she said, not letting go of the bike. I watched as her fingers found the metal levers and tapped gently on them. "You don't want to apply too much pressure or you might end up over the handlebars. Less is more."

She had such a safe, trustworthiness about her, like if anything happened, I knew she could handle it.

"Don't brake too hard, got it."

"Here, want to try?"

She let go and moved away. I was far too aware of each of her movements. I swung my leg over the bike and found a pedal. I rolled forward for a few metres. It was unlike any bike I'd ever ridden: sturdy, lightweight and smooth. I lightly touched the brakes and felt the immediate stopping of the bike underneath me. I felt Brianna's gaze on me as I manoeuvred around in a small circle, getting a feel for the bike.

"You're a natural."

"I don't feel like it."

"You look nice and balanced, that's a good start."

I stopped next to her, putting both feet down on the ground. "Thanks."

Brianna gave me a helmet and placed a bottle of water in the holder. She came super close to me as she secured the bottle underneath me.

"Essentials," she said, glancing at me almost shyly.

"Thanks," I said, my words catching in the back of my throat.

I placed the helmet on my head and struggled a bit with the straps and clips to tighten it up. There were so many.

"Here," said Brianna. "Let me help you."

I held my breath as she stepped in close and tugged on the straps by my neck. I cast my eyes off to the side as if I was indifferent to how close she was. She seemed focused on the task and adjusted various clips. It was over very quickly.

Too quickly.

"You ready, Bri?" asked one of her friends.

"Yep, two seconds." Brianna locked the car and put her rucksack on. She moved swiftly, getting on her bike, and beckoning me to join the group, who were waiting on us.

I followed Brianna out to the start of the trails. I was already lagging behind and we weren't even out of the car park yet. We approached a large map of all the trails, and it was so full of different coloured lines I could not take it all in. Plus, we were riding past it, so I didn't get a chance to study it fully. We passed wooden posts marking the start of the trails with blue, red and black markings on them with arrows leading ahead. It was all very professional and scary looking.

"Come on," said Brianna, looking over her shoulder. There was an amused look on her face, but not an unkind one.

Brianna pedalled lightly as I pumped my legs fast and did a little burst to pull up beside her. We cycled for a bit side by side. The others were already pulling away from us. Would she rather be cycling with them?

"I'm not holding you up, am I?"

She tilted her head towards me. "Of course not." She kept her attention on me, which was okay since we were on a wide path. "I'm really glad you came out with us today. With me."

I inhaled. That seemed genuine. I was thrilled to be there too, so the feeling was mutual. That was a good sign, right?

"I like your friends."

"Thanks. They're a good bunch. Plus, they know too much."

I laughed. "Now I'm wondering what they know."

"Lucy is my ex-girlfriend."

"Oh. That's cool."

"We split up a while ago. We're friends now. It's all good."

We both smiled, and Brianna looked away. I pondered this. I was naturally curious about people, it was my job after all, but with Brianna it was becoming more than simple curiosity. It felt important that I get to know her better, somehow.

Arriving at the start of what looked like a narrow path zig-zagging up the side of a hill, I frowned, feeling unsure. The others took the path and cycled up. I must have been showing my feelings on my face because Brianna read my mind.

"Put it in a really low gear and let the bike do the work for you. It's a lot easier than it looks."

I gulped, not quite believing her. "Thanks. I hope so."

Brianna slipped onto the path and floated, it seemed, upwards.

"Just follow me. And don't think too much about it."

I nodded, fully intending to follow her advice.

And upwards we went.

Through the trees, past the viewpoints, and along wide paths and singletrack. I fought hard to keep up with her, and just about managed it. My heart was pounding and my legs were burning. It was okay, though. I enjoyed a good challenge and this was certainly that. Thank God I worked out a bit, so I could handle this. Cycling up an actual mountain with the fresh air and wheels softly churning over the dirt trail felt like such a privilege. She had a knack of staying just out of my reach. I wasn't sure if she was intentionally doing this to set the pace or not. Either way, it was working. It dawned on me that I was trying to impress Brianna with my ability to keep up.

What was even happening to me?

We got to the top of the hill as I was about to pass out. By this point, my feelings towards Brianna had turned slightly resentful. Who would do this voluntarily? Who would invite someone to this? I gritted my teeth and tried not to let my heavy breathing seem too loud. I failed. I couldn't help but exhale and since it was silent it was so obvious. Brianna's breathing was a bit more laboured now too. It sounded almost sexual.

Why was I thinking like that about her breathing?

Up Against Her

She looked over her shoulder at me and gave me that gorgeous smile again. In that moment I forgot I was pissed off. Ugh, this was confusing.

The gang were waiting there by the picnic tables at an opening at the top of the hill, chatting.

"Need that granny gear to get up here again, Bri?" said one of her friends between bites of an energy bar.

"Nothing wrong with enjoying the scenery. It's not a race."

The others were drinking from strange bags with tubes coming out of them. I'd just about got my breath back as Brianna gestured for us to sit down at a wooden picnic table. I landed on the bench hard and took off my helmet, glad to be rid of it. My head felt sweaty and gross. The panoramic views of the forest and hills were breathtaking. Now the effort to get up here felt completely worth it.

Brianna got out a silver flask and a Tupperware box of chocolate brownies. She placed the items on the cracked, weathered picnic table as if this was normal. A little plastic mug wrapped in kitchen towels came out of the bag last. Had she brought the extra mug for me?

She lifted her eyes to mine. "Hungry?"

"Uh, yeah," I said, with emphasis. "I can't believe you carried all that up here in that tiny little bag?"

"It's more spacious than it looks."

"Hey, we're going. Are you guys ready?" said Lucy.

"I think we're going to rest here for a bit," Brianna said.

"See you at the bottom, slow coaches." Lucy winked. "Only joking. Take your time, we're going to hit the black route, so we'll be a while anyway."

Brianna jokingly waved her away. "She's never been one to linger at the top," Brianna said to me. "She always wants to get going to the downhill section. To the 'fun bit'," she said, using air quotes. "I think if you've taken the effort to ride up a mountain, you should enjoy the views at the top. Especially when they're as beautiful as they are today."

We held extra eye contact as she said that last part. Was she flirting? I felt a little giddy and had to look away. This was absurd, of course she wasn't. She was talking about the view.

I looked up at her and smiled then faced the view again. "I agree. It is really beautiful up here."

She continued. "Going downhill is over so fast. I like to savour the moment. Take my time before it's all over in a flash."

"You're saying you like the build-up?"

"It's the best part of anything, am I right?"

"I don't disagree."

We held eyes again. That felt like definite flirting. This was insane.

"Coffee?"

"Sorry?"

"Coffee." Brianna held up the flask. "I thought you might like some. I've seen how you get through them at work."

She'd noticed something about me. I don't know why I found this flattering. Or exciting. Possibly both. But I did.

"Please."

The little cup was indeed for me, as she poured some coffee in and passed it to me. We sat in silence for a while, just looking out at the view, sipping coffee and eating the brownies. It was comfortable. I tried not to think about having to get down a mountain in order to go home though.

It was me who broke the silence. "It's funny, I live in the countryside but consider myself more suited to city activities, apart from doing my garden. Whereas you live in the city and seem really outdoorsy. Have you ever thought about moving out to somewhere with more space? Nearer to where you can go biking?"

"Not really. I love living in the city. The people, the culture, the buzz. And I love coming to the country. For this, for walks. To breathe. It's all on my doorstep so it's not really an issue."

She sipped some coffee and turned her attention to the view. She seemed a little sad, which was at odds with what she'd just said. I really didn't know her well enough to know why, but I already knew that I wanted to, that I cared. How could I have ever been unfriendly to this woman before? How could I have got her so completely and utterly wrong for six months? The person before me now was sensitive, kind, clever and fun to be around. Not the cold, manipulative shark I'd pegged her for. I thought I was a good judge of character but apparently not. I was going to have to seriously rethink my value system given that I'd got her so wrong.

"Brianna, there's something I need to say to you."

Her eyes were hesitant. "Yeah?"

"I wasn't just a bit difficult with you when Helen announced the merger, and we both know it. I haven't been as friendly towards you as I should have been since you started. It must be tough starting a new job, not knowing anyone, and the least I could have done was be welcoming. I'm sorry."

Brianna's eyes were wide. It looked like she was struggling to respond.

"Sorry, I know that's come out of nowhere and we're not even at work. I don't mean to talk about work, but I felt I needed to further clear the air and apologise to you. You've been lovely to me since we've been working together and I'm not entirely sure I've deserved it."

"Wow. Okay." Brianna paused. "Truth be told I was a little hurt by you. You didn't seem to like me very much and I didn't know why. So, I wasn't particularly keen on you either."

That hurt. Why did that hurt so much?

Brianna looked deep in thought. There was so much more to this conversation than either of us was letting on, I could tell. I could see that I'd excluded her. That I'd made things more difficult than they needed to be.

"It's totally understandable you didn't like me either. I was a dick to you."

She gave a small smile in recognition. Her guard was down. She seemed so vulnerable and real. Why wasn't she more like this at work? Why all the armour? I wondered this, but now wasn't the time to ask.

"So what was, or dare I say, *is* your problem with me?" There was no hint of anger or malice in her voice, only interest.

"I have no problem with you any more," I said quickly. "Though you do have questionable tastes in hobbies."

She laughed. I breathed out. We were still on good terms. I could feel a safety present in it that was quite freeing.

Up Against Her

"This feels so silly, because I know you now," I avoided her eyes. "I thought you were cold and I thought you were untrustworthy."

"Oh. Go on." She was looking at me dead on, and I felt the weight of her stare. But the only way through this was with the truth.

"And I wasn't overly thrilled with your approach. You came in like you owned the place and I guess I was annoyed. I've been at Your View for years, I'd built up the relationships, and set the groundwork for someone like you to come in and flourish. You were amazing from day one and the complete opposite to me in every way and, since I'm on a roll now, I guess I felt threatened by you and your brilliance."

Oh God.

Brianna put her hands down on the table, not at all far from mine. "So you acted like you hated me but in reality you thought I was … brilliant?"

I bowed my head feeling naked. I could not believe I'd just said that out loud.

"I like this information." A smile appeared on Brianna's lips. "I wish I'd known sooner, and I would have invited you to lunch."

I grimaced. She was right. That would have probably worked. Had I just wanted her to make more of an effort with me and be my friend? And then taken the huff when she hadn't bothered. I scratched my head, feeling like a five-year-old.

Brianna crossed an arm over her tummy and was stroking her jaw with one hand as if lost in thought. "We do have opposite styles. I can see how my Type A work personality would have hit a nerve with you. I stepped on your toes and you didn't like it. It makes perfect sense now."

My shoulders felt up near my ears as I waited for a sign from her. This didn't feel over.

Brianna's face softened towards me like she was seeing me for the first time properly. "It's not that bad, really. I'd probably have reacted the same." Brianna finished her brownie and I finished my coffee. There was no breeze on this mountain top but I could have done with one. "I'm really glad we talked about this, Skye. Thank you for being so forthright with me. I like that in a person." She wiped her hands on a tissue then reached across the table and put her hand out for me to shake. There was a sincerity in her eyes that I loved. "Friends?"

I looked at her hand and took it in mine. Her hand felt strong and her skin was soft. The perfect combination.

"Yes, friends."

We held onto the handshake for a few seconds longer than necessary, smiling at each other. Slowly, she took her hand away but kept on smiling at me. I instantly missed the feel of her hand on mine.

Brianna swung her leg over the bench and casually straddled it. Strands of her hair had fallen forward, framing her face. My eyes drifted along her jawline to her mouth, and her full lips. Were they as soft as they looked? Like her hands?

This was crazy.

"Will you promise me one thing though?"

"Yes, anything."

"Can you keep on doing those eye-rolls of yours after I've said something in a meeting and it's all super tense? I've grown kinda fond of them."

"You want me to keep rolling my eyes at you?"

She laughed. "Maybe. It's our thing, right?"

I was speechless. I found myself laughing a little and doing an eye roll, but not consciously.

"See! Just like that. Keep 'em coming." Brianna was teasing me and I liked it.

"Are you ready to get going?"

She stood up and I got up too. After this chat I would have gone anywhere with her, so headfirst down a mountain somehow made sense.

"I'm ready."

She smiled, and we held eyes again standing beside the picnic table. Had she got even more attractive or was I seeing her anew? I felt my heart rate increase and noted the spark between us. The hot weather was not helping with any of this.

"So, we've been going up the red route. It's like a medium level route. The black route is for experienced riders, and the blue route is more accessible for everyone. We'll take the blue route and start meandering downhill. Just take it easy and like I said, keep your weight back on the bike and don't brake too sharply."

"I think I'd like to stay on the red route. I don't need a baby route to get me off the mountain. I'll be fine." Where had my newfound confidence in my ability to do an extreme sport come from?

"Skye, it's really steep. There are slippery root branches and narrow singletrack. I'm not sure you're ready for this yet."

"I'm ready."

She grimaced.

"I'm a fast learner. And I'm already feeling more balanced on the bike. Better to rip the plaster right off and get on with it. I wanna do it."

She looked at me as if gauging my seriousness and after a while seemed to give up. "Okay. If this is really what you want."

"It is."

"Do you remember what I said?"

"Yes, Ma'am. Got it all."

She laughed, awkwardly. Uncertain even. "Take it slowly. I'll go first, so you know how to pace it."

"I'll follow your lead."

Brianna packed up her bag, put her helmet on and climbed onto her bike.

"Right," I climbed off the bench, feeling my muscles already stiff but life coming back to them. The sugar and caffeine had given me a boost. "Let's do this." Standing up, I took one last look at the view and realised how high up we were. A momentary feeling of fear hit me, like when I was child and had climbed up something too high that didn't have an easy way down. Brianna smiled at me again, and it passed. It was such a reassuring and beautiful smile. I could look at it all day.

"There's a break in the descent not far from here. We'll re-group there and see how you're getting on."

She was worried for me, I could tell. I liked her concern, was that bad? The obstacle in front, not so much. But I wanted to do this. I wanted to show her, to prove to her, that I was also cool and capable. That I could handle this like I could handle challenges at work. Was I still competing on some level?

She set off in front of me, down the first slope, which was way bigger than I was expecting. Brianna handled her bike and the descent like a pro, going into the air and everything. I hovered at the edge while she shouted for me to come on as she took a corner with ease. I gulped and started pedalling. The ground fell out from under me and I was away. It levelled out and then another drop came up straight away, which I rolled down. I fought for balance, feeling my thighs already burning, hovering so low and far back on the bike. I found my way and began taking the descent with greater ease. The wind rushed past my cheeks, reminding me of how fast I was going. Brianna was up ahead, stealing quick glances over her shoulder at me. She seemed totally at ease, and very sexy in those shorts. I saw a bigger drop coming up and took it with ease. The sensation was thrilling – fast, exciting, and slightly dangerous. I loved it. I wanted more but we arrived at the end of the track on a flat stretch, where Brianna was waiting for me. She stood with her bike resting between her legs and her hands on her hips. The superhero pose was not lost on me. I stumbled a little as I came to a halt, which was annoying considering the stunt work I'd just surprised myself with.

Brianna clapped. "Here she is. How did you find it?"

"I loved it, and … I didn't die. I call that a result!"

"You're quite the natural."

"It was a total fluke, let's be real. But I want to go again, see if I can shift my weight back a little further and take it a bit quicker." I paused. "I think I used the brakes more than I should have."

"I knew you would."

"The way you flew down that was something else. You were amazing. And by amazing I actually mean crazy and reckless."

"I know my strengths and weaknesses on the bike and on the slopes. I only take calculated risks. I'm always in control."

"Sure, but you must enjoy the thrill of it?" I raised an eyebrow.

She laughed. "Okay, you got me. I'm an adrenaline junkie. I think on one level you've got to be to want to throw yourself down a mountain like this. To be fair, my friends *are* all nutters so that probably says a lot about me too."

"Well, I like trying a new flavour of herbal tea every now and again. Really feel like I'm living it up, you know."

Brianna laughed.

"Oh Brianna, this is all such juicy news. You're the most cool, calm, and collected woman I've ever met but a thrill-seeker at heart."

We held eyes again after I said this. I don't know if it was the wild and remote setting or the subject of our conversation, but I felt something pass between us in that moment. Something real and something flirty again. The air between us felt thicker now. Why did it feel like we'd spent the whole day flirting? Was this all in my head? I reset my pedals so my right foot was higher. Brianna kept gripping her handlebars like she was on a motorbike revving the engine.

"You look like you're dying to get going."

"Shall we?"

I stayed back for a moment and watched her pedal away a few metres. Time slowed down. I stood where I was and took a sharp intake of breath.

Oh my God.

I had a crush on Brianna. That's what this was. That fluttery feeling in my stomach, not being able to take my eyes off her, the pounding heart when she came to pick me up this morning – all screamed of one thing. The thought itself was ridiculous.

Developing feelings for Brianna was out of the question. It could not happen. There was no way I could let myself go there. No way. This was my career we were talking about. I thought about my mum and all our financial troubles. I took a deep breath and sighed. Attraction came and went; I'd have to sit this one out.

Brianna looked over her shoulder and called out to me.

"You coming?"

"Yep."

~ 12 ~
Brianna

It was Monday morning and my week was getting off to a great start. Strangely, I was happy being back at work, after a fun and somewhat unexpected weekend. I was relieved that things were falling into place with my mum's birthday party, and I felt renewed after a day on the bike with friends.

And the best part of it was the time I'd spent with Skye. I found myself thinking back to our chats and reliving the whole day again with her. I smiled to myself. I'd been doing this all last night: in the shower, while making dinner, when I went to bed. I couldn't stop thinking about her.

She was funny and open to trying new things, namely extreme sports, and I liked that. She was a trier. Everyone liked a trier, didn't they? And she was brave. I couldn't believe it when she'd asked to go down the red route. I was worried about her safety but didn't want to start our friendship with an argument, so I'd let her do it. And she'd surprised me, again, as she'd been doing so often since we started working together. She'd been so warm and positive and a pleasure to hang out with. The opposite of what she'd been like at work to me. I liked the way she got on with my friends and was so easy to be around. She was a decent person and I could see us being good friends.

At my desk trying to reply to emails I kept thinking about Skye. We were different, but that was okay. Any niggles I might have had about her approach to things at work would have to remain just that, niggles. She thought I was cold, but all I'd seen from her at the beginning was coldness. Part of me had resented her for being so unfriendly towards me when I first started. After her sincere and thoughtful apology on the matter, however, I was completely over it now. I respected the fact that she addressed the issue head on, too. Plus, we clearly had fun yesterday so all that iciness between us had thankfully thawed.

Also, we just got each other. In my experience, the workplace was dominated by boring heteronormativity. I could count on one hand the LGBTQ+ colleagues I'd known in jobs. After I'd found out through the grapevine that Skye was queer too, even though I didn't know her, I found it comforting. Even through all those icy moments, I'd still felt this unspoken understanding. That despite our differences, we knew we had that in common, at least.

Lucy had asked me at one point if we were together, which I'd waved away with an indignant, 'what makes you think that?' reply. This was after we'd got to the bottom of the mountain all smiles and endorphins. I was relieved Skye had made it safely down in one piece. The group had been waiting for us and watched us ride in on our high. Lucy had watched the situation, as she does, then sidled up next to me when I was on my own to ask her question.

I cupped my chin and jaw in my hand. I unlocked my phone and swiped to the pictures Lucy had sent around our group chat yesterday, landing on the one where Skye and I were talking. She had her head back laughing and I was gazing at her with soft gooey eyes. She looked amazing in those little shorts and vest top. I'd found it so hard not to look downwards when she was leaning forward on her bike and her cleavage was quite visible. Since Lucy was very astute and a good judge of character, her comment had got me thinking. Was there something between Skye and me?

I'd texted her last night to see if she was okay after the mountain biking but she hadn't texted back. I assumed there would be a good reason and tried not to think about it. I was trying not to let it get to me, but it had. I'd checked my phone constantly, feeling a pang of disappointment each time there was nothing there.

I got back to work and checked my calendar for the week. In it was meeting after meeting with Skye, the first of which started in less than thirty minutes. My head was no less clear by the time I got there and took a seat next to hers near the top of the boardroom table. She was busy setting up the screen for the other offices to join by video conference, but I recognised her notebook and favourite mug. She must not have noticed me because she didn't say anything when I sat down.

"Hey, good morning, Skye."

She glanced over at me as she plugged in another cable. "Hey, morning." She sounded distracted.

"How are you feeling after yesterday?" This was pretty much what I'd asked in my text. I felt stupid asking it again but my desire to talk to her outweighed this.

"I think you broke me." She winced as she bent down to move a cable out of the walkway at the front of the table. "My legs are like dead weights. I can hardly walk."

"Um, yeah, I wondered if you might be feeling it today. Sorry about that. Day two's probably going to be worse than today. You'll be fine the day after tomorrow."

"I hope so." She didn't look at me as she hobbled to her seat and slowly sat down, bracing her descent to the chair with her hands. Was she annoyed about how much pain she was in today? Did she blame me?

I swallowed, feeling like our interaction hadn't gone quite the way I would have wanted. It was as if we hadn't spent the day together yesterday getting on well and having a great time.

She felt *distant* today.

The room had filled up and everyone was ready to start. Skye stretched her arms up, opening her body out, and addressed our colleagues, chairing the meeting. "Good morning, everyone. I hope you're all well and enjoyed some of that sunshine over the weekend. Shall we get started? There's a lot we've got to cover."

This was our weekly senior managers meeting and the first time one of us had taken the lead. We'd discussed already that Skye would go first, and my turn would be next week. I noticed it was full of men, apart from us, and Hayley.

Skye went into full professional mode and remained perfectly calm. After yesterday, I felt I knew her so much better. I was mesmerised by her as she talked and the way she not only commanded the room but created a safe and light-hearted space for all of us. Before, I'd found this inefficient and wondered if it was genuine. Now, I could see that she had a way of getting what she needed from a meeting, all the while being true to herself. She seemed like she was able to bring her feminine energy into her job, and I respected her for it. I'd been wrong to dismiss her method before. As she talked, I jotted down some of these thoughts and observations in my notebook. I wanted to remember everything that happened during these two months. I needed to know who I was working with. Inside and out.

Skye turned the meeting to financial matters and presented her new approach to monitoring expenditure on existing projects. I could see from the room that our colleagues weren't happy about these changes, particularly Andrew, a manager in Skye's old team who had scowled at Skye the entire time she was talking. Even I was being put off by it. What was his problem anyway?

Andrew piped up. "Any idea how we're supposed to use this in reality? These ideas are all well and good but they don't actually make sense or look like they will be very helpful in practice." He threw down his comment and looked as if he expected this to knock Skye off her stride. He smirked at a guy to his left, and they shared a knowing look about this. Andrew had been one of the few people to openly criticise Helen's decisions – and us. So far, I'd been ignoring him, given that we were so busy getting on with it.

Skye hesitated. She stuttered a few times before asking him to explain again exactly what his issue was with it. He said he wouldn't know where to start because what she had suggested was so nonsensical.

I'd had enough. We were the bosses, not him. I raised my voice just enough to get everyone's attention. "Okay, Andrew, thank you for feedback. However, I'll remind you that this change we are implementing to managing project finances has come from both Skye and me and is not up for discussion. As Skye has already outlined, you can refer to the guidance document that we've pre-prepared and will be sending around straight after this meeting. You can also get in touch with either of us for additional support if you are struggling to pick it up."

I held his gaze and he backed down. Andrew had no comeback and simply nodded. Being the boss had to have some perks, didn't it? But I was confused by how poorly Skye had handled him. Maybe this job would be mine after all.

The rest of the meeting went well, and Skye did a better job at handling the meeting after that. I hung back to talk to her as she switched off the television and returned the room back to normal. I wondered if this was something an Interim Director should be doing, and if any of our male colleagues would bother tidying up the room up afterwards. I know I always left it to the office administrator to clear up.

"That was awesome, Skye. You did really well chairing that meeting."

She stopped clearing up the room and looked up at me. Her cheeks were flushed red and the skin on her neck looked blotchy. "Thank you, Brianna. But I think we both know I didn't, and don't, handle Andrew well."

"He was out of line. I think we need to monitor his behaviour. I don't want his attitude to spread to others."

"I agree. You sure put him in his place. It was really something. Thank you for doing that."

I checked there was no one hovering by the door as I was in the mood to vent about him. Seeing that we were alone I decided to speak my mind. We were trusting each other now, right?

"I don't get why he thinks he can speak to you like that, you're his boss."

"He's not happy about the merger or about our appointment, even though it's temporary. Neither is Peter. Peter thinks it should have been him. He's been hinting at switching departments for a while."

"They're both entitled. You completely and consistently outperform Peter. All his clients are on a retainer. Political polls are easy money. He hasn't brought in any new work since I've been here, anyway."

"True, but his clients are household names and he rubs shoulders with people who have a lot of power. Part of me was a little surprised Helen didn't choose him and merge all three departments together."

I tilted my head. "Skye, you've got to be kidding me. You're fantastic at what you do. Really. Talented. And you deserve this opportunity, just like you deserve to get an interview for the director position. You do know that, don't you?"

"Steady on, Brianna, I thought we were rivals. Anyone would think you were in my corner rather than going up against me."

"I just think we will do better if we support one another. For real." I meant it. Hopefully she got how sincere I was about this. We held each other's eyes. Not once did either of us break the connection.

"I do too." Skye said. "One of us better get this job. I'd much prefer that than someone from outside. Or Peter."

We continued to hold the eye contact. I meant what I'd said, and it looked like she did too. Her eyes were intense and I wanted to stay there, lost in them. The room filled up with the next meeting, and we were jolted out of our chat. We left the room together. Skye held her laptop to her chest. "See you for the pitch this afternoon?"

"You bet. I can't wait to see our star pitcher in action."

Skye's eyes were confident. "I've got a good feeling about this one."

***

My laptop bag waited at my feet in between my high heels. Our car was due in a few minutes. I liked being early for things. For me, it was about keeping my word with myself and others.

The pick-up area was to the rear of the office by the bike racks. I looked longingly at the sea of bikes crammed together, in their silent tussle for space, and rested on my own custom-built road bike. I loved that bike. It was another clear and sunny day, and I would have much preferred being out on it this afternoon than going to a client meeting to pitch for a new project. That said, this new project held a lot of potential, and I was excited for what Skye and I had to present. We'd worked on the pitch all week and I had to admit, it was good. Like Skye, I also had a good feeling about it.

The heavy door to the building opened slowly and out walked Skye. I felt my mouth drop open and could not take my eyes off her. She had changed, and freshened up for the afternoon, with new smoky-eye make-up, lipstick and hot-as-hell high heels.

"This look," I said, openly appreciating Skye's powerful outfit, "I approve."

"You look pretty good yourself," said Skye, taking in my well-fitted suit and matching heels. "It sucks that looking pretty and feminine makes us more likely to get the contract. But let's hope it does the job anyway." Skye said this so matter-of-factly. I adored her for it.

Our contract car pulled up. We got into the backseat of the plush Mercedes and said hello to Gary, our regular driver. It didn't take long to arrive at the government building, and as we gave our names at the reception desk, I felt nerves in the pit of my stomach.

We found seats as I fumbled to pin my pass to my suit jacket. Sitting down, pass fastened correctly, I watched the clock, grateful we were early. This pitch had to go well. We'd worked so hard on it and given that I was with Skye, who rarely came away empty handed, I was a little worried failure would reflect more badly on me.

Skye faced away from me in the reception area. The drive over was mostly silent, too. Skye had barely looked at me the whole journey. She just gave me a couple of one-word answers when I'd asked her something about the meeting. I rubbed the back of my neck. What was wrong with her today?

We were picked up by Josh, a civil servant who looked nothing like a civil servant – late twenties, casual, cool. We were so dressed up compared to him.

The room was bright and lacked any personality, but it was modern and relatively well maintained for a government building. We shook hands with our clients and got straight into it. I kicked us off, like we'd discussed, and then handed over to Skye to present her section. Our audience seemed attentive and nodded a lot, which I took as a good sign. Skye rocked her part, even I was convinced, and I'd heard it all before. She was amazing and spoke with such confidence. At the Q&A

we handled most of the questions fine, but one came in about the capacity of our company to handle such a large-scale longitudinal study. Skye flicked back to one of her earlier slides.

"This is something we've thought about already. Our company is currently undergoing a restructure, and we have set out a ten-point plan to improve efficiencies in our operating model. Through this, we will be increasing our resources and be in an even better position to take this project on."

"That's all very well but we need this project to start as soon as possible. It sounds like you won't be ready."

Skye levelled with the question asker, a man in his sixties, perhaps, with a long grey beard.

"You're correct. We won't be fully ready but we don't believe that's necessary in order to get the wheels in motion for this huge, game-changing study." She referred to another of her earlier slides to emphasise the point. I thought about contributing, but Skye was handling this better than I could have.

I stayed quiet.

"We are able to start now, as you can see from our logic model, and do have the capacity to complete the first stage. By the time the second stage is due to start we will have the capacity to run this nationwide. As I said, we believe our approach is not just fit for purpose but disrupts traditional methodologies. Yes, there is a slight risk in going with us, but you will not find a better designed study anywhere else. Our offer is progressive and the intellectual property behind it is already in place. Finding enough workers to do the grunt work will not be a problem, I assure you."

The grey beard nodded in approval, visibly impressed by what he'd heard, as was I. "Thanks for that."

The rest of the pitch went smoothly, and we found ourselves in the backseat of the car again. I was still buzzing from the thrill of it.

"I think we've got it. That went really well," said Skye.

"I do too. Skye, you were amazing. Now I know what everyone is talking about."

"Well, these are my lucky heels," she looked down at them, "I wear them to every pitch. Winning formula every time."

"Hmm. It's that, is it? Are you sure it's not your brain and your influencing skills?"

"Nah. It's totally the heels."

We laughed. It had been a success. We made a great team and it felt good. I had fun, even, and it was work. Skye did that for me, she lifted me, and I felt stronger for it.

By the time we got back to the office people were packing up for the evening. Lynn welcomed us back like heroes returning from battle. She said Helen had asked for us to pop into her office when we got back. Skye and I looked at each other. Lynn reassured us that Helen was in a good mood. She and her husband had won big at the horse racing over the weekend, and she was still in celebratory mode. Helen and her husband were big players on the circuit. And big spenders. They attended Royal Ascot every year, too.

"We'll head up now," said Skye. "That okay with you?" I was about to reply that it was when Skye's phone buzzed in her pocket.

"Just a sec."

Lynn watched us closely. I hadn't noticed before that she'd come out from behind the front desk to stand next to us. Skye took her call and held up a hand. She clenched her fist and said now was a good time to talk. Her face lit up and she thanked the caller for their getting back to us so quickly. She'd barely tapped off the call before she spoke next.

"We got it! That was them. They loved it. They want us to start as soon as possible."

I pumped my fists in the air. "Yes! That's amazing news." She raised a hand to high-five me and I didn't want to leave her hanging so I reciprocated. Our hands struck each other at the perfect angle and time, and the satisfying loud clap was evidence of this. It felt good to meet each other's energy like that. Something fizzed between us.

Lynn squealed and jumped up and down a couple of times. "Helen's going to be very happy." She beamed. "Well done, you two. Dream team."

"It was all Skye. She kicked ass in there."

She blushed a deep red then smiled such a beautiful and gorgeous smile directly at me. Was it for me? "This one was the both of us," she reached out and squeezed my arm. It jolted involuntarily. Her touch was electrifying. She saw my bodily reaction and part of me cringed, though a bigger of part of me took comfort in her affection, which after today was rather confusing.

"Come on, let's go tell Helen," Skye said.

***

Later that evening I stretched out in my bubble bath with a contented sigh. I sipped some white wine and watched my favourite candles flickering on the windowsill. Helen was impressed at our win and said we were already doing her proud. The relief this caused in me was not insignificant. Success felt good. And it was to be enjoyed.

When Skye had said goodbye for the evening, I'd felt disappointed. Like really disappointed. I'd wanted to go for a celebratory drink or two, or even dinner with her but she said she was meeting a friend.

I'd wanted to spend more time with her. I'd wanted to ask why she'd been so cold for most of the day. The impact of this was not lost on me. Could it be that I was feeling something for Skye? I dipped my head under the water then sat upright. I pondered the question as I put shampoo in my hands and massaged it through my hair and scalp. Yes, we'd got closer since working together, but wasn't that just a natural thing that happened when two people got along well and realised they could be friends outside of work? While there was a lot more to learn about each other, the potential was there to be good friends, if that was something Skye wanted. I could so see Skye joining my biking friends and me for drinks, and fitting right in. She was up for a laugh, probably more than I was sometimes. I liked that in her. She was fun and good at talking. I liked a lot about Skye now that I'd got to know her. We used not to speak at all and now we spent all day finding ways to talk. Complimenting one another. Email, instant messaging, calling, coffee runs, face to face chats that lasted all afternoon. Seeing and talking to Skye had become the highlights of my days.

Every day.

But she had been different today, which was a concern. Cooler. And I'd been a total mess about it. Had

I done something wrong yesterday? I poured a jug of water over my head a few times and rinsed my hair. I ran some more hot water into the bath and took another sip of wine. I continued to unpack my feelings towards Skye as I lay there. By the time the water was becoming lukewarm again I reached the conclusion that I wanted more than a good working relationship or a new friend in Skye. That had to be the explanation for why she was on my mind so much and why her behaviour today had almost hurt me.

It hit me square between the eyes and moved down to my chest where it settled as a big fat truth that couldn't be ignored.

I had feelings for Skye.

Big feelings.

There was a connection between us. And, she was hot. There was that. I had read recently that thirty percent of relationships started at work. I was open to it, but I couldn't see how it could work. I sighed. Our working situation was too high-pressured, and too fragile. People were watching us. We were going for the same job. That we could get together and it not affect things at work would be impossible.

I got out of the bath and dried myself down. It wasn't appropriate to like her that way. To avoid a disaster, I'd have to shut these feelings down.

This was the only logical solution, I decided.

~ 13 ~
Skye

Arlo was lying on my mum's couch next to me, snoring gently. So cute. I sipped a hot chocolate as my mum filled me in on the new friends she'd met at bridge. My mum liked to gossip, but in the most harmless kind of way. She liked people, and I think that was why she liked talking about them.

"When are you going to tell me how it's going at work?" She looked at me expectantly.

I hesitated, thumbing my ear. What was I supposed to tell her? That I was fighting a crush on the person I'd been forced to share a job with, who I openly said I didn't like before. After the mountain biking trip, I'd vowed to keep my distance from Brianna and cool things off. But I'd been completely unable to keep that up, especially after we won that huge project together. So my crush hadn't gone anywhere. If anything, it had intensified.

"Fine. It's going fine. We've got lots of interviews lined up for next week."

"Skye," she lowered her voice. Perhaps my full name was coming next. "What's going on?"

I filled her in with the latest in terms of the work and as much as I felt comfortable sharing. I had to admit it was going well working with Brianna. Great, even.

"Why didn't you say anything? This is brilliant news."

I shrugged. "It's all happened so fast. And I've been doing a lot of hours. Anyway, I told you last week things were going well."

"Yes, but you didn't say that you'd formed a new all-star alliance with your rival. It's very grown up of you both. Very collegial. I'm proud of you, Skye."

"Aw, thanks, Mum. Hearts."

She laughed. "Hearts?"

"Text speak, Mum."

"I think you're going to get the job."

In truth, I felt that the job would be mine too, but I didn't want to jinx it. "It's still very early days, there's a lot more to do, and the interviews aren't until next month."

"I know, I know. I know. I just have a feeling."

My mum loved looking for signs about things, to help with making decisions and to help with, in my opinion, justifying things after the fact. It was how she navigated her way through life, increasingly so as she got older. 'The universe has spoken' was one of my mum's favourite phrases. It usually made me laugh, but today, I found it irritating.

"Well then why don't I call Helen up right now and ask her when she wants me to start? No point in her bothering with the other interviews. She should pick me and do away with everyone else. Job done." I tried to lose the sarcastic tone in my voice. She only meant well. I sighed. I might as well relent. "I did pick up that book about achieving your dreams the day before she announced the merger, you know. The universe." I emphasised the latter, as we'd taken to just shortening the whole sentiment to it.

"Exactly," she squealed. You were on the right wavelength with Helen even before she told you. You're made for this job, Skye. I really believe it. With all your experience and preparation, and a bit of luck, it could happen. Just you wait and see."

I sipped my hot chocolate. My mum was my biggest cheerleader, always had been. No matter what I wanted to do in life, she'd always supported me.

"Thanks, Mum."

"And keep me posted."

"Will do."

***

The next day, I scanned the menu and chose my usual. "I'll have the cheese and tomato toastie, please."

Brianna sat across from me in the packed café. "And I'll have the chicken and salad baguette, please."

The waitress left us to it, and we smiled at each other before looking away. We were sat at a tiny excuse for a table so there wouldn't be a lot of space for eating. I instantly regretted ordering something I'd have to eat with my hands. I'd been feeling increasingly self-conscious eating in front of Brianna these days. A knife and fork meal would've been so much more civilised.

"Do you always eat the same food?" Brianna said, with a slight smirk on her lips.

I shrugged. "I like what I like."

We'd been going out for lunch together a lot. This café was one of our favourite places. Sitting so close to Brianna was the best part of my day. Admitting it to myself was a big deal, but I'd done it and I felt better about my crush on her now. Like if you accept something and name it, it loses its power. I was still waiting for my attraction to her to quietly leave. We had bigger problems to sort out.

"So," Brianna said. "What are we going to do about Andrew and Peter?" Brianna gave me her stern, serious face, which I now liked it. A lot.

"Sack them both?" I grinned.

She laughed. "If only. On the grounds that they're sexist pricks?"

"We can dream."

"We do need to deal with Andrew more effectively," Brianna said. "All jokes aside, it's fast becoming a team problem. Not only is he pissing us off but he's openly undermining us. I'm worried if this continues he might fuck up team morale. And that is no legacy to take into the interview." Brianna furrowed her brow. It was a very sexy look on her.

I nodded. Andrew had now taken to spreading rumours of redundancies despite that not being true. "I totally agree. It's an issue. He's a little shit. It's like he's trying to covertly sabotage our time as interim leaders."

Our food arrived and I attempted to eat. Strings of cheese hung from my mouth and my hands trembled while I attempted to hide the fact. Brianna kindly looked away while I wrestled with another offending string. We ate mostly in silence, and finished our food quickly.

As I was dabbing my mouth with a napkin, Brianna spoke for the first time in a while. "So, everyone has accepted their new roles or their interviews, and only two people have walked out. I think that's pretty good, don't you?"

"It could have been a lot worse. Things are settling down now with the team. I feel like I can finally breathe again." It was true. It had been a tough time getting the merger sorted. The worst of it was over now, which was such a relief.

"Do you like managing people?" said Brianna.

"Yeah, I do. I really like it."

"It shows. You're really great with people."

"Except when there's conflict. I'm far less into conflict."

Brianna just nodded. It looked like there was something on her mind.

"Why do you ask?"

"I've just been thinking about it a lot lately. As I've been getting to know the new team, watching the dynamics, noticing things."

"Oh really. What have you noticed?"

Brianna hesitated.

"Spill it."

She looked at me directly now. "Would it be okay if I shared an observation I've made about your management style with you? And please say no if you feel uncomfortable. I don't know if we're at that level of openness yet and in no way would I want to make you feel like I am criticising you. I've already learned loads from you about how to be a better boss, so it's really only something that I think would make you even better. Unstoppable, even."

What was she going to say? I was dying to know. The waitress came back and cleared our plates.

"I'm open to it. What's my crime?"

She laughed. "Okay here goes." She paused. "You're too nice."

I rolled my eyes. Why was everyone always calling me out on this?

"May I continue?"

"Yes."

"This is a strength, like I said. But at times I think it slows you down. You're too senior now to take on as much of the grunt work that you do. Delegate. Let them take on more responsibility. Let go a little, and free up more of your headspace and time."

"And here I was thinking you were the control freak."

"You think I'm a control freak?"

"Sorry, that came out wrong."

"No, I totally am. Maybe we're more similar than we realise?"

"Maybe."

I let her feedback sit with me a little. It was good she felt able to say something.

"I'm glad you felt comfortable enough to share that with me, Brianna. I'd like to think that we can be open like this more often with each other. Direct. I mean, we're dealing with so much at work, can we afford not to be? So thank you and yeah, you're spot on. I've had feedback like that before. It doesn't come naturally to me to tell people what to do. It's just my personality. Sometimes I revert to my default when I'm tired, or really stressed. It's caused me a lot of problems professionally," I paused, unsure if I should add this last part but did in the end, "and personally."

"I think it's great you're so self-aware. That's all anyone can do, right? Progress not perfection."

"It's true. I'm working on it. I need to be more badass, like you."

Brianna chuckled, softly. "You already are a badass, you just might want to own it a little more, in my humble opinion. Also, I am not a badass."

I raised an eyebrow. "Stop it. Yes you are. You know you are. And you're totally right. I need to delegate more. I do want my life back. These long hours aren't sustainable."

Our conversation turned back to the pressing topic of the day which was the ongoing headache we were having with Andrew. Brianna encouraged me to formalise our response to his disruptive behaviour. I could see that she was right.

"Okay, so as Andrew's line manager, I'll start the ball rolling."

"You need to tell him that he cannot behave this way in the workplace nor speak to the people he works with the way he does, especially not his superiors. It will not be tolerated. We have to lay down the law with him and make a show of strength. He's not going to respond to much else."

I tried to imagine saying that, but couldn't. "Brianna, so this is the exact thing I'm not good at." I lowered my voice. "How do I do it?"

"You just do it and don't take any shit from him. You're the boss, he isn't. If he's not going to respect that then he can find another job. End of."

"There's my badass."

She smiled at this. God, she had such a beautiful smile. I cursed the situation and the fact I'd never get to kiss her. I folded my napkin a few times. "You know, you should come into the canteen for lunch more often. It's an easy way to chat more informally with the team. I'm sure people would like to see you a bit more often."

Brianna sat up straight. "Um, okay. I might do, yeah."

We were quiet together for a while and then I couldn't take it any longer.

"So, what's new with you? What've you been up to outside of work? Any new mountains conquered? New bikes built? I could really do with talking about something other than work for five minutes. Or at least until we get back there."

Brianna smiled at me. "You want to kill some time with me?"

"Would that be such a bad thing?"

Brianna looked at me right in the eyes. The power of our connection threw me, as something unspoken hung in the air. My cheeks blushed, as heat spread through my entire body.

This had to stop.

"No."

"So …?"

"I've been doing more planning for my mother's party. My brothers are doing their bit too. We're all quite excited about it. Hopefully it'll be a special night for her."

"Good for you. One hundred good daughter points. When is it again?"

"Four weeks, the day before Halloween. And you, what've you been up to?"

Aside from crushing on her, not much.

"Not had that much free time lately, as you know, so not a lot. By the time I get home I'm just going to bed. Sleeping. I've been sleeping a lot."

Brianna laughed, good naturedly. "You must be needing it then."

We walked back to the office in a comfortable silence. I zipped my coat up fully. The air had turned noticeably colder now October had arrived.

Brianna and I had meetings together all afternoon. "I'm making coffee for the meeting. Want one?" I asked, hoping she'd say yes and I'd have another reason to talk to her. She did say yes and I skipped to my old kitchen with the better coffee maker and found Hayley there, one hand on the fridge and another on her hip. She regarded me as I came in.

"Hello stranger. Where've you been?"

"Oh, lunch. Just a quickie. Meetings all day." I shrugged. "You know."

I put two coffee cups on the counter. She eyed these with suspicion too. "With Brianna. That for her?"

"Yes. You want one?"

"No, thank you. I've had enough for today." She took out a Tupperware box after rummaging about for a few seconds. She placed it on the counter next to my cups and looked at me squarely. "You and Brianna seem to be spending a lot of time together? You got a new work BFF now or something?" Her tone was questioning, her curiosity was loaded. I hoped she didn't feel like I was abandoning her.

"Of course not. We've just been needing to spend a lot of time together. We share a job. We're merging two departments whilst managing clients. I'm sorry I've not been around as much. We should definitely find a time. Maybe next week? This week is out."

Someone came into the kitchen for some hot water from the hot water tank. "I'd like that, thanks." Hayley lowered her voice. "You and Brianna seem a bit ... joined at the hip? Like, lunch every day? Practically sharing an office? All from two people who never used to like each other. It just seems like a total transformation and you haven't said anything about it."

"What can I say? We get on now."

Hayley scanned my face. "What are you not telling me?" Hayley knew when I was withholding something from her and that I was a terrible liar.

The colleague finished filling their cup and left, although he did cast an inquisitive glance in our direction as he went out the door.

"Follow me. Too public here."

Hayley followed me up to my office and shut the door behind us. I had a coffee mug in each hand. "Just quickly, as I've got to go to a meeting—"

"Yeah, then, what is it?"

"I might have a little crush on Brianna."

Hayley's mouth fell open just enough to know she was shocked. She let it sink in for a few seconds.

"Skye, that is huge."

I shrugged. "No it's not. Crushes come and go. I'm sure it will pass."

"As HR I'm slightly concerned, it could not be more awkward given the work situation, but as your friend I'm really excited for you. Does she know?"

"What! No, of course not. I'm not planning on telling her. Ever."

"Hmm."

"I know. Look, it's fine. It's just a harmless infatuation so I have no problem working long hours with her and staring into her beautiful face all day. I'm really not thinking too much about it."

"Right. You're not thinking too much about it. Said no woman ever."

I laughed. "I've got to go. I've got to get to the boardroom and pretend I'm the consummate professional."

"Well now I know where my work bestie has been." Hayley shook her head, amused. "No seriously, I'm here if you need to talk."

I smiled at her as we parted, thinking I really wanted her to drop the word 'work' from that sentence.

***

Arriving thirty seconds late to the meeting, which had started early, I did my best not to make any noise or disrupt it. I mouthed the word 'sorry' to Helen as I tiptoed to my seat, very aware of the icy glare she was giving me. The boardroom table was full. I found the last seat after placing Brianna's coffee next to her. She acknowledged me only briefly, giving me a quick and functional thank you before returning her attention to the speaker. Someone was presenting although I found it hard to focus on what they were saying. My eyes settled on Brianna turned slightly away from me further down the table. Her neck was slim and elegant. A few wisps of hair hung down from her low ponytail. I liked the shape of her shoulders, elegantly and effortless back and relaxed, and her forearm resting on the table. Her skin seemed so smooth. I traced a few freckles all the way up her arm, to the line of her short-sleeved shirt. I wondered what it would be like to caress the skin along her arms, all the way up, under her sleeve until I found her bra stap. I'd slide my fingers under it and tug it off her shoulder. She'd watch me as I did this, with that look in her eye.

"And that's why Skye will be overseeing the transition towards the new operating model."

I looked up and everyone's eyes were on me. Shit. Why had he brought me into it? Couldn't I just coast in one fucking meeting for once?

"Yes," I began, thinking on my feet. "I've drafted a timeline and shared it with the relevant people. Everyone who needs to know about it at this stage should know."

Peter sniggered and spoke under his breath. "Famous last words." My heart sank and I felt hollow. He was blatantly disrespecting me in front of the senior team and I didn't know what to do about it.

The presenter continued, ignoring Peter's comment, as did everyone else. Part of me was glad in that I didn't have to respond, but here it was showing up. An alpha male needed dealing with. If only I knew how. I sighed, quietly, and returned my attention to Brianna. She'd turned around so that she was facing the table now and not the speaker. She looked up and we shared a little eye contact. For a second, I forgot we were in a room full of people and at work. She broke the connection slowly and then fiddled with her notebook. I felt better about Peter and his shitty remark. Brianna and I had a plan. We'd play it tough. We were a team. We had each other's backs. And she got me.

The next day I was eating lunch with Hayley in the canteen, shamelessly wondering what Brianna was up to. Before long, Brianna appeared. She scanned the room and stopped when we caught eyes. We held eye contact for a little longer than necessary, and then she tentatively made her way through the tables and chairs in our direction. My heart pounded a little faster as she approached.

"Mind if I join you?"

Hayley's raised eyebrow was far too obvious. I gave her a quick glare and she reset her face.

"It's great to see you in here." I smiled.

Brianna sat down and smiled back at me. "It's about time I showed a face."

~ 14 ~
Skye

About a week later all the talk in the office was about David's retirement party. Overall, he was a good guy and deserved a proper send off. I was proud Your View was going all out to provide him with one. As head of the social committee and with my new-found powers, I'd signed off on extra champagne and a free bar. Helen was so extravagant and had spared no expense on other office parties and celebrations over the years, so I figured she wouldn't mind. She once took the whole of senior management to Royal Ascot and flushed everyone with fifty quid to bet on the races. I couldn't think of any other office party as important as this one. David was a legend. He wasn't perfect but he'd helped me develop in my career and I'd be forever grateful to him for that.

At the end of yet another intense day Brianna and I were still there. We'd been interviewing applicants for the last few roles, and it had caused a major backlog of work. It was late. This had become such a pattern. I had a sneaky suspicion this wasn't by necessity at times. Brianna barely resisted my invites for late night takeaways and tonight was no different given we'd just finished a pizza between us in the canteen again. I'd been doing my best to ignore my feelings for Brianna but spending so much time with her through work was making it difficult. It was okay to look and dream, right?

As part of the merger, Helen had told us we both needed to know more about what the other did on a day-to-day basis. For this, we'd need to take refresher training courses in the other's discipline. I'd done some quantitative research before, but I had to re-learn basic statistics and survey analysis, while Brianna needed to learn how to use talking to people as a form of social research. I'd spent many an afternoon huddled over a computer with Brianna, fighting boredom over the numbers and my persistent crush on her. It had been a struggle.

We were both passionate about what we did, and I liked sharing that with her. In one encounter, Brianna had said that 'statistics were like bikinis, what they reveal is interesting, but what they hide is vital'. I kept thinking about her saying that and whether or not she was trying to flirt with me.

Tonight, we were sitting on my couch at opposite ends. My laptop and notebooks and papers were scattered around me. Brianna just had her laptop and one notebook.

"You know your new office is kind of growing on me." Brianna said.

"I thought you said it was messy and not conducive to clear thinking, just like my old office?"

"Well it is. But it's also warm and cosy, and well, lovely. It makes you want to spend more time here. Which means you stay at work longer and get more done. I see it now."

"I've nurtured some of this stuff for years. You've got to have a good workspace. It's so important."

Brianna smiled. Her lips were full and rosy tonight. It looked like she'd freshened up and re-applied her make up at some point. I noticed earlier on and it had given me a little boost all evening.

"So, you ready for your training session?"

She groaned. "Of course. I love qual. Words, feelings, opinions. My favourite things!"

"Brianna, I know you're a numbers person. And I'm the complete opposite here. But we need to do this. It's already been pushed back too many times."

"Okay, okay. What special form of torture do you have in store for me?"

We'd already briefed each other on how we ran our departments, so she knew the processes and she knew the shape of what we did but not so much the techniques of the methods we used.

"I've prepared some slides on some of the tools we use and how we go about them. I know you understand the way we're structured and how we function, but what you need to know more of is the theories underpinning our methods and how this translates into the useful findings our clients need and can do something with. What brings in the money, so to speak."

"That's correct. The whole dark art of it."

I laughed at this. "You know the lingo. Yes, colloquially we hear that sometimes in our sector. The reason people think that is because there is a high degree of subjectivity built into it."

"As opposed to the objectivity that the numbers give you."

"Exactly."

Brianna made a face at this, as if she hadn't expected me to agree with her.

I continued. "That's the whole point. That's where the skill of the researcher will either shine or fail when it comes to social research. That being said, coding and analysing qualitative data is still a science."

She frowned, again.

"It'll make more sense. Bear with me. The trick is to create a well-structured sample of the target population. We put similar groups of people together and essentially look for consensus, and for the deeper meanings. I'll show you how we analyse the qual data, and how it gets distilled into something meaningful that answers the core objectives. Like any project, we need to know why we're doing it in the first place. What do we want to get out of it? What problems are we trying to solve? Once we know this, we can begin."

"Uh-huh."

I picked up my laptop. "I've got the slides on here. Did you want to share the screen sitting here? Or we could fire them up on the monitor or move to the boardroom if that's easier?"

"It's okay, I'll scoot over."

It was way more comfortable and chilled out in here than the boardroom, so I was grateful she didn't want to go there instead. Brianna sat closer to me on the couch so she could see my screen on my lap. She was so close that I could smell her hair. I became aware of her slow, steady breathing.

This was my torture.

I took Brianna through the slides and talked about the different contexts and situations we'd use different types of focus groups, interviews, workshops, on-street surveys, and online focus groups for. Brianna listened well and appeared to have dropped her earlier attitude. She turned to me after a while and asked me what I liked about this line of work as she put her arm on the couch behind me. I don't think she was conscious that she'd done it, but the move felt intimate. "It seems chaotic."

"I like bringing order to the chaos." I paused. "But I think the thing I love most is that it forces you to have an open mind and to really listen to what people are saying. You have to be naturally curious about people and seek the truth. Always the truth."

"That's beautiful, Skye."

We quietly looked into each other's eyes for a few moments. I felt a fire in her eyes and it did things to me, down low in my body. I turned my head away, feeling my cheeks burn. "I call it radical listening."

"That's inventive." Brianna said, softly. "I like that."

"Do you want to know the technique?"

She nodded a few times. I took that as a yes.

"You must approach the research participants with open, and non-leading questions. It's all about creating a safe space for people so they can open up and you can get to the core of the issue at hand. Your body language matters too, as the energy you bring to the table can influence the findings you get. You have to listen with your whole body, with your entire being, and focus it one hundred percent on the participants. It's not just what they are saying that counts as a finding, it's also how they are saying it. You use each of your senses to build up more of a picture than just words alone could ever provide." I paused. "Sometimes it's all about what they are not saying."

"So you're an observer. Does this mean that all this time you've been secretly analysing my body language?"

I gulped. "Of course I have. You're very easy to read."

She laughed a little. "And what am I saying right now, with my body?" She removed her arm from behind me and moved slightly back to her side as if she'd only just noticed.

"That you're comfortable and relaxed."

She just nodded.

"Right, so let me demonstrate what active listening is and how we use it in qual. I'll pick a topic. I don't know. Health. That's very on point right now."

"Okay." She sat back, folding her arms.

"Defensive about something?"

"Ah." She unfolded her arms. "Very good. It's not some sort of role play, is it? I hate role plays."

"It isn't, don't worry." I paused. "So, Brianna, how would you describe your health on most days?"

She crossed her legs and folded her arms again. I didn't say anything about it. She looked off to the side and down at the floor, before glancing over at me, cautiously. "I'm already thinking too much about this but in general my health is good. I've not been to the doctors in a couple of years. I don't smoke or do drugs. I drink more than I probably should, but who doesn't, right? I'm quite active with all the cycling although I work too much and it stresses me out sometimes. I could do more to get my stress levels down I guess. My BMI was healthy last time I checked, and I don't take any medication for anything. When I was seven I had meningitis. The bad kind. I nearly died. I don't know. What else?" Brianna dropped her head back onto the couch and took a deep breath. "Since I have the floor, I'd say we focus too much on physical health in our society, and we should place as much importance on our mental and emotional health. You know what I mean?"

She looked over at me and bit down on her lip. God, she was sexy.

"Very good. Now I'm going to try and repeat back what you said to demonstrate I was listening and then I'm going to ask you if you felt that I was listening or not as you spoke. If you felt that I 'got you'."

"I can't wait."

I repeated what I had heard.

"Wow. You remembered pretty much everything."

"And how did you feel when you were talking? Did you *feel* like I was really listening?"

Brianna found my eyes and held them. "Yes. I felt completely under your attention. You didn't fidget or get distracted. And it didn't look like you were just waiting for me to finish so you could speak. You looked at me the entire time, like I was the only person in the whole world. I liked that. You do that a lot to me."

She smiled, shyly, and so did I. What were we, eighteen? My heart rate picked up. She thought I looked at her like that a lot? Did I? Brianna blushed. Oh my God she was blushing.

"And I am utterly impressed by how much you remembered. I hope you're not remembering all the stuff I say on a daily basis."

"I remember everything." Shit, that came out wrong. I ran my fingers through my hair. "I mean, sometimes I can't switch off very easily. I can wake up during the night reciting stuff word for word or obsessing over what people have said and what they might have meant by it. I guess it's the way I make sense of things."

"That must be hard."

This was going in a direction I was less comfortable with. "I'm the boss now so I do way less primary research these days. As you know, this can be delegated to more junior colleagues. I come in to do the high-stakes interviews and focus groups with clients viewing behind a screen."

"Well, you expertly demonstrated how to radically listen. Thank you. I bet you don't forget any birthdays."

"Um, I've forgotten one or two in my time. I'm sorry to hear you were so ill as a kid. That must have been scary."

Brianna shrugged. "I think my parents were more worried than I was. I remember enjoying having their attention for once."

"Sounds pretty rough, Brianna. Such a lot for a seven-year-old."

"I learnt that life could be taken away at any point. So you might as well make the most of it."

"You learned that so young. Is this why you're into an extreme sport?"

She looked off to the side. "I hadn't made that connection before. It probably is." After a few moments, she faced me again. "Can I have a go? Ask you an open question?"

"Sure."

Brianna uncrossed her legs and repositioned herself so she was facing me more. She put her arm back up on the couch and rested her hand close to my shoulder. The side of her knee was only a centimetre from the side of my thigh. My tummy fluttered.

"I'm trying to think of a question."

"No problem. Take your time." I sounded way cooler than I felt. I shut down the laptop. The training was over. This was just chatting.

"What are you most afraid of?"

Fuck. That was her question? My mind went blank.
"What? Too direct?"
"No, I just wasn't expecting it."
"I'll pick another one."
"No it's fine." I sat up straight. Did I want to tell her something real or something kind of silly? I chose silly. "Losing wi-fi connection."
"That can't be it." Brianna said. "What are you really afraid of?"
I was quiet for a moment. "Okay. I think I'm *most* afraid of dying alone."
"I get that. It's not too dissimilar to mine."
"Oh really? What are *you* most afraid of?"
She was quiet for a while. I stared at her.
She spoke softly. "Living a life surrounded by people, family and friends, who didn't really love me."
Ouch. That was a painful idea. And possibly even worse than mine.
"Sorry, I took us down a really depressing route here. Let's lighten it up a little. Can I try again?"
I nodded, feeling even more empathy for her now than I ever had. That was such a sad fear. I hoped it wasn't true for her.
Brianna perked up. "What's your morning routine?"
"My morning routine? Oh, I'm a beast."
She shook her head and smiled. There was no hint of judgement, which I appreciated. "Fair enough."
"I get up early. I meditate, do my affirmations and some journaling. Then I work out for twenty minutes if I have time. I'm a little obsessed about productivity and being successful, as you might have guessed."

"You're a high-achiever." Brianna continued. "What's your perfect day?" She paused. "I think I'm getting the hang of this."

I smiled. "You are. Let me think. Okay I'm going to sound very much like a cliché but I don't care. I'd wake up from a long deep restful sleep feeling amazing and happy to be alive next to the woman I love. We'd spend the day laughing, hanging out," I lowered my voice, "doing other things too, then meet up with friends for food, drinks and party times. Probably in a hot place next to a beach, sea views and good vibes." Had I gone too far? Woman I love? Really? I was on a roll tonight.

"That's nice. I like it."

I raised an eyebrow. "Do you?"

"It's not far off mine."

"No way. We can't have similar answers for both. That is not normal."

"Well, I'd add in an afternoon spent biking or hiking in some beautiful mountains—"

"Ah see that's where we differ. Strenuous exercise definitely does not feature in mine."

Brianna laughed. God she was even more gorgeous up close. Her hand was still behind me. Did she know what this was doing to me? I squirmed, in a good way.

"Sorry, I think we veered off topic there."

"It doesn't matter. I might not put you in front of a focus group yet but hopefully you get the drill now."

"I get the drill. Talking, listening, asking questions."

"There's a lot more to it than that."

"I know." She put her hands in the air as if surrendering. I missed her arm so close to me. "This was just the very basics. Thanks for taking the time to give

Up Against Her

me a glimpse into your world. If I'm going to be in charge of a team doing this stuff then I need to know."

I raised an eyebrow at this. "If you get the job of course."

Brianna grimaced and looked down. "True."

A tense silence followed. I'd been so engrossed in the merger and in getting to know her more and indulging my secret crush I'd almost forgot about our rivalry for the top job.

"You did great with the questions, Brianna. You were patient and inquisitive. Two key skills for any researcher." In reality, this felt like just an excuse for us to talk. I'd never shared that about my perfect day with anyone before.

"Thanks. This stuff really works. I don't open up like that normally."

So it wasn't just me who thought we'd been sharing more than usual. I liked it. I liked talking to her. I wished she would open up more.

"Yeah, about that. You're like a closed book sometimes, Brianna. What's with that? If people around here only knew how thoughtful and sweet you are …"

Oh my God I'd called her thoughtful and sweet. What was I doing?

"I thought you said I was a badass?" She shifted back up the couch and started packing up her laptop.

"I know. Your sensitive side will be our little secret."

Brianna was quiet. I hope I hadn't overstepped. Was she going to leave now? I really didn't want her to.

"Are you going to David's leaving party tomorrow night?" I could not wait for the party. I had my dress and shoes all picked out.

"Yep."

"Great, that's great. I wasn't sure if you would be."
"Oh. Why?"

"I wasn't sure you enjoyed the social stuff as much. You seem to leave early a lot, keep to yourself."

"You been keeping tabs on me?" She raised an eyebrow, but from her tone she was only teasing me.

"No, no, I guess I just noticed."

"It's okay." Brianna smiled. "I keep to myself at work mostly. I like to keep work and my personal life quite separate."

That was disappointing. I thought we were getting along quite well recently. We could be friends, like for real. If only my crush would go away. I sighed, my crush wasn't going away, and this meant our friendship would never have any legs. We might not know each other in the future and that made me sad. Not unless something did happen between us.

In my dreams, maybe.

Making a move on Brianna seemed impossible. She seemed happy to be around me but could I name it as interest in me too? Ugh. I imagined her rejecting me if I said something. The prospect was unbearable.

"But I am really enjoying getting to know you better, Skye. Working together has been super fun."

I must have beamed at her because she reached over and squeezed my hand. The touch felt electric. From the look on her face, I think she felt it too. Brianna took her hand away, sat up straight and got to her feet. She checked her watch. "Look at the time. I'm going to cycle home."

Every inch of my body wanted her to sit back down. This was getting out of hand. I just nodded a little, and I must have looked seriously disappointed. I had to get a grip.

"Thanks for everything today, Skye. I'll see you tomorrow?"

"Yeah. See you tomorrow."

She put her laptop in her leather satchel. Was she bolting? Was she flustered? Did it matter? She picked up her coat from my coat-stand and folded it over her arm. My feet carried me up to see her out. This wasn't my home but I felt I needed to be polite. She swung the strap over her shoulder and reached for the doorknob. Fuck it. I didn't want her to go.

"Brianna."

She turned to look at me. Her eyes were dark but also a little scared. I dropped my eyes to her lips and I know she saw me do it. I bit my bottom lip. She stared at this. The moment stretched on. I wanted to kiss her, but what if she didn't feel the same?

I took a deep breath and came to my senses. "Are you a hugger? Can I give you a hug goodbye?"

Her shoulders relaxed and she smiled, holding out her arms. "I am, if you can believe it."

"Yay," I said, stepping into her space. We clashed a little, as she was still holding her coat and went low behind my back but I did the same to her. Then I went in high as she tried to readjust. We laughed.

"Shall we try again?" said Brianna.

"Yeah."

I sent my arms high this time as hers went to my lower back. I rested my arms around her shoulders and inhaled her scent. Our bodies barely touched but I loved it all the same. I pulled away out of politeness but felt a gentle but firm tug on my lower back keeping me there.

She took a deep breath as she pulled me closer. I felt our bodies touch more fully as we sank into one another, her arms enclosing around my waist. The soft bulge of her breasts pressed against to mine and my whole body tingled. We just stayed like that, locked together. It was so nice. Her coat was draped behind me and I cursed a little that it was still there. That any clothes were still blocking us. Her arm dropped down my back a little. Oh my God was she going to feel me up? I prayed she couldn't feel my pulse race in my neck. After what felt like an eternity but was probably only fifteen seconds Brianna let her arms drop away and stepped back.

She smiled but didn't hold my eyes. "I'd better get going."

I mumbled something in response and said for her to take care on her way home. The fact we'd hugged like lovers hung heavy in the air. She told me not to stay too late and I said I wouldn't be far behind her which was true. Why we weren't leaving together I did not know.

"See you tomorrow, Skye."

"And you, tomorrow. See you then."

Once the door was closed I sat back down on the couch all on my own.

What the fuck?

~ 15 ~
Skye

Hazily I became conscious of the feeling between my legs as I woke up from a dream that Brianna was straddling me, naked, saying 'I know you want this'. I could almost feel the weight of her body on mine, yet I knew it wasn't real. What was real was the same intense throbbing that I'd been aware of in my dream as wave after wave of an intense orgasm ripped right through me. It was so powerful and pleasurable and not in my control. It was as if my body was operating through me, not asking me for permission. As it came to an end I wanted to be back in my dream having sex with Brianna. In a way I still felt like I was.

What the fuck was that?

I lay in my bed, still turned on. This had never happened to me before. I checked myself. There was wetness, a ridiculous amount. I'd had a wet dream. What the hell was the name for it in a woman, anyway? My body had literally thrown an orgasm at me to wake me up to the fact that this was more than just a crush. This was my intuition calling to me. A sign. The universe. Super-hug had happened, and that was all on Brianna. She'd kept me there. She'd pulled me in and held me against her body. I'd never had a hug like that with a friend or colleague before. No, that was a sex hug. We'd been like magnets, closing in on each other. It had felt so inevitable. It was only a hug but felt like so much more.

I lay on my bed staring at my window. Would it be awkward at work today? My feelings for Brianna were now jeopardising our working relationship. Should I just tell her how I feel? After last night, could we really just ignore the spark between us any more? She'd had that look in her eyes when she pulled me in. It was the same look as in my dream. It would have been so easy in that moment for one of us to kiss the other. We deserved a medal for not taking it further. Even though I was just lying in bed, my body was tense. The dawn chorus was happening outside my bedroom window. The heating hadn't come on yet, so it was a bit cold in the room. I doubled the duvet over my body to get warmer. I was in no rush to get up and start this day.

I knew how I felt. But would Brianna be open to something happening? Would I? My thoughts swirled. I thought about how something might happen between us, still feeling turned on from my sex dream. I let my imagination run wild, and then felt a little sad. It was highly unlikely anything was going to happen between us. Last night was testament to that.

If I made a move on her and she rejected me wouldn't that be so much worse than talking to her about it and seeing where she was first? What was I going to do, lure her into my office and pounce on her? Stay late at the pub together and blame it on the alcohol? No. Talking it out like emotionally mature adults felt safer all round. My dignity would be *slightly* more intact if she didn't feel the same or want to go there. I could brush it off and say it was nothing. That I'd misread some signals. We'd laugh it off. We'd forget about it.

I never made the first move, anyway. How would I even go about it? This had hurt me in the past, and I'd missed out. I'd had enough of being so passive. In dating and in my life in general, outside of work. At least at work I'd learned how to call the shots, although that had been a hard lesson and I still had a lot to work on. If I wanted things to happen in my life, I had to take charge and do something about it. I had to push things forward and drive change. I couldn't sit about and wait for things to come to me, when I had so much to offer. So much to give. That was an old thinking pattern that I was ready to let go of. As a woman in her mid-thirties, in her prime, now was the time to take control of my life and own my future. Starting with honouring my feelings for Brianna and doing something about it.

I got up and took a shower, ignoring my morning routine, excited about my decision to tell her. But when? Perhaps I could broach the subject after our interviews? No, that was too long to wait. If I waited until one of us was the other's boss, wouldn't that be way more difficult for something to happen between us? It could get really complicated. A million scenarios ran through my mind, none of them without consequences. Throughout my shower I analysed the situation and did my best to problem solve. This was exactly the sort of state I'd stay in unless I took action and moved things forward. I didn't have the time or inclination to live in angst for months only to end up heartbroken over something that never happened. I'd been there before. No. In my heart, I knew I had to do something about this. I needed to know if she felt the same. It had to be addressed.

Like, today.

***

The train into work was quieter today because it was a Friday. David's party was tonight. I could have done with more sleep. The way I'd woken up this morning had been such a shock. An immensely pleasurable shock that connected me to myself in a way I didn't know was possible. The open-plan office was quiet. People were probably pacing themselves this morning due to the party tonight. Brianna's door was closed when I got in. I glided past it, nervously, into the safety of my own office. At my desk I lay forward resting my head on my forearms, unable to focus on anything except what I was going to say to Brianna and how I was going to do it.

I was glad I had my own office, and this new one was turning out well. I liked being so close to Brianna during the day. When I'd got promoted to head of department and got my own office, I thought I'd miss the buzz of the open-plan office but in reality my focus and productivity had sky-rocketed. Being able to take moments like this to fully zone out without fearing someone would think I was slacking was such a privilege because it was after moments like this that I felt super-charged and able to get back on it.

Today, however, my mind was not on work. I gazed at the couch. Last night was so wonderful. Just sitting together felt so right. Peeking out from under the couch was Brianna's notebook. I hadn't noticed it before. I approached it with caution and picked it up. Should I look inside? Of course I wouldn't. It would be an invasion of her privacy and that was not my style. My tummy did somersaults as I realised this was now the reason I had to go and find her.

I took a deep breath and fixed my hair, then put on some lip balm. I opened my door but hers was still closed. There was no noise coming from her room either. My heart pounded. The butterflies in my stomach almost made me turn back. But I didn't. I took a deep breath and knocked on her door a few times. Not getting an answer, after a while I opened it gently.

Her office was empty.

I couldn't find her in the kitchen or on any of the other floors. Not wanting to make it obvious that I was looking for her I was careful not to ask anyone and instead just walked around. I even hovered at the sinks in each of the toilets in case she was in one of the cubicles. Feeling like a stalker now, I went back to my office to contact her. I chose a text to distance myself from the work email given this felt more like a personal message. However, an email from her had come in when I was out looking for her. I clicked on it. She was working from home today. She never worked from home. Was she avoiding me? Why would she be avoiding me?

I knew why.

An email from Jacinda came in requesting Brianna and I meet with Helen and her in Helen's office at ten thirty. I checked the meeting invite and Brianna had accepted. Butterflies swept through my tummy again.

In Helen's office the sun was shining in from the skylight. Brianna was there already, of course, on the screen facing the table via video call. Only when I had seated myself next to Helen and put my professional face on did I allow myself to look into the screen at Brianna. She was wearing a casual T-shirt and her hair was down and wavy. She was sitting near a window with some books and a plant in the background. This snapshot of her home reminded me of her office: minimalist, stylish, tidy. I hadn't seen her on a video call before.

"Good morning. Thank you for being able to meet with me at short notice. I just wanted to check in with how the merger has been progressing recently. I've been very happy with what I've seen and heard but I wanted a more formal update from you both."

Neither of us said a word.

"Nothing to say? Nothing at all?"

"It's going well, Helen," Brianna said.

"Things are coming along well. We have completed most of the interviews and are starting to move to the new operating model," I added.

Brianna and I didn't acknowledge each other at all. Did Helen notice?

"Good. Happy to hear it. The interviews for the director position will take place on the fourth of November. It goes without saying that you will both get an interview, but you will both have to submit an application, so everything is done properly. I wanted to let you know before the job is advertised externally."

"Thank you for letting us know, Helen," I replied.

"Yes, thank you," said Brianna.

"There is one other thing. I will need an interim report first thing on Tuesday morning, so I can share it with the board on Tuesday afternoon."

What the actual fuck?

It was a bank holiday weekend, and I had this afternoon booked off as annual leave, and it was David's retirement party tonight. Was she taking the piss? I frowned before catching it and resetting my face back to neutral, I hoped. What could I do? Say no and risk getting on the wrong side of Helen before the interview? What if Brianna was fine with it? I glanced up at the screen and Brianna looked like she was about to say something.

"That's no problem, Helen." I said, getting in there early.

Brianna closed her mouth. Then she spoke. "Actually, Helen, that's going to be quite hard. It's a bank holiday weekend. We've already got a lot on our plates today and we're supposed to be off on Monday for the public holiday."

"Oh. I didn't realise it was a holiday weekend, my apologies. Unfortunately, I can't budge on the deadline. I had dinner with the board last night and I promised them Tuesday."

Brianna backed down and agreed to the deadline. There was nothing more she could have done. I respected her for trying, though, and wished I had her confidence.

The meeting ended and I headed downstairs. Coffee. I needed coffee. Hayley was in the kitchen talking to one of the kittens. This was where Hayley did her best work, she often said, because people tended to open up more in the kitchen about how things were really going than in performance management meetings. She liked to know what was going on and was good at finding it out. She'd handled many personnel situations before they escalated, all from just making herself available and caring enough about the people who worked here to go that extra mile.

I spilled milk on the counter then tripped over the recycling boxes. I found some paper towels and cleared it up before taking my coffee to one of the tables, hoping Hayley would pop over once she was done with the kittens.

The caffeine went straight to my head. Why did Helen have to make my life so much more fucking difficult than it already was?

"Hi," said Hayley, hovering above me. She sat down. "You okay? You seem distracted."

"Hey. I'm fine. Thank you. How are you?"

"Don't ask."

"What was that about?" I nodded in the direction of where she'd been having her conversation.

"There's been some drama among the kittens ahead of the party tonight. Nothing I can't handle though."

"Let me know if I can help."

"I will. Should be okay though. I've had a word with all involved."

"You've worked your magic."

"We'll need to wait until later to find out, but yes. If they take my advice and if they value their jobs they'll do well."

"Ouch. Hard-talk." This was no time to talk about me and Brianna.

"This is a place of work, not a hall of residence. They've got to learn that at some point." Hayley got up. "I've got a meeting. Whatever happened to our long boozy lunches and carefree lives?"

I grimaced. "Thing of the past."

I stayed in the kitchen for a few moments after Hayley left looking at the whiteboard full of calls for nights out, craft nights, sports teams and what not. As head of the social committee, I'd got the whiteboard paid for and installed but the more senior I got in Your View the less and less I was able to do socially. They all looked like fun things, but it would be odd for me to attend. No one wanted to hang out with their boss, that was just a given. It seemed like only a minute ago it was me organising these types of events and being the one to get everyone chatting and having a good time. Seniority came with drawbacks. It was indeed lonely at the top. And now I was going to complicate things with one of the only other people on my level that I would want to hang out with.

I got back to my desk and there was an email from Brianna. She'd already divided up sections of the report so we could share the load between us. Her ideas were clever and would cut down the time needed to write it. She said she'd find some time today and on Monday afternoon. Her email was short, formal, and signed off with 'best regards'.

Was that it?

What did I expect though? This was exactly the kind of mess I'd be in if I didn't address the situation between us. But it wouldn't be today. Helen's report had ruined that. And she was hiding at home. It'd have to be Tuesday. I could wait that long, right? Or there was David's party later? No, that was a bad idea. Not safe or mature or dignified in any way. Clicking the report open, I put my feelings to one side and got started, grateful I had that to focus on instead.

~ 16 ~
Brianna

Happy to hover at the bar and people-watch, I nursed my glass of wine and scanned the room for Skye. She was nowhere to be seen. I smiled to myself. I could imagine her getting ready, all energy and enthusiasm and then fashionably late.

The massive hotel function room also did weddings. The high ceilings and long ornate windows gave it a grandness that I enjoyed. I had an excellent view of the band with Matt from my team on bass. He had the same swagger of any bass guitarist and wasn't bad either. So far, he'd delivered the funk and soul classics very well. The party was loud, but not too loud. I'd been able to hold a normal conversation with Lynn earlier. The dance floor in front of the band was empty for now. I had no intention of gracing it.

It was nice to see my colleagues all dressed up, and I was glad it wasn't black tie. It seemed as if all David's family and friends were here too, and there were a lot of them. This gave the party a different vibe to your typical work night out. A much better one.

One thing that remained constant, however, was the queue at the bar.

As Matt and his band started the chords for another song, Skye arrived with Hayley. My head involuntarily swivelled around. My heart rate immediately picked up as I saw her and what she was wearing. She had on a figure-hugging blue dress with the lowest neckline, and her hair in a stylish up do. Skye was stunning and hands down the sexiest woman here. I could not stop looking at her and imagining what it would feel like to slip that dress off her. A warm heat spread through my lower body. There was no controlling it. I took a large gulp of wine and looked away. When I looked back up, we caught eyes across the room and didn't look away. Had she been looking for me too? A slow smile crept onto her lips. Hayley said something to her and she turned away slowly.

God she was hot.

We hadn't even spoken yet and I was all fired up and turned on. How was I supposed to do this? To play down the impact Skye was having on me? Could I do this for much longer? Something had shifted between us last night. I was thrilled when she'd approached me at the door. I'd wanted to kiss her, or for her to kiss me. Instead, I'd held onto her for ages in that hug.

Was that not a dead giveaway?

Skye was on my mind when I fell asleep and the first thing I thought about when I woke up. She was there with me throughout the day, even when we weren't together.

I couldn't face her today after last night and had worked from home instead. I stared into my glass not knowing how I was going to handle my feelings for her tonight.

It was a little overwhelming.

When I looked up, Skye and Hayley were standing right in front of me, flute glasses in hand. Hayley initiated air kisses on cheeks as she said hello to me. We'd never done this before, but it fitted with the event.

Skye took her turn. She moved much slower than Hayley, or maybe time slowed down. I inhaled her and the delicious smell of her perfume as she glided into my space. Instead of an air kiss she planted one slow kiss on my right cheek. The smooth fullness of her lips left an imprint on my skin as she slowly pulled away.

"Nice to see you," Skye said.

"And you."

"You two look great together," said Hayley.

We both turned to her. I was lost.

"Your outfits." She pointed. "You're both wearing shades of blue."

I looked down. She was right. My dress was a darker blue and we did go well together. "Oh yeah."

Hayley smiled at us both with a hint of something in her eyes. Was it a knowing look? Had she and Skye been talking about something? "I'm going to go and find David. I'll be right back."

Skye looked at me. It was the same look she had last night in her office. Her pupils were dilated; I could hardly see any blue.

"Brianna, you look really gorgeous tonight." She then lowered her gaze and subtly ran her eyes over my body so that only I would notice, before tilting her head towards my ear. I felt goosebumps rise on my arms. I let my eyes follow the low neckline of her dress as she leaned in closer, lowering her voice. "I don't know which I prefer you most in, a suit or a dress. You look really hot in both."

My breath caught in my throat. Did she just say that? I felt almost naked standing there, which was unusual for me. I was normally the one undressing people with my eyes. What was she doing to me? Who was this newer, bolder Skye?

I liked it.

I allowed myself to trace my eyes all over her body. I did so in the full knowledge that she had just checked me out so it would be okay. Had I let myself do this before? We were in a crowded room but all I could see was Skye. No one else mattered. Skye licked her lips as she raised her glass to her mouth then sipped her champagne. Her lips looked so full and inviting. I wondered about kissing them. I was so turned on and this was just from looking at her.

"I have your notebook by the way. You must have left it in my office last night."

Last night. Why was she bringing up last night? This was flirting. No doubt about it. "Thanks. I'll get it on Tuesday." I paused then smiled flirtatiously. "Did you peek?"

"I would never."

"I would. Only joking."

Skye blushed. Why was she blushing? She smiled and took another sip, as did I. We were quiet for a minute.

Skye broke the silence. "How shit is that of Helen to drop that on us this morning?"

"So shit." I shook my head.

"And not to know that it's a bank holiday weekend, I mean, come on …"

"It's very out of touch."

"I know, right? She could have given us more time. She must think we're her bitches."

I burst out laughing. "That's an interesting way to put it."

Skye's tone turned more serious. "Um, I was hoping to talk to you about something."

"Yeah, sure. What about?"

She looked at me and then away, and then back at me and then away again. "Never mind. It can wait."

Now I was really intrigued. But I didn't want to probe her for more. She seemed quite sure that it could wait. "Okay. No problem. Just let me know."

Skye seemed a bit unsettled after that. All around us were people mingling and moving from group to group. Peter was making a beeline for us. His tall frame was as lanky as a high-jumper's, or should that be a pole vaulter's.

I nudged her elbow. "Brace yourself, here's Peter coming."

"Brianna. Skye." He looked between us, not smiling with his eyes.

We made banal small talk for a few minutes. Even though I was standing with Skye, I seriously considered excusing myself to go to the bathroom.

"Have you heard about the kittens?" Peter tried to sound casual about this but failed.

I wished he would leave us alone. "What about them?" I spoke flatly.

Peter's eyes sparkled at knowing something we didn't. His ego was so huge and so painfully obvious. What a little gossip he was.

"Two of the kittens have been seeing each other. Then one of them found out the other was cheating with their flatmate and is now refusing to work with them."

"I saw Hayley dealing with this in the kitchen earlier." Skye said. "Who is it?"

"Oh, I'd better not say. Confidentiality and all that. Thought Hayley would have told you."

Skye bristled.

I snapped. "Peter, you'd do well to stop stirring things up like this. If Hayley knows then I'm sure she's dealing with it from a work perspective. The last thing we need is you or anyone else getting involved and causing more drama, especially at David's big night. You should know better. Shame on you, Peter. For fuck's sake."

He slinked off after that. Pathetic, he was.

"Wow." Skye said. "That was magnificent."

I shrugged. "We're not at work but our plan's still our plan. You're still with me on it, right?"

"I so am."

"Good. Also, I don't agree with calling the junior researchers kittens. It's dehumanising and dismissive and, frankly, weird."

Skye nodded, listening to me.

"I'd like to put a stop to it if we can."

"You know what. You're so right. It is weird. It's just what we've always said. I'd never questioned it before," Skye paused, looking thoughtful. "I want to change it too."

"That's awesome, Skye."

We held each other's eyes for a second too long again. I took a deep breath, snapping at Peter had tensed me up. "Okay, how's about we take it down a notch or two and just focus on having a good time tonight?"

Skye beamed at this. "More drinks?"

"Always."

From my spot in the bar I was able to get the bartender's attention. I got us some wine but didn't have to pay. It was still open bar.

"Did you know about this?" I asked Skye. "People are well onto their second and third by now."

She was sheepish. "I might have paid for it to be open all night."

"All night? That was you? Does Helen know?"

Skye shook her head, no longer looking sorry at all. "David deserves it." She looked over at him. "This is his night."

"True. Hopefully Helen doesn't notice the bill. Also, aren't we supposed to make these kinds of decisions together?" I wasn't bothered by it, but felt it still needed to be pointed it out.

"God you're right. I'm sorry. And after I accused you of doing this before."

"I'll let you off. This time."

Skye blushed. "I'll keep that in mind."

My head went somewhere it shouldn't have, and I bit my lip. "Anyway, here's to a good night."

We clinked glasses and spent the next half hour or so mingling with others. My eyes kept wandering in Skye's direction. More than once, she caught me looking. All she did was hold my eyes then do her little smile. All right in the open. This whole thing was crazy.

The band stopped playing and Helen stood at the microphone next to cool Matt and his bass guitar. Was she about to sing?

"Please can I have your attention for a moment, lovely people?" It sounded more like an order than a question. This wasn't just a work function and it seemed out of place. She thanked people for coming and said a few words about David and what he meant to her and Your View.

"He has had my back for longer than I remember, and I wish him every bit of joy and happiness as he starts his retirement."

Her speech was short but sincere. She did well.

"And now for the man himself."

David joined Helen by the band and took the microphone from her.

"If I get as good a turn out for my funeral I'll be a very happy dead guy." The audience chuckled, non-committedly. Mass humouring of the old white guy had its own distinct sound. "No, seriously. Thank you all for joining me and my wife Sandra tonight. This is the best possible send-off I could have imagined. I've had my time, and I know I've benefitted from certain things and my path has been fairly easy in life. I'm leaving you now but I know Your View will continue to succeed because you have some very capable young women leading you into this new and challenging future. I believe things are going to get better. I know it. I've always known it. The old ways won't last, that's for certain, and it's women like them who are going to get us there." He pointed at me and Skye. A hundred heads turned to look at us. "While they've been temporarily at the helm, I've been able to wind things down and wrap up a lifetime. Thanks for letting an old man go easily." He looked emotional. Oh God, was he going to start crying? "But I've got you all for one more night. So please, join me on the dance floor and show an old man a good time, won't you?"

He got a cheer and a long clap for his speech. Despite myself, I was moved by his optimism and show of faith. Skye glanced my way and we caught eyes briefly. The strength of our growing connection both personally and professionally seemed to pass between us as understood.

We did make a good team.

The dance floor filled up as the lights dimmed and the party entered a new phase. Families with children said their goodbyes, and David looked like his heart was about to burst. His wife Sandra was by his side the whole time. They were a pair, and they would be starting a new phase of life after this party. It must be amazing to have that kind of partnership with someone. Someone who was there for everything.

A new song started and people sprung up and headed towards the dance floor.

"Would you like to dance?" Skye's eyes sparkled.

"I don't dance at these things."

"Brianna. It's a party. People dance."

"You go. I'll be fine here."

She gave me a scolding look.

I wasn't budging. Not with everyone here. I'd look a fool. I shook my head.

"Don't make me drag your ass up there." She insisted.

Again, I would normally dig my heels in but Skye just had an effect on me. I caved.

"Okay. But just this one song."

Skye nodded. "One song."

She was already up and gliding towards the band. Her hips started to sway to the beat, and I might have lost my mind at that point. Had I seen anything sexier in my life I wasn't sure. She turned around to face me as she stepped onto the dance floor, still moving, still doing things to me, and encouraged me to dance with her. Despite myself, I followed suit and forgot I was dancing at a work do. Thankfully, it was packed enough for me to feel less watched. All I could see was Skye and her smile, and slightly flushed cheeks. She really got into it and let loose. She was free, co-ordinated, and goofy enough to melt the hardest of non-dancers like myself.

She stepped a little closer towards me. "Just admit it, you're enjoying yourself. I can see it."

I smiled. She was right. I was. I'd never have got up here had she not persuaded me.

"Thanks to you."

The song ended and I turned to go. She caught my wrist. Her touch sent a wave of electricity right through me.

"Where you going?"

"One song, remember?"

She held my eyes and shook her head in disagreement. Fuck, she was so hot.

"Uh-uh," she pulled me closer. "You're going nowhere."

There was nothing I could say to that. We stayed, as did most people, as the next song took over. Even Helen was up dancing. She finally let me sit down a few songs later. I left her there dancing with Hayley and Lynn as I went to the bathroom to regain some composure. The quiet was momentary relief. I washed my hands at sinks which were like a tropical rain forest, complete with waterfalls for taps, giant ferns and atmospheric lighting. I dried my hands with a thick paper towel. The lighting was kind to my face in the mirror. I'd worn more make-up than usual tonight and it had lasted well. Tonight was going really well. Possibly the best work do I'd ever been to.

"There you are." The door closed behind Skye as she appeared out of nowhere.

"Were you looking for me?"

She hesitated. "No." She slipped into a cubicle.

I squirted some tasteful moisturiser onto my palms and massaged it into my skin then waited outside for her. When she came back out a few minutes later she seemed surprised.

"You waited on me?"

"Yeah. Is that weird?"

She thought about it. "No."

We walked back along the wide corridor of the hotel together. The plush plum carpet enhanced the feeling of luxury that the hotel was going for. The ceiling felt even higher out in the grand entrance hall for some reason. Art hung on the walls in magnificent frames. People dotted around, chatting or saying their goodbyes for the night. Two of the junior researchers were having a fight by the looks on their faces and raised voices. Skye and I looked at each other as we passed. These must be the two Peter had been talking about.

"I don't even want to know about that," Skye said.

"Yeah, me neither. At least not until Tuesday."

Skye laughed. "Totally."

We headed back into the party which was still going strong. We got another drink and then Skye went off to speak to David. She looked apologetic as she went, but she had nothing to apologise for. I hovered beside some people from the office and made a little small talk. As the night wore on, I remembered this was still a work function.

Skye appeared by my side a little while later. "David's having the time of his life."

David was back on the dance floor now, surrounded by people.

"Looks like it." I smiled, and Skye followed my gaze.

"You softie," she teased.

"Am not." I pretended to be pissed off. She didn't buy it. Her hair was a little looser, and her skin was glowing. She looked more lovely now than when she first arrived.

Skye grimaced. "I have to go soon."

"Oh no. Why?"

"To catch the last train. It leaves in like fifteen minutes. I've had a great night, and I've said goodbye to David. Better to leave on a high, right?"

"Do you have time to catch it?" The train station was close, but it'd be tight.

"If I leave now I do."

"I'll walk you."

"You don't have to do that."

"I'm happy to leave now, and it's on my way home."

"Um, okay. That would be great. Are you ready to go like now?"

"Yes."

"Don't you want to say goodbye to David?"

Not particularly. I wished him well, but we weren't close. Plus, he had a ton of people around him.

"I'm okay. We spoke earlier and sort of did it then. He's going to have a million goodbyes tonight so I'll just save him one."

"Okay. Let me find Hayley."

"Find Hayley for what?" said Hayley, appearing beside us.

"We're leaving," said Skye. "Brianna's walking me to the train station."

Hayley gave Skye another funny look. That was the second time this evening. Did she think there was something going on between us? Was there?

~ 17 ~
Brianna

We parted with Hayley and strode towards the cloakroom. The cool night air was a relief after the heat of the party. My feet were getting sore, but I still wanted to walk with her. We fell into step heading towards the station. I was slightly concerned Skye was going to miss her train.

"It's really nice of you to walk with me. And in this cold."

I glanced over at her. Now that we were out of the party something had changed. She looked a bit nervous. It was like we'd created this tiny pocket of time where we were just two people leaving a night out. Her train was in minutes so our parting would have to be brief. The station came into view, and the sight of it was an instant downer. What was I doing letting her go home? The night was still young.

"Skye. What if you came back to mine right now instead of going home?" The offer was out of my mouth before I could stop it.

She looked surprised but kept on walking. "Oh. Um."

"It was just an idea."

There was a long silence that nearly killed me. We reached the entrance to the station. She turned to me with a questioning look in her eyes. Our eyes locked. I got that feeling again in my chest.

"I'm having the best night with you. I don't want it to end. Come back to mine. We'll spend some more time together. I have wine. And a spare bedroom."

I still hadn't thought it through and now it was all out there. I wanted her to come home with me and she knew this now. Did she know I wanted more than just to hang out? After last night in her office and the sparks that were flying between us it had crossed my mind she might very well be on the same page as me.

Was this a good idea?

"I'd love to."

I smiled and she returned it. Her eyes were dark, and a little unsure. I forgot all about the party we'd been to, about where we were. That we were colleagues.

A heavy silence hung in the air as we walked the rest of the way to mine, making me think this was more for her too. We entered my building and I led her up to my flat. She didn't say much when we entered my flat and seemed more interested in looking around at my living space. We hung our coats up at the door, then kicked our heels off.

"I'm so glad to be out of those." Skye neatly placed her heels on the ground next to my shoe rack. "They look good, but they do come at a cost."

"They looked really good on you."

"Thanks. I like your place. It's classy. It suits you."

"Cheers. Wine?"

"Yes please."

She followed me to the kitchen. I scanned my apartment and my counter tops, checking things were clean and presentable. They were. Phew. I switched on the low lights instead of the brighter ones since it was late and to set a nice vibe. I took out my best wine glasses and poured some Sauvignon Blanc. Skye leant against the counter, with both hands on the edge of the counter behind her, looking incredibly sexy. She watched me the whole time, which made me blush a little.

"It's homelier than I expected."

"How so?"

"I thought it might be more neutral, like your office. But this feels warm and cosy, despite how tidy it is."

"I *guess* I'll take that as a compliment?"

"Sorry. I think I'm just a bit nervous."

I handed her the wine. Our fingers brushed, sending a wave of electricity up my arm. I leant against the kitchen island facing her.

"Why are you nervous?"

She looked shy. My breathing was uneven. We both sipped our wine as I waited for her response. This felt nothing like just hanging out.

"Brianna." She paused, putting her wine down on the counter. Her hand was trembling. "There's been something I've been wanting to talk to you about. And it's not about work. Well, it is a bit about work, but it's definitely not work related. Earlier, when I said I was hoping we could talk about something …" Her voice was shaky.

The energy in the room completely changed. With every word she'd already spoken I knew what she really meant. What she was about to verbalise. I felt it in my bones. I willed it to happen. I wanted to hear her say it so bad. Skye then fell silent for a ridiculous amount of time, which became kind of uncomfortable.

"Skye, what is it?"

She found my eyes. There was a total and utter rawness in how she was looking at me. I'd never seen her quite like this before. So real. We'd gone into that zone that only lovers know.

She took a deep breath. "Brianna, I like you. Like, *like you* like you." Her eyes darted away. I wanted them back and for her to look at me like that again. She blushed.

"You like me?"

"Look, I'd planned to be much cooler than this. It's totally okay if this is all on me. It's just a harmless crush. It doesn't have to be a big deal. I'm sure it'll pass. I'll be okay. I just thought it'd be better if we got it out in the open, whatever's going on between us, given that we work together. It's been getting very … distracting lately." She scratched her head. "Especially because I feel like it hasn't just been me who's been feeling something recently, so …" She looked up and found my eyes again, searching for my response. Her vulnerability was so sexy, and so powerful, and so honest. I was in awe of her courage.

"Skye, I like you too."

A smile appeared on her lips. "You do?"

"Yes."

She gulped. Did she grip the counter a little tighter? I became very still, conscious of the gravity of what we were saying to each other. There was a safety in discussing it like this, in my kitchen, so matter-of-factly. So emotionally mature. I was grateful she'd addressed it head on. I don't know that I could have put myself out there like that. I'd probably just have kissed her.

But this was also kind of hot.

"So that's us both said it." She put her hands over her mouth like a big secret was out. And it was. I had no idea she actually liked me too. I took a deep breath, feeling more sure about the situation with each passing second.

"Thank you for saying something, Skye."

Skye was quiet. "Sorry. I'm still just processing this information."

"There's no need to apologise. I am too."

"I mean, it doesn't have to get in the way of anything at work, right?"

"It's got nothing to do with work." I agreed. "What we do in our free time is private."

"Exactly. Private. It happens all the time."

"All the time."

Skye brushed a few strands of fallen hair away from her face and looked back up at me. There was a long silence as we held a ridiculous amount of eye contact. The invisible boundary between us disappeared, and a new dimension came rushing in. I put my glass of wine on the counter and stepped right into her space. She inhaled, then her eyes dropped to my mouth. I placed my hand over hers on the counter and she smiled at me, shyly. I caressed the skin on the back of her hand. Every touch felt electric. When she bit down on her bottom lip a jolt of pleasure rushed through my body.

I took another step so that our lips were just inches apart. My heart pounded as I placed my hands on her waist. She cupped my elbows, gently at first, then pulled me into her. The soft curve of her body pressed into mine through the thin fabric of our dresses. I dropped my head and planted one kiss on her neck as I inhaled her sweet perfume mixed with her unique scent. Skye let out a shaky breath, then ran her fingers along the underside of my forearms. The soft touch of her fingers on such a delicate part of my body gave me goosebumps. I rested my forehead on hers, and bit down on my lip.

We stayed like this for a few moments. I couldn't believe we were finally doing this.

Our heads tilted and then our lips were touching. Skye's lips were so soft. Everything about her was so warm. She had this irresistible feminine energy. The kiss was so slow, tender and meaningful. But I needed more, and pulled her closer before parting her lips. As we opened ourselves to each other something clicked and we kissed and kissed like nothing was holding us back any longer. I lost myself in the kiss, her mouth, feeling her tongue probe mine and the hot need I had for her between my legs.

Skye pulled back, cupped my face and looked me in the eyes. "Why haven't we done this before?"

"I don't know."

I shook my head, aching to have her lips back on mine. We found each other's mouths again and our kisses intensified. I moved my hand to her chest, feeling the soft bulge of her breast underneath her dress. Between hot urgent kisses and gasps of breath I slipped my hand inside her dress, feeling the buttery skin of her breasts and found her nipple. She moaned, which sent another jolt of pleasure through me.

"God, that feels so good," she said, into the side of my face.

"This dress." I mumbled.

"Mmm." She breathed, between kisses. "Take it off then."

I reached behind her back and gently unzipped so that the top half of her dress fell down her body and pooled at her waist. My eyes roamed over Skye's naked breasts, and she watched me look. She was beautiful. We kissed again, slowly, as I touched her breasts, feeling a hunger take over me. I lowered my hand to her thigh and ran my fingers up and down her leg, gently teasing how high I was going to go. She moaned softly, sending a burning heat through my entire body. I slipped my hand under the dress and found the bare skin of her leg, then her inner thigh, then higher still. She put her hands in my hair and tugged slightly. Our kissing continued and deepened the closer I got to where I knew she needed me. Using my knee, I nudged her legs open wider. She gasped when I ran my hand over her underwear. Slowly, I slid my fingers under the thin fabric. I found her, and my fingers got completely covered in her wetness. I stopped and looked at her with my fingers still in the same place. "You're so wet."

"Yep, please ignore."

"No, I love it." I kissed her neck and started touching her.

"Yep." She put her arms around my shoulders. "You can continue."

I touched her lightly. She dug her fingers into my back and I felt her body tense up. I parted her lips and slid my fingers deep inside her. I did this very slowly at first then faster, pulling her towards me almost. Her soft moans sent me wild. I returned to her clit and within a few seconds her whole body tensed up and she came loudly into my shoulder. Her face, neck and chest were flushed completely red.

"Skye, would you like to, um …" I looked towards my bedroom, "come to my bedroom with me?"

"Yes. Yes, I would."

~ 18 ~
Skye

Brianna held out her hand and led me to her bedroom. My feet carried me but my brain was two steps behind. I couldn't believe this was happening. She was quiet as she turned on a little lamp in her room. The bed was made. There was a book on her bedside table, and two candles on her windowsill. It was a lot softer than I thought her bedroom might be. A particularly sexy painting of a naked woman's body faced her bed.

She held out her hand again. "Come here."

We stepped together and held each other like we did before, my hands on her elbows, hers on my waist. I still felt a bit nervous. What happened in the kitchen felt like a warm-up. We locked eyes again. I bit down on my lower lip. Brianna kept her eyes on mine as she stepped out of her dress and got completely naked. My breath caught in my throat. She was stunningly gorgeous.

"Now you."

A little self-consciously, I took my dress off and let it fall to the floor, then slipped my underwear off in the most elegant way I could manage, unsure if I succeeded.

"Skye," she held my hands, "you're so sexy." She lowered her voice. "Like *so* fucking sexy."

I melted into her as we kissed. She pulled me down and we sat on the edge of her bed still kissing. Her body felt firm and toned. I ran my hands over the forearms I'd been watching for so long and gripped them. Just that was enough to send tingles all through me. Our arms clashed as we almost fought to touch each other. Out of pure lust, I got down on the floor and knelt between her legs. I reached up and gently pushed her tummy for her to lie back down on the bed. She lay back. I spread her legs open and stared at her below me, vulnerable, full of want and so hot. I kissed the soft mound of dark hair, and down the sides. She moaned as I teased her again then found her with my tongue. Her hips bucked at this one touch, causing me to smile. I gently licked her up and down. When I looked up she was looking at me and we held eye contact for long enough that I knew even then that I would never forget that moment.

Her breathing became ragged as I worked faster and she put her hands in my hair, possessively. Her legs tensed and her orgasm began to build. I put both my hands on her hips and felt her build and build in my mouth then explode, moaning loudly as she did so. My tongue never left her as she came down from her orgasm.

There were a few moments of silence except for Brianna's heavy breathing. She sat up on the edge of the bed again, and I climbed onto her lap and straddled her. Her cheeks were flushed. We looked deeply into each other's eyes. There was nothing else in this world than our connection in this moment. Brianna wrapped her arms tightly around my body as I cupped her face and softly kissed her on the mouth, hoping she could taste herself on my lips. The kiss soon became something wild, breathless, and hungry.

We rolled sideways onto the bed, our limbs entangled. Her head being so close to mine was so new and so amazing as we lay side by side. I still couldn't believe I was in her bed. Gently caressing my tummy, she tilted her head and planted slow and deliberate kisses on my neck. I tingled at her touches and loved the feel of her soft cheek against my skin. Her tenderness surprised me a little. I didn't want her to stop.

I moaned as she lowered her kisses, slowly moving down to my chest, and then my breasts. Her finger traced the sensitive skin along my lower abdomen. When she kissed my nipple I moaned again, unable to help it. I ran my fingers through her hair as she lowered her hand to my clit. She touched me so lightly, like before, that my need for her felt desperate now, bordering on ridiculous. I cried out her name. We'd hardly said a word so far so saying something felt kind of a thing in itself. Her mouth left my nipple and she turned her head to look at me, all the while still touching me.

"Is this okay?"

Oh my God she was so sexy. "Yes, yes, this is very okay."

The combination of talking to her and what she was doing sent me over the edge. My heart raced in my chest and my leg muscles burned. My whole body let go as wave after wave of pleasure surged through me. I cried out her name more than once.

She lay her head down on the pillow still facing me and my body turned towards her like a magnet. She pulled the covers over us from her side, wrapping us up in a sort of bubble. Inside this little cave we just smiled at each other.

She tucked a few strands of my hair behind my ears, affectionately. I could only imagine what state it must have been in. "You like my sex hair?"

"Best I've seen it." Brianna stroked my hair, smiling broadly. "It's soft. Healthy."

"I eat my greens."

"And other things."

"Yes. About that …"

She raised an eyebrow.

"I would like to do that again. Like very soon."

"Well, who am I to stand in your way?"

"Quite."

Brianna's expression turned more serious. Was there a problem? Did she want to tell me something bad?

"Skye, that was amazing."

I relaxed, feeling relieved.

"You're so delicious." I cringed at myself. "I mean, you know what I mean. It was incredible." I was a tad mortified at my awkwardness and just how much I'd obviously enjoyed myself.

"It was."

She leant over and placed her lips against mine. We kissed a little, brushing our noses together. I loved the feel of her skin against mine. When she started caressing my waist and running her hand all the way down to my hips, I felt things ignite again. I kissed her deeper and we pressed ourselves together. This was going to be a long night.

***

Opening my eyes and realising I was in someone else's bedroom was rather disorientating for a moment, then I remembered last night.

Brianna.

I turned around and she was lying right there next to me facing the other way. The duvet had fallen down so her bare back was half exposed. She stirred, then faced me, pulling the covers with her as she turned.

"Hi." I smiled at her.

"Good morning." She smiled back. Seeing her like this, first thing in the morning was just lovely.

"How's your head?"

"My head is okay. I only had about three drinks." She reached over and squeezed my hand. "You?"

"I'm a little tired. When did we go to sleep?"

"Not until after ... four?"

I was quiet for a while as I bathed in the awesomeness of our night together. We'd stayed up for hours making love and just exploring each other. We just couldn't get enough. I don't know how we decided to go to sleep in the end, that was a little blurry.

"Brianna, I had a wonderful evening with you."

She picked up my hand and kissed it. "I did too."

"I think I'm going to go home. Get myself sorted out. You know."

"But you look so sexy this morning." She leant over to kiss me.

"Ah. Not so fast. I have morning breath. I need to shower. Get cleaned. All the things."

"You could have a shower here if you want?" She kissed my hand again and raised an eyebrow. "Or maybe we could have one together?" Her eyes were dark again. I had a feeling if I stayed we'd never leave this bed.

I put a hand on her waist, then thought better of it because of my impulse to start it all up again, so I moved it to her arm. "I hadn't planned on staying out. I feel a bit all over the place. I need to get back home, get myself together. Then maybe we can talk later?"

"I understand." She smiled back. "You can borrow some of my clothes to go home in if you want?" She got out of bed, completely naked and totally confident. Was she trying to make it impossible for me to leave? She threw on a dressing gown and fished out a pair of trousers and a nice jumper. I sat up and brought the sheets up to cover myself. She placed the clothes at the end of the bed, then perched at the side.

"Wearing your clothes is going to feel kind of sexy."

"Yeah. I won't be thinking about it. At all."

I laughed, softly. "I like this side of you." I wanted to say more but then maybe I wanted her to say more first. It was quiet and I felt her hesitation too.

She squeezed my thigh then stood up. "I'll leave you to get ready."

My hair was wild, and I looked terrible. I used a facewipe of hers to make myself feel a basic level of clean and presentable, then scooped up my dress from the floor. I was a little stiff from all the sex as I put on the clothes that smelled of her. Brianna's dressing table was filled with expensive looking bottles and creams. She had about five different types of hairbrushes. A warm heat went through me as I thought about how I'd run my hands through her hair last night. The chunky wooden bedframe was like something out of a magazine. The bed itself took centre stage with its messed up white sheets, and cushions on the floor. There was a large rug underneath the bed, giving the whole space a styled feel. I wanted to drink in this moment. I hoped it wouldn't be the last time I was in here.

I passed a room full of bikes and parts, like some sort of bike repair workshop that smelled faintly of bike oil and tyres. God she was hot. I found her in the kitchen. She looked up and smiled as I stepped across her open-plan living space.

"Are the clothes okay? They look good on you. Can I get you anything before you go?"

"They're perfect, thanks. Maybe a glass of water?"

Brianna had cleared the counter and emptied our glasses of wine. A faint smell of wine lingered near the sink. Seeing the place where we first kissed in the cold light of day was like a wake-up call. This was real. This had really happened. The pull I felt towards her was so strong, even now. She got out a jug of filtered water from the fridge and poured us each a glass. She handed me the glass and our fingers touched, sending tingles through my body.

I downed my water in one, then tried to ignore the brain freeze, aware of her eyes on me.

"Here," she handed me a canvas bag. "For your stuff. I thought you might need something bigger for your dress."

I took it. "Thank you. That's very thoughtful."

At the door I put my heels back on. They didn't go with the trousers, but I didn't care. It was all a little surreal. There was no doubt we'd be seeing each other again at work, but what about for other reasons? Did she think this was just a one-time thing? Surely not after the way she'd touched me and her pleas for me to stay this morning. How she couldn't get enough of me. It was something more, right?

"Skye." Her tone turned more serious. She stepped close, putting her arms around my waist. "Last night meant a lot to me." She kissed my cheek once. "Can I see you before Tuesday?"

I kept a straight-ish face but inside I was ecstatic and scared and overwhelmed and excited. "I'd like that."

She smiled then pulled me in for a full-body hug. She smelled of sex. I squeezed her hand as I moved out of the door, neither of us dropping the touch until our arms reached their full lengths.

Fuck. I had it bad.

***

On the train home I think it really sunk in. The enormity of it. I checked my phone. It was lit up with a few messages on my home screen. Two from Hayley asking if I'd got home okay and another about how hungover she felt this morning. I left them for a bit, and just looked out the window. My lips felt bruised from all the kissing. Even between my legs felt a little tender. Our desire had been insatiable. Our sex had been ferocious, and I think that's why I'd been so shy this morning and left.

I was about to reply to Hayley when a message came in from Brianna.

Hey you. Thank you for a very special night. There's this feminist open mic night tonight. Spoken word and live music. Would you like to go? I thought maybe we could have dinner before? Around seven?

Adrenaline rushed through me. Hell yes I wanted to see her again today. Thank God she got in touch so soon. My earlier need to process suddenly disappeared. I typed my reply instantly:

Yes to that!

Seconds later:

Wonderful. Enjoy getting clean. I hope it's short lived ;) See you tonight xxx

I re-read her message a few times. Who was this new flirty and open Brianna? If I'd just met this woman, I would be on the phone to Hayley right now proclaiming I'd had the best sex ever with possibly my future wife. But I couldn't. I couldn't tell Hayley, not just yet anyway. The arrival of the countryside out of the window helped calm me down a little. Some things never changed. It was a comfort.

When I got home, I had the distinct feeling that something was different. I was going about my routine, using my things, yet something felt like I was doing it all for the first time, post-first-sex with Brianna.

Later that afternoon I tried to order groceries online but just couldn't focus on it. I put my laptop down and made a cup of coffee and gave up trying to downplay the significance of sleeping with Brianna. It wasn't just that we'd had sex and it was amazing and I was still elated that Brianna liked me back – we had a connection. If she wasn't a co-worker, things would be different. She would be perfect. Yes, I had needed to thaw her out a bit, but that was done now. There was no iciness between us any more. I might not have known where this was heading, but it was worth exploring. And that was terrifying because my job was the most important thing in my life.

I was due to call my mum this weekend. Given that my mum could always tell my emotions from my voice, I decided to keep my distance for a bit longer, as I always did when I was getting involved with someone new. That left only one other person I'd want to share this with – Hayley, but I just couldn't. Not yet, anyway. Only when it was time to get ready for the evening did I start to perk up.

~ 19 ~
Skye

I saw Brianna waiting for me in the station before she saw me. She was wearing black skinny jeans, a blue denim Sherpa jacket and dark tan boots. To think that we were doing this was still kind of blowing my mind. The train station wasn't that busy. When she recognised me and smiled I melted inside. I swear we were smiling differently at each other now we'd cracked through the layers. I held my breath the last few steps with butterflies in my stomach.

"Hey." Brianna was the epitome of cool. Did nothing faze her?

"Hi. Were you waiting long?"

She leant in towards me and planted a kiss on my cheek.

"Not long. You're on time. You know me, though, always early for things."

"Yes, painfully early."

"Better to be early than late."

"Better to be on time and everybody wins."

She grinned at our playful jousting, thankfully not looking offended.

"You look gorgeous, Skye." Brianna looked me up and down.

"Thank you." I inhaled, loving her attention. "You do too. I love your Doc Martens."

"Oh these? They're so old."

"I've never seen you in them before."

"I don't wear them to work. Work is suits and heels."

"Well, you rock the rock chick look. I like it on you." She was hot. I could have just said she was hot, and nearly did, but we'd only just met up and I didn't want to come on too strong too soon.

"Thanks. So, there's this lovely little Italian restaurant I want to take you to. It's near the venue. And I know you like pizza so—"

"Sounds perfect."

At the restaurant, we got seated in the corner and this suited me fine. All the more space to stare dreamy eyed into Brianna's beautiful face. The restaurant was full, and the tables were close together, with just enough space for the waiting staff to dart about. On the way over to the table I took a quick scan of the room, thankfully no one from work was there. Smells of garlic and herbs and oven-cooked pizza circulated the room. Before long we had a bottle of red wine and bread and olives on the table. Brianna was quiet. Hopefully she wasn't having regrets about us sleeping together.

"It's so great to see you again today," Brianna said.

"I know. It's so scandalous, right?"

She smiled at this. Every time she smiled it did something to me.

She bit down on her bottom lip. "You kind of ran away this morning. What was that about?"

"Oh you know, minor freak out. But I'm over it now."

"What were you freaking out about?"

I held her gaze. As if she didn't know. Did she really want to address it all so early on in the evening?

"I think you know. We work together."

Brianna furrowed her brow at my comment, looking so sexy. Not distracting at all.

"It just all felt very real this morning. It was a lot to process."

"It's okay. I know how you feel. It is a lot to unpack. But like I said, I'm glad that you said something last night." She put her hand over mine. "What we do outside of work is no one's business."

Not strictly true. That being said I didn't want to spoil the moment. I didn't know where this thing between us was going, and I didn't want to ruin any of that potential by focusing on the negative right away. Her hand on mine felt so good.

"You're right. Let's not focus on work. It takes up way too much of our attention during the week as it is. I just want to have fun tonight."

"Excellent plan."

I laughed. "You do love a plan, Brianna."

"I thought you said no work talk?"

"Sorry, my bad. Let's make a deal not to bring it up again tonight, yeah?"

"Deal. So tell me about your family."

"Okay." I took some wine, buying some time to decide how much to say. "My parents are divorced. My mum lives alone, which she pretends she's happy about, but I know she gets lonely sometimes. That's why she's in so many clubs. I swear, she has a better social life than I do."

"Does she?"

"I used to have a big circle of friends, different groups, you know. And work, I'm quite social at work. Or used to be. All this extra stuff to do with the merger has really obliterated my social life lately."

"Ah. You brought up work."

"I keep doing it. Sorry. Anyway, I don't have any siblings. But I do have lots of cousins that I'm close to. One of them used to work at Your View in Digital." I knew my mistake. Brianna tilted her head and raised quite the pronounced eyebrow at me. I hung my head in shame. "Sorry. Maybe you should talk now. How's your mum's party coming along? Booked the stripper yet?"

Brianna burst out laughing. "No. She's getting spoiled but not that spoiled."

"Yeah, I don't think your dad would be too happy about that."

Brianna became quiet. Was it the mention of her dad?

"I don't think he would care much."

What could you say to that? Were they unhappy? And why wasn't he helping to plan it, anyway?

"He just does his own thing these days. He's paying for her party, at least."

Ouch. "And your brothers, how are they?"

"They're good. I'll be seeing them all tomorrow. It's my niece's fifth birthday party. Ollie's daughter. He has a three-year-old son, too."

"Awesome. You're an aunt. I wonder what that must be like."

"It's great. I get to see them for fun things then escape to my child-free life."

"You don't like children?"

"No I do. But in small doses. I think it'd be different with your own. But I'm not there yet."

"So you want to have children one day?"

"One day. What about you?"

"Yes, definitely. One day. I've frozen my eggs already."

"What? Seriously?"

"Two years ago."

"That's very organised of you. I'm impressed. I hope you get a chance to use them one day."

I inhaled. This had got deep very quickly. Had we really just talked about whether or not we wanted children? A long minute or so passed in silence.

"I have another question for you. One of your open questions." She grinned.

"Yes?"

"Tell me about a time when you were a complete badass and gave zero fucks about the consequences."

This was a strange question. Why did she want to know this? "I can't think of anything."

Brianna shook her head. "Skye, what am I going to do with you?"

I flashed back to last night. She could do anything she wanted with me. I blushed. Fuck, she noticed.

Brianna sipped her wine. I watched her swirl it around a little. The waitress came over and took our order. We both ordered a fresh pizza. The waitress gave us a look, but I couldn't place it. Did she think we were a couple? Was it that obvious?

"So back to my question," said Brianna, ripping off a piece of bread. "Surely there must be something?"

"Does shoplifting a magazine at fourteen count?"

She laughed. "Yeah, that counts. Which magazine?"

"Star Trek: The Next Generation."

"Now *that* I did not expect. That makes it not count. Give me another example."

I racked my brains. "I once got into a proper road rage fight."

"What happened?"

I put on my best American accent. "Bitch cut me up so I let her know about it."

Brianna chuckled. "And how did it go?"

"I shouted obscenities at this poor girl, so not great. Given the fact that I was in the right and a few days before my period, I blew up. It was a hot day and my air-conditioning wasn't working so I had the windows down and then we came to a stop side by side at the next red light. We got out of the car. I squared up to her like a rude boy. She backed down when I threatened to trace her number plate and report her to the police."

"I love that story. I so can't imagine you ever doing anything like that but then I can the more you talk."

"Being in the right helped. She was driving dangerously and nearly caused an accident."

"You kicked ass. You stood up for yourself."

"Or nearly got stabbed. That was always a loose possibility. Why do you ask, seriously?"

"I just think you should channel that attitude more. Stop being so nice all the time. Take some risks, like that one. Although maybe a safer one next time. Telling Peter where to go, for example." She put her hand over her mouth. "Oops, I did it too."

"It's the main thing we have in common, so it's bound to happen."

Brianna frowned at this. Or was it a wounded look? It was the whole point of what we were doing tonight, to get to know each other better, and I'd just invalidated it. Why had I done that?

"I do know how to be a badass and take risks. I told you how I felt about you, for instance."

I took a few sips of wine and avoided her gaze. Wasn't I more of a risk taker than her in that respect?

And didn't I throw myself off a mountain with minimal bike skills?

"You're right. You did do that and it was so brave." She reached across and held my hand. "I am so happy you did. I don't know that I would have been so—"

"So badass?"

She smiled in defeat. "Exactly."

My head was still in a more serious place. I didn't want to gloss over or blindly accept this advice she kept insisting on. I removed my hand from hers, feeling a little triggered.

"I think I can come across as a bit too nice because I was socialised into it. I do think it's good to be a kind person in the world. If people want to try and take advantage, that's on them. I can spot that behaviour a mile off nowadays. Trust me. I've had therapy on this. I know why I always used to be such a people-pleaser." A waiter served the table next to us. I waited for him to leave. "Basically, my dad was a pretty difficult character growing up. He's a very manipulative and controlling person, and I guess over the years I learned it was easier just to let him be right. He's the sort of person who wants to own the narrative of any situation, and if he doesn't like something he just denies it or gaslights you. Pandering to that was the easier choice when I was younger, so when you say I'm 'too nice' or can't handle Peter or Andrew at work it kind of pisses me off." I took some more wine. I'd had no intention of talking about my dad this evening, or ever really. He'd abandoned me, we no longer spoke, and I did my best never to think of him. "I know exactly what you're talking about but I don't want to go there."

Brianna looked alarmed. "I didn't mean to push your buttons. I'm sorry."

"It's okay. You mean well."

"Skye," she squeezed my hand again. "It's probably your biggest strength." She paused. "And your biggest weakness."

"Are you talking about work again?"

"Not specifically, no. I think you are kind and generous *and* strong and powerful. There have just been a few times when I've wanted you to step into your power more. But now I realise I have no right to be saying any of this. I've overstepped. I'm sorry."

"You're just saying what you see. You don't need to apologise."

"That stuff with your dad sounds really hard."

This was still going way deeper than I thought it was going to go tonight. I'd wanted a fun date, not to discuss my most painful topics. I picked up some bread, not quite ready to change the subject though. "You know, we talked about this before. You said you thought I was too nice, and I said you needed to open up more at work."

"True." She nodded.

"Do you mind if I elaborate, now that I know you better too?"

"Sure."

"You're so fun to be around outside of work, and, more recently for me, while we're at work. And yes, we're talking about work now."

"Okay."

"You've gotta let people in more, Brianna. You need to be more vulnerable. Let people see the real you. That would make you stronger."

Brianna looked stunned. "I can't do that."

"Why not?"

"I don't want to let my guard down. To be successful in business I've had to adopt a tough persona."

"Why?"

Brianna pursed her lips and rubbed the back of her neck. "I've always been competitive and determined, and high-achieving. My parents encouraged it. Or maybe they just expected it. Whatever. It's just who I am."

"Does it really help you work with your team and create good work?"

She was quiet for a few moments. "Yes, I think it has. I don't think there's anything I need to change."

"Brianna, people don't know you at work. You keep to yourself. Some people are afraid of you. You can be quite intimidating."

"Something we'd never say about a man."

"True. But there are plenty of men who are open and sociable in the workplace. Don't you want to know things that might help you take your team to the next level? That's why I took your feedback so well. And don't you just want to enjoy yourself at work a bit more? Have a bit more fun?"

"I'm not sure you took my feedback that well, but I get what you're saying. I'll think about it."

"We completely failed at not talking about work, didn't we?"

"I'm okay with it if you are?"

Despite the nature of our conversation, I still felt a level of safety in it and that we trusted each other enough that we weren't going to take it personally. It also felt refreshing to have such a frank talk. I nodded. "I am. I'm glad we can be this open and honest with each other."

The waitress finally came back and we got started on our gigantic pizzas. The table was only just about big enough to hold everything, so some concentration was required.

"So, what films and TV shows do you like?" said Brianna, cutting her pizza. "What are you into? You should know, I have an irrational dislike of reality television. Or so I'm told. I think it's perfectly rational."

"Love Island."

Brianna put down her knife and fork, and half got out of her seat to leave. She wasn't being serious though. Neither was I. As dates go, this was already one of the best I'd ever had.

***

The venue was further down the same street, so it didn't take long to get there. The ground was wet and the relatively warm air had that after-the-rain aroma. We entered an old municipal building of some sort, with a grand archway leading to a massive doorway that was open. People were milling about, mostly women. Brianna spoke to the person in the ticket booth, a small glass panelled room overlooking the entrance walkway. I hung back as she sorted the tickets. The space opened out into a large high-ceilinged room, with pillars leading to more rooms at one side. It was an unusual space for a gig but full of character.

"Cool place, huh?" said Brianna, joining me in the archway.

"Yeah. I like it."

"They do lots of events and open the place out to different arts and creative industries, and community groups."

We strolled further into the venue, towards the tables and chairs, and bar.

"Do you go to many of them?"

"Sometimes."

I just nodded, still taking in the place.

"They're also a city arts festival venue. That's where they started. Empty spaces in this part of town rarely go unused these days."

There wasn't so much a stage but a designated performance area with a full band set-up: drums, three guitars, keyboard, piano, trumpet and main mic at the front. It was busy, with a mixture of people standing and sitting, in anticipation for the performances.

"Do you want to find a table and I'll go get us drinks?" said Brianna, half turning away.

"Okay, thanks. Another red wine please."

I managed to get one of the last tables in the back corner. For a Saturday night, the atmosphere was remarkably calm. Brianna came back and took the seat to my immediate left. Her choice of seat was sweet. We couldn't be closer to each other.

"You seem happy about something," said Brianna, taking a sip of wine. She rested her elbows on the table and leant forward, gazing into my eyes. I unashamedly looked down at her mouth. Brianna was beautiful. I loved being able to properly look at her now, without feeling like I'd be caught staring.

"I'm just happy that we're doing this tonight. That we're here, together."

"I'm happy that we're here together, too."

"I didn't realise you were such a feminist. But now that I think about it, it makes sense."

"How so?"

"You aren't fazed by meetings when we're the only women in the room. You hold your own well."

"Thank you."

We were interrupted by the compere asking us to quieten down and prepare for the first act. They were an all-female four-piece punk-rock band from the local area. Vulva Verses. Brianna and I shared an amused look. I loved being this free and myself around her. Sharing things with her. Connecting.

The crowd had mostly settled and were ready for the night to begin. It had a part gig, part conference feel. As if we'd listen to a performance and then have a Q&A afterwards. I hadn't been to an event like this before, come to think of it. It was all very conscious and thoughtful and intimate.

The lead singer took the mic. She was tall and fierce-looking. Her voice was angelic and soft. "We're Vulva Verses, and we're so pleased to be here this evening. We hope you like our songs."

What came next was the loudest, screamiest, angriest four minutes that I'd ever heard in a live act. I loved it. I had no clue what the lyrics were, my ears were red-hot from the volume level. I didn't need the lyrics, though, as their energetic rage chimed with something deep inside me.

Brianna was engrossed too. I stole a few looks at her as we listened. The band finished their first song to a round of applause from an audience that looked shocked to their core, except for their friends near the back who cheered the loudest.

"Thank you. Our next song is called Trials and Tribbing-Relations."

Brianna burst out laughing, but I didn't know why. She saw the look of confusion on my face. "I'll tell you later," she said.

The gig passed quickly. Performer after performer graced the stage. The intimate venue created a safe, respectful, and even loving atmosphere. The performers and the audience were as one sat together at the venue, indistinguishable. I could do with more gigs like this, if Brianna was up for it. The compere announced a short break and then we'd come back for the final three acts. Almost as one, everyone got up and headed to the bar.

"This is awesome. Thanks for suggesting we come here tonight."

Brianna reached for my hand under the table and held it. I quivered at her touch. "I'm so glad you're enjoying it. It is a bit different."

It was only nine thirty. By the time this finished, all I wanted to do was head straight back to Brianna's and pick up where we left off last night. I trembled at the thought of repeating what we did last night.

"Hi."

I looked up and Siobhan was standing in front of us with a curious look on her face. Had she seen something? Were we being too affectionate? Brianna let go of my hand under the table.

"Great seeing you both here," said Siobhan, stepping out of the way so someone could get past, and smiling broadly. She looked much more relaxed than she normally did in the office. She had a stern, 'something's about to go dreadfully wrong' look about her most of the time despite having little to no real responsibility. But she was hungry for it, and I could tell that she'd go far. Some people just had a quality about them that you could see would take them a long way in their career.

"And you," I said quickly, perhaps too quickly, "these performances have been fantastic, right?"

"Yeah, they're spot on. Absolutely first class. I'm here with my friend Tara. She's performing in a bit."

"That's fantastic, I'll look out for her," said Brianna. "What's her thing? Her genre."

"Spoken word."

"Nice."

"She's getting pretty big on the scene around here. I hope you enjoy it."

Brianna and I both just nodded.

Siobhan must have picked up on our hesitation. "See you at work next week. Hope you both have a fab bank holiday weekend."

We waved at Siobhan as she left, as a knot gripped my stomach. She could easily have seen us holding hands. I didn't want to think about other people right now and the consequences and complexities of being seen together with Brianna.

But it was hard not to.

"Do you think she saw something?"

Brianna shook her head. "Why would she? We're just sitting here, enjoying the gig." She leaned in closer to me. "And our hands were shielded under the table. She couldn't have seen."

I trembled at her closeness and loved any talk of us being physical together. Did I really care if Siobhan or anyone knew anything at this point? Reality felt a long way off. This was the weekend after all.

"You're probably right."

"I'm happy to forget about it, if you are?"

I smiled softly. "Already forgotten."

Brianna gazed deeply into my eyes with a questioning look in hers. "Would you like to come back to mine after?" She cleared her throat. "For some coffee?" She was clearly trying to act cool, but I saw her vulnerability, which was rare. I loved having that effect on her.

My smile widened. "For coffee?" I teased. "Just for coffee?"

She squirmed in her seat. "No, not just for coffee."

We held eye contact as Brianna squeezed my hand under the table again. She stroked my hand with her fingers, and each stroke sent warm tingles right through me. A new band came on after a short intro from the compere. Damn. We wouldn't be able to make a quick exit now. We listened to the rest of the song but all I could think about was what we were going to do when we got back to Brianna's. I was hyper aware of her next to me and couldn't meet her eyes given the nature of my thoughts.

When the song finally ended Brianna tugged on my hand. "Do you want to get out of here?"

I took a deep breath. I did want that. But I also enjoyed making her wait like this.

"I do," I bit my lip. "But I was kind of wanting to see Siobhan's friend play. She sounded great."

Brianna nodded slowly and her eyes narrowed slightly. I think she knew that I was playing with her.

"Of course. No problem," she said.

***

Things escalated quickly once we got back to Brianna's flat. Almost as soon as we got into the safety of her hallway, she was pushing me up against the wall and kissing me. She tugged at the sleeve of my jacket, and I slipped out of it in a hurry.

"I've wanted this all day," breathed Brianna, in between her kisses.

She wrapped her arms around my waist, and we deepened the kiss. I shivered in pleasure. It was like we were drinking each other in, frantic and raw. She felt both familiar and like totally uncharted territory.

She guided me onto the leather couch, and we lay down beside each other, face to face. I felt her breath on my lips and trembled slightly. We both knew where this was going. Even though we'd slept together less than twenty-four hours ago it felt like a big deal that we were doing this again, and so soon.

My earlier confidence suddenly disappeared. What if it wasn't as amazing as last night?

I pushed that thought from my mind as Brianna planted kisses along my jawline and shifted her weight so that her thigh pressed against my centre. My body went into overdrive as a wave of tingles rushed through me. Rational thought was off the table. I was completely in her control.

She gave me a smouldering look. Her eyes were full of desire. She pushed herself up and pulled her top over her head. I quickly did the same. Her eyes settled on my body, and she slowly ran her hands over the lacey fabric of my bra. I quivered as a warm heat spread through me. When she paused, resting her hand in between my breasts on my chest, and looked into my eyes, I felt the strength of our connection. It was so powerful. I swallowed. My heart raced. Could she feel my heartbeat? Did she know how much I liked her?

I ran my fingers through hair. She looked down at my body, and then found my eyes again. She kept her eyes on me as she reached down, undid the button of my jeans, and pulled down the zip. I lifted my hips and moved the jeans down a bit. She slid her hand over my centre, moving the fabric of my underwear to one side, urgently. I gasped, hyper aware of how turned on I was and how she now absolutely knew this.

She leant in and whispered in my ear, her lips brushing the side of my face. "I've got you exactly where I want you."

She did have me. We both knew it. We found each other's lips again and kissed with a hunger and a thirst that left me breathless. I ran my hands over her bare back as her fingers slid over my clit. Warm tingles rushed through me. She stopped, suddenly, her fingers hovering over me.

"Hey," I said, frustrated.

The look in her eyes was downright naughty. "That's for all the flirting you did."

I opened my mouth in protest. "What …?"

"You know what you did. Kissing my cheek at the party. Constantly checking me out. Making me wait tonight … I could go on."

I gave her my best innocent look. "I thought you liked it."

"I did." She kissed me again. I quickly felt breathless.

"Actually," Brianna broke off. "I want you in my bed." She got up, holding her hand out for me. "We need more space."

As we moved into her room, memories of last night came flooding back but were quickly pushed out by the immediacy of being here with her again. My fingers reached for the button of Brianna's jeans. We slid each other's jeans down and then stepped out of them. I nearly tripped as I pulled my socks off. Smiling, she reached out to help me.

Steadier now, I put my arms around her and unclipped her bra. She let the straps fall forward, off her shoulders. I kissed her again, feeling my head spin. Brianna took my bra off as we were kissing then tugged at my underwear. The kiss deepened as we let our panties fall to the floor. We pressed our bodies against each other. The full skin-on-skin contact was so intimate.

Brianna guided me onto her bed in what seemed like slow motion and straddled me, before bending down and kissing me deeply. She was so naked and so ridiculously hot. My dream had literally come true.

"I want to be close to you," Brianna breathed.

"You're lying on top of me naked and I'm naked. I think this is pretty close."

"Closer," she whispered into my ear as she expertly positioned herself onto me. I felt the heat of her wetness on mine as she rolled her hips against me. She let out the sexiest moan I'd ever heard. This was definitely closer and felt out-of-this-world amazing.

I dug my fingers into her hips. A tiny droplet of sweat gathered at her temple. Her arm and leg muscles were really working. My whole body was trembling. My heart raced. I didn't want this to end. She slowed down and we moved together more deliberately. An almost painful tension built inside of me as tingles spread throughout my entire body every time she rocked her hips.

"Skye." Her breathing was ragged. "I'm really close."

"I am too. Fuck. Brianna don't stop. Don't stop."

Our bodies glided over each other in a frantic search for release. She looked into my eyes and came, sending me over the edge at the same time, together, in an uncontrollable frenzy.

We melted together as one in a pile of sweat and racing hearts. She lay on top of me. I didn't know what to say and apparently neither did she. She broke away and pulled the duvet up and over us then put her arm on my waist. I leaned in and kissed her gently on the lips, before resting my head on the pillow again. I ran my thumb over her cheek. "How do you feel?"

Brianna shrugged. "Yeah, not bad."

"Hey." I slapped her, playfully.

She pulled me onto her in one swift movement. She laughed as I cried out in mock protest. Our eyes locked and I felt her breathe deeply. "I feel amazing. How do you feel?"

"That has never happened to me before. So pretty fucking incredible actually." That sex was mind-blowing. I'd never thought it was possible to come in that position until tonight. And only the second time we'd slept together, too.

"Me neither. Not like that."

"We fit together perfectly."

"We do." Brianna smiled.

I grinned. "You're very athletic, so that helps."

"It's all in the hips and glutes."

We lay there dreamily gazing into each other's eyes. I put some strands of hair behind her ears and stroked her cheek with my thumb. Something in the quiet moments like this felt very special. Our connection went way beyond just sex. All I wanted to do now was hold her, talk, and see where the mood took us next.

And that's exactly what we did.

~ 20 ~
Brianna

Only after morning sex did we finally make it out of bed. And by make it out of bed I mean Skye sitting upright, naked, wrapped in the duvet, watching me throw on a T-shirt and jogging bottoms by my chest of drawers. As soon as I'd set foot on the floor I regretted the end of our time together. I could have stayed there forever with her. The only reason I insisted we got up was because I had my niece's birthday party to get to. I tried extra hard to reassure her that I wasn't kicking her out.

"Brianna."

"Yeah?"

"You look beautiful."

I blushed a little and then looked around for her clothes then handed her all that I could find.

"Did you want to borrow anything again? It's not the nicest wearing yesterday's clothes."

"Could I borrow a T-shirt please?"

I handed her a T-shirt from my chest of drawers. "Would you like some coffee?"

She said that she did and would just go to use the bathroom. I left her in my room, noticing how lovely it was to do so. It didn't feel strange at all. I let that sink in. Like yesterday, she was in my house, in my clothes, in my bed … To think Skye was wandering about my room, probably looking at my things, my space, was in its own way kind of hot. She was a work person. But she was so much more than just a work person now.

She was Skye.

We sat on the couch with our coffee and some toast, and talked. Skye sat opposite me with her back to one of the arms. She was sitting in the same spot where things had heated up last night. For the life of me, I couldn't stop thinking about it, even though she was still here. I forced myself to be present with her, so as not to miss the here and now. Her hair was down and slightly messy, her cheeks still flushed.

She took a big bite of toast. "I should have Nutella for breakfast more often. It's so good."

"It's really moreish though. I once ate a whole jar."

"What? Never. You're such a healthy eater."

"I'm so not. The brownies, remember?"

"Oh yeah." Skye took some more bites. "What else do you like to indulge in?" There was a naughty look in her eyes. She rested her foot against my shin. It felt so normal, and so right. Her eyes now reminded me of the raw sexual intimacy that we'd shared. It was hard to look in them now and not think about us having sex.

"I think last night was a pretty good example of where I allow myself to indulge."

"Yep, you indulged all right."

We laughed. It felt expansive. Limitless. Like we were friends as well as lovers. Were we lovers?

"What time is your niece's party?"

"Um," I checked my wrist. "Shit! It's in an hour. And it's a thirty-minute drive away."

Skye put down her plate. "I'm so sorry. I should get going and let you get ready. You should have said. I wouldn't have made myself so comfortable and had breakfast."

I leant over and held her ankles as they were nearest to me. "Skye, I asked you to stay. I want you to be here. You don't need to apologise for anything. You apologise too much. What's with that?"

"I'm sorry."

"See! Apologising for apologising. Look, my brother's house isn't that far from yours. Let me drive you home. You've been on the train for most of the weekend."

Skye smiled. "It's been some weekend."

"And you don't deserve to have to take the train home again. Plus, I really want to keep hanging out with you."

"Well, if you're going to put it like that then I'd be really grateful for the lift. Thank you."

In the car a bit later Skye and I fell into a comfortable silence. Sunshine poured into the car; its heat amplified by the glass and black paint. Skye was glowing. Her skin, her hair, her eyes. I glanced over again out of the corner of my eyes.

"Hey," she turned her head to me and smiled. "Eyes on the road."

I blushed, looked straight ahead and took a deep breath.

When we pulled up outside her house, I turned the engine off and turned my body towards her as she turned hers towards mine. She bit down on her lip. I was lost for words. This was ridiculous. We were like lovelorn teenagers.

"I would invite you in, but I don't think you have time."

"Yeah, I have to go, it sucks. I'd love to see inside one day."

"I think you'll like my bedroom." Skye raised an eyebrow.

"Skye. So naughty." I put my hand on her thigh. "I love it."

"Just so you know, my house is a bit more … rustic than your place. I have a lot of stuff."

"Shocker."

"It's a clean and organised mess. I know exactly where everything is."

"Of course you do."

"But it's charming, and homely. In my humble opinion of course."

I squeezed her thigh. We found each other's eyes and I tucked a strand of hair behind her ear. Skye gave me a look that I couldn't quite make out. I wasn't sure if she was going to invite me around later or if this was going to be the big goodbye before work on Tuesday. God, work on Tuesday. We'd discussed literally nothing about it.

Skye leant forward and placed a super soft kiss on my lips, and paused for a second. I opened my eyes to find hers open too, but too close to focus on.

We laughed. She kissed me again on the cheek this time and I just smiled. My heart felt like it was going to burst with happiness.

"Enjoy your afternoon, Brianna." She pulled back and held onto the door handle. "Will you text me and let me know how it's going? I want to know how good the cake is."

"I will."

***

"Ah, there you are. I was just saying how unlike it is of you to be late."

"Mum, I'm only five minutes late."

"Well, everyone's already here. We've already started."

I took off my denim jacket.

"You're looking well, darling."

I thought she didn't like me casually dressed. "Thank you."

"Would you like some wine? There's a vintage malbec on the go."

"I'm good, thanks."

She gave me a withering look. "Brianna, must you be so sensible all the time."

"No, Mum, just when I'm driving."

"One glass with food isn't going to hurt. And it's a Sunday for Christ's sake."

I gave her a don't push me look and she rolled her eyes and left me to it. Her small frame was still somehow larger than life. I'd never quite been able to work that one out.

"Thanks for coming, Bri," said Ollie. "Good to see you." He regarded me a little longer than necessary. "There's something different about you. What've you been up to?"

Typical Ollie. More of a parent to me than Mum or Dad. I smiled. "Not much."

"I know that look. That smile. You're seeing someone, aren't you?"

I shook my head and bashed him away, directing him into his own house, where everyone was. I don't think I'd seen this many children in the house before. They were everywhere, dashing about, jumping, screaming, and tugging on adults' hands. My niece spotted me and came running towards me with her arms wide and a delirious sugar-fuelled look on her face.

"Aunty Bri!"

I knelt down to her five-year-old height and welcomed her into my arms with a bear hug. "Happy birthday, Isla. You're getting so big. Here." I squeezed her shoulders. "This is for you."

She became transfixed on the gift-wrapped box I pulled out of my bag.

Isla ripped the paper off and her jaw dropped. "A watch? Look Mummy, Aunty BriBri got me an Apple watch."

Joanna, my sister-in-law, came over. "Isn't Aunty Bri generous? What do we say to Aunty Bri?"

"Thank you."

I had no children and a good job. If I couldn't spend it on the people I loved, what was the point? I would have got her more, if that wouldn't have involved upstaging her parents. I'd learned that lesson last year.

"You're so very welcome."

Joanna looked pleased. I'd already asked Ollie if it was okay for me to get her one and he said that it was. "Are these all your friends, Isla? What a lovely party."

"They're all my friends and they are all here to play with me. We've got a bouncy castle in the garden. Want to come play on it?" She put the present down at her feet, already forgotten in the excitement of her party. I didn't blame her. "Why don't you go ahead, and I'll be over in a few minutes?"

"Okay." She ran off. I put the present on the sideboard.

"Have you eaten?" Joanna asked. "There's plenty of food."

I wasn't very hungry as I'd had such a late breakfast but didn't want to disappoint my host. "I'd love some. Smells delicious."

I followed Joanna to the buffet, waving hello to James, who was playing a computer game with the children. I recognised Ollie's friends and their children immediately, as they'd all bonded through having children around about the same time and were nearly always together at big events. My mum was in the garden opening another bottle of wine while entertaining her counterpart, Joanna's mother. My dad was nowhere to be seen.

"Have you seen my dad, Joanna?"

"Oh, he's not here yet. Had to work." Ollie said, swooping in and grabbing a sausage roll. "Apparently he works on a Sunday now and it's more important than his granddaughter's fifth birthday." He popped the rest of the sausage roll into his mouth and chewed it rather aggressively. He always did stress eat.

I frowned. His granddaughter's birthday for fuck's sake. Dad's avoidant and withdrawn behaviour had gotten worse in the past few months. No, years. But this was a new low.

Out on the garden patio, Mum stumbled as about five children raced past her. Granted, they were like mini tornados but if she was steadier on her feet it wouldn't have been an issue. My mum responded by emptying her latest glass of wine. Joanna's mother did well pretending not to notice.

My nephew appeared and hugged me around the knee. We had a little chat about his new dinosaur Lego then he left to go back and play in the garden. My brother handed me a coffee, I hadn't asked for. "Ah, thanks. You know me so well."

"You're welcome." His face turned serious. "I'm so pissed off at Dad."

"Yep, I thought you were. It pisses me off too. But you know what, he's always done this. Just suiting himself. Acting like he doesn't even have a family. There's no point in letting it keep getting to us."

"I know. I guess I hadn't really believed what you had been saying about him all this time. Until today."

"It can't be easy being the golden child. I get that now."

"I don't want to let it ruin Isla's day."

"It'll be okay," I said. "You've got people who love you. Who love Isla. Try to focus on that."

He scoffed and turned away a bit. "Easier said than done."

I looked at him. He was bothered about it. Excessively so. "Ollie."

He turned back towards me, shrugging his broad shoulders. "What?"

"You're nothing like him, you know."

His face softened and for a second there was a glimpse of his unguarded younger self. "I know."

I smiled at him and saw the weight lift from his shoulders. "But you are a greedy bastard."

He laughed. "We were going to bring out the cake soon. Get it going early, so it gets eaten and it's not too close to the kids' dinnertime."

"Very sensible."

A short while later the party was asked to decamp to the garden and children were seated on the floor. Joanna and Ollie came out of the house with the massive cake singing 'happy birthday' to their daughter. Mum was singing happy birthday louder than anyone, which was sweet. Isla clapped her hands in anticipation. I got my camera ready.

Dad was missing this.

Isla blew out her five candles and looked like she might burst with happiness. Joanna helped her cut the cake and I waited until the children had theirs before inching towards the table and waiting my turn for a slice. I found a seat on the garden wall and people-watched while I ate. I thought of Skye, and wished she were here. I messaged her, without overthinking it.

Cake tastes delicious, but not as good as you. Wish you were here with me to enjoy it.

It was forward. Was it too forward? I got butterflies in my stomach. Three little dots appeared instantly.

I wish I was with you too. But not just to eat the cake...

I was about to reply with something outrageous, but my mother appeared in front of me, blocking out the sun. I put my phone down.

"You're awfully quiet sitting all the way over here by yourself. What's wrong?"

"Nothing's wrong."

"Then why aren't you talking to anyone?"

"I just sat down for a second to eat some cake, what's the big deal?"

"It's a party, that's what. You're supposed to talk, mingle, have fun. Not sit on your own in the bloody corner."

"I am having fun. Why do I have to have fun in the way you want me to have fun."

"It's anti-social. I've been telling you this your whole life. Had to force you to go to things. Had to help you make friends."

"And I've never listened. Mum, I'm my own person. I'm not you."

"No, you're not."

"What's this really about? Why're you having a go at me? It's not like I've ignored anyone here. A five-minute time out to recharge is hardly too much to ask for."

She gave me another one of her withering looks.

I finished my cake and placed my paper plate on the wall underneath my cup. "Where's Dad?"

She dismissed the question with an exaggerated tut and shake of her head. She threw her silk scarf over her shoulder and looked away, disgusted.

"Your father is hiding on that golf course or in that club lounge sipping single malt with his cronies. Useless twats, the lot of them."

"And how are things?"

"Why don't you come home once in a while and see for yourself? When was the last time you visited?"

I couldn't remember. Visiting World War Three was not exactly an appealing way to spend a weekend.

"I've been busy."

"You're always busy. Just like him."

"You know how it is, Mum. I have work. A life."

"You work far too much, darling. Far too much."

I shrugged. She knew about the director opportunity and fully approved of me getting it. I couldn't get my head around her sometimes.

"And what about in other areas?"

I rolled my eyes. Was she really trying to go there?

"You look good. You're attractive, darling. Surely there must be someone you like?"

"Mum, for fuck's sake can we not do this again? This is not the place."

"Hey." James joined us, can of beer in hand. "What you talking about?"

"Nothing," I said.

James came with a train of young children behind him, so the conversation was over. It had bothered me though. I forced a smile on my face and spoke with the children, ushering them towards the bouncy castle that I hadn't had much of a look at yet. Looking over my shoulder as I walked away from my mum and brother there was a pained look in my mum's bloodshot eyes. Fuck, that was depressing.

"Aunty Bri, watch how high I can jump! See! See!"

I caught Ollie's eyes as he mouthed 'thank you' at me, I guess for playing with the kids, then turned to chat to his dad friends. I shrugged then felt a tug at my hand from Isla, who had fallen on the bouncy castle and wanted to tell me this in no uncertain terms.

It was going to be a long afternoon.

***

Logging on to my work laptop in my living room on a bank holiday Monday was not my idea of fun. It was a beautiful and crisp October day, perfect for a day of mountain biking with my friends. I punched in my password. Helen was Helen, and if I wanted this job, I had to make some sacrifices. I thought of Skye. I hadn't been able to stop thinking about her since the second I left her on Sunday afternoon. She was visiting her mum for dinner last night. Otherwise, I'd probably have asked to see her.

I craved her. Which was crazy, since we saw each other all the time. My head was spinning like the ring on the start-up screen. Was she working on the report now too? I wondered what it was going to be like working together now that ... I didn't quite know what to call it. I knew that something about this felt special and the time we'd shared so far had been incredible.

I knew that.

I wasn't the least bit interested in working today. Or in this tedious report for Helen. Still, it had to be done. I kept telling myself.

There was an email from Skye. Just seeing it gave me butterflies. It was already feeling weird. We had so much to do, and yet I was now so beautifully and painfully distracted by my attraction to her. I sat back in my office chair looking at the unread email from her wondering how this was going to work. I clicked on it. Her email was completely professional. You wouldn't know a thing was going on between us.

She was being sensible.

Was I a little disappointed at that?

I replied completely formally. We had so much to do. It turned out we both had a full day of work ahead of us to get this report right. If our first checkpoint report to Helen was shit, all our hard work would already have been for nothing.

I got my head down and got on with it. There was nothing else for it.

~ 21 ~
Skye

Exiting the station through the same doors we stood at on Friday night before deciding to go back to Brianna's felt like looking into an alternative reality. Had it all really happened? The whole thing had been such a delicate process. What if she hadn't asked me to come back to hers? Would we ever have found our way to each other? Was it just a wild weekend of sex or was there something more? Our eyes locking as I was going down on her was probably the sexiest thing that'd ever happened to me. A powerful wave of tingles ripped through me as I walked along the pavement. Fuck's sake, I was so attracted to her. I hadn't fancied someone this strongly before. Nerves of our first meeting at work since getting very naked together plagued me all day yesterday and intensified as I neared the building. How could I look into her eyes and not think of our sexy time together? I blushed just thinking about it. Intense sexual attraction and nerves were a powerful and uncomfortable combination. I barely even looked at Lynn as I rushed past and mumbled good morning at her.

It wasn't until my office door was closed behind me that I felt a bit calmer about the situation. I hadn't seen Brianna on my way in. Part of me was relieved but another part of me was disappointed. And this emotional upheaval, I could not have. Not at the start of the working day.

What was happening to me?

In the kitchen, Hayley and I did our morning routine while chatting about the party on Friday. I gave nothing away. There was no way I was going to fess up in the kitchen at work. I hated lying, but I had no choice. I'd tell her later. She'd understand.

"How's the counselling going?"

Hayley leant back against the kitchen counter. "Not great. I didn't realise it would be this hard. At least he's talking now. He started off grunting one-word answers to the therapist. It was so embarrassing."

I could feel the strain in her voice, so chose my words carefully. "But you're talking more now during the sessions?"

"Yep, we are. I think he just needed more time than me to feel comfortable enough to open up in them."

"That's good."

"How did you get on after you left the party on Friday?" asked Hayley as she cleaned the kitchen counter of coffee grounds. "Did you and Brianna … you know?" She raised her left eyebrow suggestively and lowered her voice. "Did anything happen between you two? Those sparks were flying. Don't worry though; you were very discreet. I just say because I know you, and I know about all the feelings."

So much for me keeping it private. "There's no feelings." I retorted.

"If you say so."

"And nothing happened." I didn't sound very convincing.

She shook her head and smiled. "You are such an awful liar. Skye, I'm happy that something happened between you two. This is hot goss."

I went pale. This was the opposite of gossip. This could be career ending. Perhaps that wasn't true but now was not a good time for anything to get out.

"Sorry. Shit. Not gossip. Just news. News. Please don't worry, I would never tell a soul."

I breathed again. "Now is not the time. But I'll call you later. No wait, I'm working tonight. I'll call you tomorrow."

"I can't wait. Skye, this is huge."

I shook my head at her, unable to deal with her powers of perception or a serious conversation about it. I hadn't even talked yet to Brianna. Besides, I was still in that hazy faze where all I really wanted to think about was the next time Brianna and I would be naked together. I kept to myself for most of the day. Thankfully, I had no meetings and could just focus on editing a report. There had been no word from Brianna. Not a thing. Then again, I hadn't contacted her either, apart from copying her into some emails. So not about anything to do with us.

An email came in. Helen wanted to see both of us in her office about the report we'd sent her last night. My heart rate picked up almost instantly. No doubt about it, this was stressful. I cursed that Brianna and I hadn't made the time to have a proper chat before now. Our lack of facing up to reality was like a brick to the head as now the first time we would see each other at work post-whatever-the-hell-was-going-on was going to be in Helen's fucking office.

Brianna was already there by the time I got up. She had her back to me as I went in. I traced the outline of her shoulders then her profile as I took my seat. I remembered wrapping my arms around those shoulders and nuzzling into her neck. She smiled at me briefly but her eyes said so much more. I don't think I'd ever felt as awkward in my life as I now did sitting across from Helen, beside Brianna.

Helen had on a loose white blazer and bright pink lipstick. She looked fantastic. Vibrant. And with something on her mind she wanted to say. I had no idea what this meeting was really about.

"I wanted to discuss your interim assessment report with you both in more detail and fill you in on my conversation with the board earlier today. First and foremost, the report is fantastic. Absolutely perfect. Exactly what we needed. Thank you for working on it over the weekend. I can tell you collaborated, it's good."

We'd collaborated all right.

I looked straight ahead at Helen rather than acknowledging Brianna in any way.

"That's great," said Brianna. "Was there anything else?"

I agreed. Why had Helen hauled us in just to say well done?

"Yes, there is. Two things. First, you signed off on an open bar for David's party. The fee was too high and I question your judgement. The first hour would have sufficed."

I took a sharp intake of breath and kept my eyes straight ahead at Helen. "Brianna had nothing to do with that. That was all me."

"Well then that's worse. You should have known what she was doing, Brianna. Where was the communication?" Helen paused. "The board has overlooked it in the end, because it's David, but I am not entirely impressed. It's minor, however, so I will move on."

Thank God for that. To think I'd got Brianna in trouble made me feel sick.

"Second, and most importantly, there is a major problem in the way you are running things."

What?

"You've given me a thorough and honest account of the department. However, I've finally spotted a key issue." Helen paused, doing that dramatic suspense thing she does. "The question is, have you?"

For fuck's sake, why was she talking in riddles?

"Not sure I'm following you. You liked the report but you think we have a problem?" This time I did look over at Brianna, who looked as confused as I did. We briefly glanced at each other, purely in work mode.

"I see. You haven't clocked it. And you don't know the bigger picture. Okay. Right, here it is. The people in your department aren't working hard enough."

My mouth fell open and my face contorted into a look of disbelief. Brianna's was much the same, which was a relief.

"These are the tough conversations that we have at this level. If you can't handle them, then maybe senior management isn't for you."

Give us a chance. She'd only just made her statement.

"Your team doesn't belong to you. They have no leader and they're not pulling together as one. We're a sinking ship."

I cleared my throat. "Helen, if I may. You appointed us to fix the situation on a temporary basis. You can't surely suggest that we are now the problem."

"You've taken charge of the ship and found the source of the leak. That doesn't mean the ship still won't sink."

Brianna sighed. I felt her frustration.

"I should never have let it go on for as long as it did. Simon and David have been completely useless these past few years, and I say that with all due respect to what they achieved overall. But they've nearly run us into the ground."

"We aren't going to run into the ground, Helen. The numbers. They're good. Our client list. They're happy. We're improving things. We've got a plan." I insisted.

"Yes but your team aren't with you. That's the problem at the centre of all this. And only you two can fix it. I don't work with my employees on research projects any more. I'm just a sponsor, even though the company is mine. I can give motivational speeches and rubber stamp the direction we agree to go in, but ultimately, they must work for you."

I disagreed with her. She was supposed to be the leader of this place. Not us. Or one of us.

Maybe she was the real problem.

"Now that we've got to the root of the issue, I should think now is a good time to tell you that I am planning on stepping down soon. I'll stay on as a board member, but I want to effectively hand over the reins. And preferably to you two, with one of you as director."

Now that made sense. She wanted us to run her company for her. How had I not seen this before? "Are you going to appoint a new CEO to replace you?"

"I see no point. I'll have each of the directors report straight to the board. That way I can split the burden and have more time to go on my cruises and travel." In time,

I might consider appointing a Chief Exec, but only if I can fully trust them."

"Why are you telling us all this right before the interviews?" I asked. "Is it not favouritism?"

"Because I need you both to realise that this is your company if you want it. You are both well placed to get the job. And if you want it to succeed you must find a way to bring the best out of your employees and inspire them to do great work. There's little greatness happening around here except from the two of you."

A rare compliment from Helen. She must be serious.

"So from our joint-assessment as co-interim directors you now feel that the issue is a resource issue?" Brianna said.

"It's a team issue. You're not a team. We were fractious even before the merger. There're too many big personalities all pulling in different directions. And from what I can see, not enough are pulling towards you two."

Ouch. I thought my team were pretty awesome. They respected me, right?

"Skye. You do too much. You've got to delegate more. And you've got to get those big personalities under control." Helen paused, looking between us. "Brianna, your team don't belong to you. You need to meet them more on a human level."

We both just sat there.

"See, that's the problem. Even I've just referred to the team as two different teams. We still need to integrate and get everyone working together as one. Until we do, we're doomed."

God, she was dramatic.

"You've both done admirably, but there is more still to be done to turn this ship around. As you know, interviews for the director position are in three weeks. If you can further strengthen us before then I will be very grateful. I really appreciate all that you are doing, and I hope you can see where I'm coming from."

I just felt stunned. And pissed off. All Helen ever did was dump stuff on me and tell me to sort it out.

"And before you go. As I've said, you two are my favourite candidates. But it has to be a board decision who gets the job, and we've had some very strong external applicants."

I wanted to get out of her office. Out of the building, even. I'd worked so hard yesterday getting that report ready for today. I'd given my all to this job only to be met with these accusations.

Fuck this.

Brianna spoke up first. "We need time to think this over. If it's okay with you, we'll gather our thoughts and start addressing what you've said. See what difference we can make in the time left." I felt like Brianna spoke about us like we were a true team. I liked it.

"Do what you must."

***

Brianna came to my office with me without discussing it. We always seemed to have meetings in my office. I shut the door harder than normal then fell back onto the couch. I was in no mood to jump through yet another of Helen's hoops.

"Helen can fuck right off," said Brianna, standing in front of me, hands on hips.

"I know, right? After everything we spelled out in the report and giving up our days off to work on it and she picks up on issues with the team again. We could have just told her that in five minutes. And like any team is perfect anyway."

Brianna pursed her lips. "But what if she has a point? Haven't we already talked about the fact you're too nice and I'm too detached or something?"

"We're already aware of the issues. We're already trying to address them. We don't need Helen to tell us."

"You're so right."

Brianna sat next to me, much closer than normal, but she hadn't exactly straddled me, which would have been preferable.

She took a deep breath. "Neither one of us might get the job, so I don't see why we should stress about it."

"No stress. I like that." I paused, lacking in energy. This whole situation wasn't easy. "I think I've had enough of work for the day."

I waited for Brianna to follow up with something about us but she didn't. She just sat there, looking at the floor. We still hadn't mentioned our amazing weekend together. Was that weird? I was starting to freak out about it the longer this went on. I checked my watch even though I didn't need to.

"But I have to work tonight. I'm facilitating a viewed group with clients."

Brianna just nodded. Was she nervous?

I put my hand on her thigh. She flinched at first but then relaxed. She looked at me properly then. Her eyes spoke of a truth that only we knew. I liked that. I liked that a lot. A slow smile crept onto her lips and reached her eyes. I entwined our fingers. We just sat there quietly with each other, holding hands. Things didn't materialise into the conversation we ought to have had and I was okay with that.

Why spoil the moment?

I kissed her cheek, which she leant into then brushed her face next to mine. Brianna found my lips and kissed me softly. We leant into each other and fell deeper into the couch. Her embrace was like falling into a warm luxurious bed. Her lips already felt so familiar. The soft and slow kiss just continued, I didn't want to jeopardise it and apparently neither did Brianna. She touched my face, which felt very loving, then kissed me deeper and I reciprocated, wondering how far this could go and feeling easily that it could go all the way. My desk caught my eye and it jolted me back to my senses. Thank God the door was closed properly. But it wasn't locked.

"Brianna?"

"Yes?" she breathed into my neck.

Every fibre of my being wanted to stay there with her and keep doing what we were doing, but this was the office and people would be walking past right outside the door.

"Perhaps we should stop."

I watched as her eyes cleared out of a mist of lust, and she sat up, pulling me up with her.

"You're right. Sorry. Fuck. I don't know what came over me. I didn't mean for anything to happen here."

"Neither did I. Are you free later? I won't be long with these groups."

"I could stay and watch? I've never seen a focus group before."

"You've never seen a focus group? Don't say that to Helen in your interview."

The interviews. God, why had I brought those up. Why?

"Thanks," she hesitated. "I'll try not to. I'd like to stay and see you in action. And see you afterwards, if that's okay?"

I fixed my hair then found her eyes. "You can see me afterwards."

"I can't wait."

"Also," I got up and fished her notebook out of my desk drawer. "This is yours."

Brianna raised her eyebrows, then took the notebook from me. "Thanks."

It had only been five days but so much had changed since that night and our long hug at the door.

I smiled. "I'll see you later."

~ 22 ~
Brianna

I was very aware that it was strange that I was hanging around the basement viewing studio in my free time. Thankfully, no one seemed to notice. Except perhaps Siobhan, who had clocked my presence. Her job was to meet and greet the respondents and clients, and ensure the whole event went to plan.

Three clients and I occupied the room. We were behind the mirror, like detectives in a police department albeit a much more stylish and comfortable one. I did good small talk and made sure they all had wine and knew they could help themselves to the cheeseboard. I was there for Skye and not to entertain the clients, but it had proved unavoidable.

Skye headed up a table of eight carefully selected people who all shared a similar socio-economic background and set of behaviours around health. Getting something constructive out of this situation did not seem like something I'd be good at. Skye made it look easy. She was warm, friendly, chatty, clear, quick, charming, relatable, and most of all, fully in control. She brought everyone into the discussion and handled the one asshole in the group admirably.

"Thank you, John. We've heard a lot from you already. Would anyone else like to comment on the question?" John piped down but you could see that inside he was fuming.

The wine tasted sharp and cheap. Helen should know better than to feed this to the clients. Perhaps she didn't know. I made a mental note to get better wine in stock for clients. That might well have gone in the report too, given the level of things she'd picked up on. One of the clients poured a second glass; it didn't seem like they were too bothered. Free stuff did always taste that little bit better, I guessed. I scratched the back of my neck then let my eyes rest on Skye. Her clothes were sensible and fitting for the situation. Still, I found her as sexy as she'd looked on Friday night in her gorgeous dress. I loved watching her as she facilitated the discussion – the way she talked, the way she listened. Her smile. I was mesmerised.

The first group ended and the second group got started. Skye was busy the entire time and we never got a chance to talk. The second group lasted forever. My eyes would have been shutting had it not been for my relentless desire to watch Skye and take her all in. I had no idea how she found the energy to do this. The shit people came up with was exhausting. And Skye had to pretend it was all very useful and very interesting. I was tired just watching. By the end, I couldn't care less what people were saying. Finally, Skye brought the group to a close and the respondents began to make their way out. A long chat with the clients ensued about what the initial findings were, which Skye also made look effortless. I mostly confirmed what Skye was saying by nodding emphatically in places. Siobhan raced around sorting out the guests and helping them get away. She even tidied up after the clients, and I found myself helping her with it as Skye cleared up the table in the room.

"They liked that wine," said Siobhan. "Bit harsh for my taste."

When Siobhan left, the place was finally silent and empty except for us. Our eyes met.

"Come here." Skye held out her hand and I took it. "I want to show you something."

We walked all the way up the stairs to the top of the building, then up the old crooked staircase to the roof. She unbolted the window and gave it a gentle push, and we climbed out onto the asphalt. I could hardly see my feet on the roof, it was so dark. The sound from the road below felt closer than it was. My hearing must have been heightened by the dark. I walked around a little, then found a spot beside the wall. I felt Skye's eyes on me as we moved to the edge. The skyline was lit up all around us, the buildings, old and new, large and small, peppered around.

"I love this view. I've never been up here at night."

"Yeah," said Skye. She rested her elbows on the wall, looking out. "It's peaceful too. I used to come up here a lot when I was first starting out."

"What for?"

She stood up straight, facing me. "To clear my head. I had a lot to learn back then. Every day felt like a battle. There's just something about it up here. It helps you gain perspective."

She turned back out towards the city looking pensive. Her hair was tucked behind her ears. She was so beautiful.

"Hey," I said. "You look so pretty."

A smile spread across her lips, and she faced me again. Her eyes sparkled and poured into my soul, touching something inside of me. "So do you." She paused, scratching her head. "Brianna, I want you to know, this is more than just a sex thing for me. I really like you."

The smile that grew on my face began to hurt my cheeks. She was so brave and so incredibly in touch with and open about her feelings. I admired that. I touched her arm, wanting to hug her madly, but it looked like there was more on her mind.

"I've been feeling this way for a while."

"Oh yeah? Since when?" I sounded way more nonchalant than I actually was.

She hesitated. "A little while."

"So, you've been my secret admirer all this time?" In truth, I felt the same, but I wanted to get more out of her on this.

"Not all this time." She playfully slapped my arm. "I didn't like you very much at the start."

"Yeah, you were a delight the first time I met you."

She nodded.

I held her hand and squeezed it. "No, seriously. Some things are too important not to recognise." I looked down, then back up her. "This means a lot to me too." I searched her eyes. "You mean a lot to me."

She smiled and brought my hand up to her lips and planted a gentle kiss on the back of it. "Why didn't you say anything?"

"You were my arch enemy. I couldn't risk it."

"Yeah, same."

For some reason we laughed, hard. It was a cleansing sort of laugh, deep from the belly. I felt so connected to her. I stepped towards her and kissed her. Her mouth opened and it quickly turned heated as we pressed ourselves against each other.

"Brianna," she pulled me in closer and whispered in my ear. "I want you."

I led her towards the building and pushed her against the wall. It was darker away from the edge, but I could just about see her face and the desire on it.

We kissed again, this time more slowly and intentionally. I leant on the underside of my forearms on the wall by her head. She gripped my arms and tried to pull them towards her but I resisted. I enjoyed the fight for power between us. She gave up and put her hands underneath my top, onto my skin, causing me to shiver. Her touches were hungry and bold. I gave in and did the same to her, feeling her soft breasts underneath her jumper and the hardness of her nipples.

"Are you cold?"

"What? No," she breathed, in between kisses.

I pinched her hard nipple. "Something else then."

She moaned. "Ow."

"Sorry."

"Don't be."

I ran one finger from in between her breasts down to the button on her jeans and back up again.

"Stop teasing me," she whispered into the side of my face. "I need you."

Kissing her again, I pressed my thigh in between her legs. I felt her move underneath me, trembling slightly. She moaned quietly, sending a warm heat all through my body.

"Here." She took my hand. "Let's go."

She pulled me back into the building, down the stairs, and into her office. After locking the door, we were all over each other again. We kissed passionately knowing we were in a private space. She tugged me down onto the couch, still kissing me. I struggled out of my blazer. She slipped off the couch and got onto her knees, keeping her eyes on me the entire time. My heart pounded. She bit down on her bottom lip as if asking for permission and I nodded. Silently, she pulled at my trousers, and I let them be taken off. My breath caught in my throat when she tugged at my underwear and slipped them off too. I was naked from the waist down on her couch in her office while she was fully clothed. The rush of it was such a turn on. She gently opened my legs wider, drinking me in with her eyes. She adjusted herself to get more comfortable, tucking her hair behind her ears, and held my hands. When she started kissing the area around my clit I swallowed hard, staring down at her. Lightly, she flicked her tongue in just the right way, sending a flood of warmth all over my body. Heat rose within me as she explored me, probing gently and hungrily. I gripped her hands and she settled into a rhythm. My whole awareness was focused on her mouth and what she was doing to me. She took her time and I was in no rush for it to stop. I didn't want it to end. After a while I couldn't fight it. My muscles burned and I was ready to come at any second, which I think she knew. I moaned and let go of her hands, gripping the couch now instead. I couldn't control it any longer as I raised my hips upwards so that I was on my tiptoes, holding out for a few seconds longer as she licked me and I couldn't take any more. I cried out when it finally happened, as wave after wave of pleasure went through my whole body. My heart raced. The fact this was at work was crazy. Skye knelt up and leant between my legs, kissing me on the mouth. I tasted myself on her lips and found it hard to focus. She was all I could see, and all I wanted to see. I wrapped my arms around her waist and our eyes locked. There was a depth to our connection that almost overwhelmed me. I swallowed, feeling more vulnerable now than I could ever remember. As if she sensed as much, she picked up my clothes and helped me put them back on. I didn't know what to say, it was all so hot and sexy one minute, and tender and intimate the next.

"Come here," said Skye, leaning back on the couch now and gesturing me to cuddle into her. I rested into her as she put her arm around me. We hugged like that for a while, neither of us saying anything. In her arms I let myself fall, and as she stroked my hair and kissed the side of my head I think she knew that she had caught me.

***

Glancing at my watch my heart rate was high but not for a good reason. We were in a team meeting that had gone off the rails almost as soon as it started, with Andrew openly disrespecting everything Skye and I said. It would be funny if it weren't so awful.

"You two girls have no idea what you're doing. It's embarrassing to watch. This department needs some firm, and yes I will say it, *male* leadership."

"I'm going to stop you right there. That is an inappropriate way to speak in the workplace," said Skye, seething but still managing to sound professional.

"See, this is the problem. You can't say anything any more. No one can really speak their mind, so we don't get anywhere. Nothing of any value is ever shared any more. PC gone mad. I'm sick of it."

"Okay that's it. This meeting is over. I'm calling it to a close. Andrew, I want to talk to you in the boardroom. Now. Brianna, you will join us."

Skye had switched on the inner badass I knew she always had. Within minutes, we were sitting across from Andrew at the long table. He still had that smug look on this face. If Skye didn't sort this out, I would.

Skye's look was steely. "Why do you think it is that we called you in here, Andrew?"

He sniggered, but still managed to shoot us a patronising look. "Because you want to slap my wrists and try and tell me you're the boss."

"We are your bosses."

"Not for long."

"What do you mean?"

"I'm applying for the job you're in the process of letting go pear-shaped. Soon, I'll be on that side of the table and you'll be taking orders from me, as it should be."

I took a deep breath. My nostrils flared and my forehead scrunched up as I regarded this pathetic excuse for a person. I snapped. "What I don't understand, Andrew, is how you've been allowed to get so far in your career with the attitude you have and the mediocre, at best, performance you offer."

"I've had no problems. I reject the term mediocre. Especially coming from you."

Skye sat forward, clasping her hands together on the table. "Your conduct has been out of line for years now. Actually, the whole time you've been here in my opinion. I agree with Brianna, it is a scandal that you've been allowed to stay at this company and get into a management position. For that, I will take the blame.

You have been insubordinate and disruptive, which I have noted on your performance record. You've already been given your first official written warning. I have a second written warning already drafted and that was for yesterday. It's on my computer ready to get sent to Helen. But I'm not going to share it with her any more."

"Not got the balls?"

"I'm firing you for gross misconduct instead. Andrew, you're fired."

"You can't do that."

"Just watch me. Get out."

"I'm going to speak to Helen."

"No. You are not. I am your boss," Skye glanced over at me but I took no offence. She was killing it. "We are both your bosses until a new director is appointed. We have full authority to handle resourcing matters as necessary and I won't hesitate to execute this. You're toxic. You are not good for this company and I want you out. Helen will have my back. She's already given me the permission to sort this out. If you so much as send her an email about this I will make sure you are blacklisted from every research company in the country. I have a lot of friends out there, a lot of favours to cash in. You so much as tweet out one pissy little message about unfair dismissal and I'll ruin you, you piece of shit."

Skye held his eye. I felt the intensity of her stare and she wasn't even looking at me.

"You can't just fire the competition."

"Oh I think I can. And who's to say you were ever even going to get an interview anyway? Why would Helen want to promote someone whose behaviour has been flagged as an issue? Who has never single-handedly won any new business? Who hasn't an ounce of empathy and lacks the ability to lead by example? You are really bad at your job and I'm sick of other people making you look good and you taking the credit."

Andrew's face had gone red and a vein was bulging in his neck. If he got violent, I would take him down. While I might not win, I'd put up a good fight and protect my Skye.

He stood up, towering above us, knowing full well how physically intimidating he was. As a person, not so much.

"Fine. I quit. I don't want to work with either of you any more anyway."

He slammed the glass door on his way out nearly taking it off its hinges. I was impressed that it hadn't shattered. Just like Skye hadn't.

***

The rest of the day was spent dealing with the aftermath of Andrew getting fired – talking with Skye about it, talking with Hayley in HR about it, then talking with Helen and the other directors. It turned out this was the first time anyone had been fired at Your View, except for offers of voluntary redundancies over a decade ago. Helen had Skye's back and Hayley didn't think there would be any cause for him to claim unfair dismissal. To say I was proud of Skye would be an understatement. The message she had sent to the rest of the department was clear – she was not to be messed with.

Back at mine, the door hadn't even shut yet and Skye was leading me towards the bedroom. This had become a daily situation – sex before work, sex after work, and, I guess, not much talking about where this was going. I wanted to have that conversation with her, but we were too busy, it seemed. I think neither of us wanted to break the spell. We were having sex all the time. The more sex we had, the more we wanted. We'd agreed not to let anything else happen while at work, to at least try and keep that boundary. She'd been sleeping over at my place most nights, and when we parted at the office I would long for her despite spending most of the day in her company. I'd never felt this level of craving for another human being before.

I wasn't the clingy type.

But Skye was different.

She made me feel different.

She undressed as she made her way into my bedroom. At the foot of the bed she turned to face me, wearing nothing but her underwear. She had on a royal blue lacey matching set, which set off her hair and eyes beautifully.

"Sit on the bed."

I obeyed and sat down, my arms out behind me. She leant over me, unzipped my trousers, and pulled them off, all the while looking right at me.

"Take your top off."

I did as I was told, loving this more dominant side of Skye. She walked away towards my cupboard and pulled the belt off my dressing gown.

Okay. This was happening. I lay back onto the bed, wondering what was coming next. At the foot of the bed she took her bra off and let it drop to the ground before slipping her panties off.

"Arms up."

I put my arms above me and gripped the slats on the headboard. Skye moved swiftly above me, keeping her concentration on tying the knot, her brow furrowed.

Clearly, she'd done this before. I gazed at her body, so boldly poised above me. When she finished, she looked down at me below her, then lowered herself and kissed my lips. We kissed for longer than I would have liked, as I was eager to get to the next part. She broke off and planted slow kisses on my neck and chest as I ached for her already.

"You should know," she paused, "I'm going to take my time with you tonight."

She had a commanding look. I simply nodded, resigned to the fact that she was going to torture me with this. She ran her hands down my arms and undid my bra. She pulled it up to join the knot at my wrists, leaving my bare breasts in front of her. I was already wet for her, desperate for her to touch me there. Lowering herself down my body, she slowly kissed my tummy, down towards my hips, placing kisses nearer and nearer my centre. I could feel her hot breath through my underwear before she kissed the waist band and tugged at it with her teeth. Then, she rolled my underwear down my legs. We locked eyes for a few moments. I felt exposed and vulnerable, and not just physically. It was like Skye was seeing into the deepest parts of me.

She straddled me and I felt her wetness on the lower part of my tummy. I just stared at her beautiful body sitting on top of me. I still could not believe I got to be with her like this. She ran her hands down the underside of my arms above my head. I attempted to break free so I could touch her, but the tight material binding my wrists stopped me.

"Uh-uh." She shook her head and rested her hands in between my breasts. I took a deep breath, wondering what was coming next. Skye moved her hands from my heart and placed them over my breasts. Gently, she brushed my nipples with her thumbs. I gasped, feeling goosebumps pepper my skin. She leant down and took my nipple in her mouth, lightly flicking it with her tongue. I moaned, not knowing how much more of this I could take.

Her breathing became ragged. She undid the knot, and my arms were my own again. She moved up higher still so that her knees were either side of my head. She looked down at me from above.

"Is it okay if I do this?" she asked.

"Yes."

I licked my lips as she lowered herself and hovered above my mouth. When she finally gave herself to me, she quivered and held onto the headboard. I rested my hands on her hips. I felt her relax into it and the world fall away. The only noise came from her soft moans. I let a hand drop and touched myself as I flicked her with my tongue. My fingers were soaked in my own wetness. Skye glanced over her shoulder at me touching myself then let out a deep moan as she gripped the headboard and tensed up. Her thighs squeezed the sides of my head as her moans became uneven, desperate even. This time we both really let ourselves go. My muscles tensed up so much I ended up in a bridge pose as the most intense orgasm ripped through me as she came into my mouth and cried out my name. It lasted and lasted, and I savoured every second.

She stroked my arm as we lay sprawled out on the bed together side by side. I swung a leg over her hips to get closer to her. But it wasn't enough. I wanted to be inside her, next to her, on top of her, and all at once. The sex was helping, but I wasn't done and still wanted more. A lot more.

"Your neck." She rested a hand on my chest. "It's all a rash."

"So is yours."

She placed a hand on her upper chest. "Oh yeah, it's all hot." She paused, her eyes sparkling. "I love it when we come together."

"I hope the neighbours aren't in."

"What's your heart rate?"

"Huh?"

"Your watch. You rotated your wrist and it flashed up. I thought I saw it over a hundred. I'm no fitness expert but that seems quite high to me, especially for someone who cycles up and down mountains for fun."

I brought my wrist up and checked. "It's one hundred and eleven. In all fairness, I've just had the most amazing orgasm and we're naked in bed together. I am bound to be ... somewhat excited."

"And that's the correct answer." Skye smiled. She kissed me on the lips, then rested her head on my shoulder and nuzzled into me. "You're fun to tease."

"You know you were amazing today. The way you stood up to Andrew. It was really something."

Her chest rose and fell from her deep breathing. "Yeah, it really was."

~ 23 ~
Brianna

A week later I visited Skye's house for the first time. We were celebrating having handed in our final report to the board. After a delicious three-course meal, which Skye had left work early to cook, we moved to Skye's living room. I ran a finger along her records, scanning the sleeves with my head tilted. She had an eclectic taste. Lots of genres. I came to a rest at one and pulled it out slightly. The sleeve was wrinkled and felt of a different time.

"Tracy Chapman?"

"Yeah, do you like her?"

"I love her."

Skye picked up the old record and removed it from its sleeve, being careful to avoid touching the tracks. She placed it on the turntable and lowered the pin. Acoustic music filled the room. She put her hands around my waist, and I put mine on her shoulders. She smiled. "This is a classic."

We swayed softly to the music.

Skye turned her head towards mine, momentarily taking her hands away. "Oh, sorry. I thought you didn't dance?"

"I do now." I found her hands and put them back where they were. Our bodies moved together so easily. I sighed and rested my head on her shoulder. "I'm so happy. And so tired. Is happy-tired a thing?" I was exhausted from a full-on week at work and frankly from all the sex as well. It was a good kind of exhausted.

"It is when you're having fun." She brushed some hair away from my eyes. "How do you want to relax? How would you relax right now if you were at home on your own?"

"I'd have a bath. It's how I unwind."

The next song started. "I have a bath." Skye's eyes sparkled. "We could take a bubble bath together."

"Together?"

"Yes. Together. Now. Would you like to?"

I thought about it. "Okay."

She kissed me on the lips briefly. "I'll go run it."

Skye went off to start the bath and I looked around a bit more. Her house was cosy and warm. I pictured her sitting by the fire, reading a book, a million miles away from our high-powered office environment. She had Post-it notes on her fridge with things like, 'believe in yourself!', and 'success comes to those who work smarter not harder'. I liked that she hadn't hidden them before I came around. She called for me and I made my way upstairs after turning the record player off.

Skye was sitting on the edge of the free-standing bath. The bathroom was surprisingly large, with black and white square tiles and a separate shower cubicle. She'd lit lots of candles and scattered them around.

"Come." Skye held out an arm. "It's nearly ready."

"It's lovely in here."

"Thank you. My roof might be falling in but at least I have this room."

I stepped into her arms. She rested her head against my waist. Lavender-scented steam filled the room, and we watched the bubbly water climb until it was ready.

Skye dipped a few fingers in the water then turned off the tap. She caressed my arm causing the tiny hairs on my arms to stand up, which was an achievement since we were in a hot room. She did this move quite often. Her caress continued up my sleeve. She slipped her hand under my bra strap and started to guide it off my shoulder.

"Are we really going to have a bath together?"

She stopped. "Do you not want to?"

"No, I'm …" I stuttered. I took a deep breath. "It's just a little awkward is all."

"Awkward?" Skye looked at me sceptically. "After all the things we've done?" She raised an eyebrow.

"You know what I mean. That was in the heat of the moment. This feels …"

"Feels what?" Her eyes were kind.

I shrugged slowly. "More intimate somehow. Scarier."

She nodded. "You feel vulnerable."

I folded my arms across my chest.

"We don't have to," Skye said, tenderly. "It was just to try and help you relax. I figured we were comfortable with each other enough but it's totally fine if you're not feeling it."

She'd lit so many candles and the bubbles were all fluffy and ready to be enjoyed. What was I doing? This was a romantic moment and I was spoiling it. I just wasn't used to anything like this kind of intimacy. But I wanted to be.

I took my top off and threw it on the floor. "Forget what I said, I'm all in." I slipped my trousers off quite unceremoniously. "Don't look."

Skye had a pleasantly surprised look on her face, and she just shook her head and then nodded. She closed her eyes as I got out of my underwear and carefully got in. I felt myself relax as I adapted to the hot water and the bubbles engulfed me.

"I'll be back in a second," Skye said. "We need more wine."

She dashed off leaving me in the tub by myself. I heard her go down the stairs and faint clattering from the kitchen. When she came back she had two glasses of red wine and the bottle under her arm.

"The essentials," she said, handing me a glass.

"Thank you." I took a sip. "This is delicious. So smooth."

"Yeah, it's my good bottle. This is a special occasion."

"Yep. I certainly wouldn't have predicted this two months ago."

We both laughed, softly.

"No, I can't say that I would have either," Skye said. "A fist fight in the car park maybe, but not a romantic bubble bath together."

"True."

Skye placed her glass on a shelf beside the tub then got undressed. I would never tire of watching her do this. Seconds later her foot was in the water, and it touched my leg.

"Sorry."

I drew my legs up so she could get in, she took her spot at the other end of the tub and then we stretched our legs out. There was just about enough room for us both. I rested my arms along the edge of the tub, enjoying how our legs were entwined. Skye splashed some water on her face and ran her wet hands through her hair which was tied up, flattening it down a little. She looked very sexy even surrounded by bubbles. We sat in silence for a little while.

"Thank you for going to all that effort with the meal tonight. It was really delicious. I feel very spoilt."

"You're welcome. It was my pleasure."

"Yes, about that. It seems your pleasure is my new favourite hobby."

She grinned at me kind of goofily, which was adorable. "Yes, it is."

"I did say I liked extreme sports."

"Hey." She mock splashed some water my way, then took another sip of wine. Her skin was peppered with tiny water droplets and she looked serene. I put my head back and let out a contented breath. "I feel so peaceful right now."

"Wouldn't it be nice to just stay here forever?"

"And get super wrinkly?"

"Super wrinkly. You wouldn't recognise us. When is your birthday?"

"The thirteenth of November."

Skye smiled. "You're a water sign. Like me. That's another thing we've got in common. I'm July. The seventh. Our star signs are highly compatible."

"Please tell me you don't believe in all that rubbish?"

"I love it. I'm a Cancer and you're a Scorpio. Makes perfect sense."

I sighed, jokingly. "Okay. Tell me why, then promise never to speak of it again."

"I can't promise that." Skye laughed. "Scorpios are fierce motherfuckers who'll sting you with their tail if you cross them. Cancers act like they've got everything together but they're just soft and warm homely types who want to snuggle up. And we both love water."

"Well, I did do a lot of swimming at school."

"See. It's accurate. That and your whole personality."

"Hey," I splashed some water on her legs. "There wasn't a lot that was very flattering in your description of Scorpios."

"They make the best lovers."

"I take it back. I'll be a Scorpio."

"You already are."

"The best lover or a Scorpio?"

"Both."

We held each other's eyes, which sent a gentle throb down low in my body.

"Hey," she said, excitedly. "Want to know something crazy?"

"Always."

She pursed her lips, and hesitated, as if regretting her suggestion.

"What?" I half-laughed.

"Have you ever …"

"Have I ever what?"

"Have you ever had a wet dream?"

"A wet dream? Like, coming in your sleep?"

"Yes. And waking up from it while – you know."

"Like a teenage boy?"

"Women have them too, apparently. I googled it. It's a sleep orgasm, and the medical term for it is 'nocturnal emission', which is less nice."

"No. I haven't. Have you?"

"Yes." She paused. "Recently."

I narrowed my eyes. "How recent?"

"A few weeks ago."

That was around the first time we slept together. Was there a connection?

"Tell me more."

"It was about you."

I stopped breathing. My mouth hung open but I didn't care. That was the best thing I'd ever heard.

"I was having a sex dream about you and then I woke up having an orgasm."

"That's fucking amazing. Dream me has *game*. What was it like? What was the dream about?"

She blushed. Even in the heat of the bath I could see her skin redden.

"I'm so embarrassed telling you this but I just had to. It was like a normal orgasm but there was nothing physically going on. I had been sleeping. It's been blowing my mind ever since."

"Literally. Your brain did that to your body? That is crazy."

We held eye contact. "I don't know, I kind of felt like it was you doing it to me."

I swallowed, feeling turned on.

"What was I doing?"

She bit her lip, then looked away. "Now that would be telling."

"That's the best news I've ever had." I held out my arms. "Come here. I want to hold you."

"Aww. That's so sweet."

"I can be romantic."

Skye held her hands up. "I never said you couldn't. Shut your eyes then so I can turn around?"

"Not going to happen."

"Brianna. Close them. This isn't going to be pretty."

"Nonsense. But Okay." I closed them as requested.

The water sloshed as she shifted herself around and leant back onto me as I sat up straighter and wrapped my arms around her. I put my head on her shoulder and gazed down at her body. Her knees were bent up and her legs pressed together. I loved the shape of her thighs and the shape of her breasts. I rested my hands on her tummy, just under the water. We were quiet for a while, just enjoying the moment. I took a long and slow deep breath and Skye's body rose and fell with mine. I was suddenly very aware of how naked and intimate we were. As we'd been in the bath for a little while, the water level had gone down a notch but it was still warm. The candles flickered. I caressed her low down on her tummy and planted a few slow kisses on her shoulder. She backed into me a little harder. I touched her breasts, taking their fullness into my hands and squeezing them possessively. She leant back and turned her face towards me and we kissed. I traced my fingers down her body and touched her in between her legs. She moaned and rested her head back on my shoulder, sending a jolt of electricity through my entire body. My fingers glided over the soft flesh of her clit just underneath the water, causing a bunch of ripples. I knew what she liked most by this point, and I teased her with it. Her breathing became uneven. She dug her fingers into my thighs and tensed up. Her moans increased and I could feel she was close. She turned her head and kissed me again until she came in my arms. The water splashed as her body shuddered. When her breathing came back to normal, I returned my hands to her tummy, kissing the side of her head. She was so beautiful. Seeing her like this was such a turn on. Being responsible for it was such an honour.

She closed her legs and we kissed softly before she broke away with gooey eyes and a satisfied look on her face.

"I love what you do to me."

"I love doing it." I squeezed her with my arms and legs.

Skye whispered. "This feels so good."

The line between us completely disappeared. I was her, and she was me. We were just two souls living in the moment. I wanted this. I wanted her. I was falling so hard for this woman. I took a deep breath with my head resting on her shoulder, inhaling lavender mixed with her scent. I was ready to talk about what was going on between us. We still hadn't, and it was becoming silly. I wanted her to be mine. To be in a real relationship with her, out in the open, even at work. But clearly, we weren't even serious enough for Skye to broach the subject. My heart ached. What if she didn't want what I wanted? I couldn't carry on like we had been forever. I didn't voice any of this to her. Instead, I replied with a small voice.

"It does."

~ 24 ~
Skye

I liked getting dressed up. Always had. Tonight I had on my favourite little black dress. A dress that made me feel classy and just the right amount of sexy for events like this. A line I'd need to straddle tonight being that I was meeting Brianna's family for the first time. Brianna and I were walking towards the venue for Brianna's mum's sixtieth birthday party in the expansive country estate. The path was lit up with green lights along the side, and the grand house was majestic, lit up in orange and purple. The grounds were littered with orange and golden leaves, just about visible beside the path in the green light. The other guests were all dressed up, even the children, who were playing in the gardens as their parents mingled.

My heels clicked as I walked. Glancing at Brianna, she seemed tense, and had also been quiet on the way over. Brianna had been here earlier and helped set things up, before going home to get ready and then picking me up. The fact she'd invited me had been a surprise, albeit a wonderful one. She asked me last night, after our bath together. I instinctively said yes, because I wanted to go with her. I wasn't sure if she was regretting inviting me now, given that her invitation had been so last minute and she was being a little off with me.

Brianna stopped in her tracks, drawing me to a halt beside her. She was slightly pale.

"Skye, I was wondering if ..." She hesitated. Her eyes were uncertain for a few seconds then she seemed to snap out of it. "I'm so happy you could be here with me tonight. It means a lot."

I smiled. "Thanks for inviting me."

She took my hand and entwined our fingers. A smiled formed at my lips and this seemed to cheer her up.

"And you look gorgeous. Did I mention that?" The sparkle was back in her eyes now, and I felt a heat down low in my body.

"Once or twice. But stop it. I do not want an incident in a spare bedroom or something at your mother's party. Not the sort of first impression I want to make."

Brianna held her hands up in the air. "I hear you."

"I know I said I liked water, but this is throwing me in at the deep end, no?"

Brianna beamed. "You have nothing to worry about, you're so loveable."

Loveable. Did she just say that? We held each other's eyes as something passed between us. It made my breath catch in my throat.

Brianna took a deep breath. "Skye, how should I introduce you tonight? Can I say you're here as my date?"

Her date? Was I not more than that? I swallowed. "Of course you can. Or you could say I'm here as your girlfriend? Aren't we ... girlfriends?"

Brianna raised her eyebrows and then smiled, reaching her eyes. "Yes, yes we are." Her eyes had widened and dilated. "That's good because I want to show you off tonight, this beautiful, clever, and amazing woman. You."

I cupped her face and kissed her softly on the lips. "Girlfriends." I beamed, feeling equal parts excited and terrified.

Brianna started towards the house and I followed her, my head spinning. There was no doubt I felt elated at the conversation, but the thought of how we were going to manage things at work made me feel uneasy. I had been trying not to think about it these past few magical weeks with Brianna. Perhaps that was foolish. I pushed these thoughts from my mind. This was no time to think about any of that.

As we entered the grand house, Brianna picked up two glasses of champagne from the waiter's tray and thanked him. Brianna and her brothers really had gone all out. Almost immediately, Brianna and I were spotted.

"Hello! Look who it is!"

"Aunty Esther, so great to see you." Brianna and her aunt did air kisses on each cheek, then her aunt turned her attention to me.

"And this is my girlfriend, Skye."

Her aunt's face lit up and she hugged me.

"Welcome. So nice to meet you, Skye." She stepped back a little to regard us in the way aunts do. "And don't you both look stunning together. You make such a beautiful couple."

"Thanks, Aunty Esther. That's very kind."

"It's true. You look like models. Also, Brianna, you and your brothers have done very well putting all this together. It really is something. What a special treat to give your mum."

Brianna blushed. She was so adorable.

I sipped some champagne as they shared some words and caught up briefly before we moved on. Her aunt commented again on how lovely we were together before she left.

"See," said Brianna. "They're gonna love you."

The atmosphere was a nice mix of formal, elegant, and homely. The antique furniture was something in itself to look at. Pictures of Brianna's mum had been placed all over the walls, along with gold balloons. There were pictures of her mum at all ages. She was striking. Brianna was right, they did look very alike. Same dark hair and intense brown eyes. She led me away from the pictures, not saying anything about them, and pointed things out about the house, and some of the people there. I really just followed her around and found it hard to look at anyone else in the place but her. She was wearing a suit and looked incredibly sexy. I half wanted her to ignore my comment earlier and whisk me away to some stately bedroom.

There was a lot of mingling and picking up fresh champagne flutes and nibbling on canapes. I was introduced to her immediate family, brothers and their partners, and told the children's names. When we finally found her, Brianna's mum was a little cold. For a second, I could see where Brianna got that part of her personality from. She spoke only briefly to Brianna and barely registered me when Brianna introduced me. She wasn't rude, she just wasn't warm. Brianna brushed this off, which I found a little sad.

Speaking with her brothers was much better. Brianna changed around them. She became a little harder and more sarcastic. And a lot more gay. Something about the jokes she told and the way she acted. I loved psychoanalysing this. Watching and reading people was my thing.

"Are you having a good time?" said Brianna after a while. We'd spoken to so many relatives, I almost wanted to get a notepad out and take notes. Even with my memory, there was a lot to take in.

"I'm having a good time. I'm enjoying listening and people-watching. I love family parties. Everyone looks the same, walks the same. Same mannerisms. Take you and your mum, for example. Spitting image. You and your brothers hold yourselves the same and you and Ollie have the same laugh. It's so cute."

"I think you become blind to the similarities when it's your own family, don't you?"

"It's easier to notice it in others, yeah."

"I think you've met nearly everyone."

"Not your dad. Where is he?"

"He is here. I've seen him floating around. He loves mingling at parties like this. They've known a lot of these people for decades, so I guess he chooses to focus on them more than us."

This was strange to me, but Brianna didn't seem to think it was.

"Point him out to me next time you see him?" I asked, my voice going up at the end.

"Well that's him over there." Brianna gestured in the direction. "Tweed jacket."

He was tall, perhaps in his seventies, but looked in good shape despite a slight stoop. He had the same air about him as Brianna and her brothers, but they didn't look particularly alike. Actually, Ollie and he looked quite similar. His hair was almost white. He was too far away to get a feel for his eyes though.

"Handsome," I said, and smiled.

Brianna just shrugged.

We wandered around the grand house for a bit hand in hand, which was making me even more smitten than I already was. I felt so safe and protected with her but would park that feeling for later analysis. I don't think my heart had stopped pounding since we'd briefly talked earlier.

I had a lot to process.

Brianna found an empty table.

"Want to sit for a while? Take a time out?"

"That would be lovely, thanks."

I was grateful for the breather, although it was in the main room, which was like a hall, near the band. The band had been playing non-stop.

Brianna pulled out a chair for me and I sat down. She really rocked that suit. I think it was the best I'd seen her look yet. She sat close to me and we just smiled at each other for a bit and sipped more champagne. I could look at her forever. The shape of her mouth, her warm and steady gaze, her lovely arms.

"Who are all these other people?"

Brianna subtly pointed out the various people, who was related to who, who her mum was friends with, neighbours, or colleagues. I got a real sense of the life her mum had lived and the world that Brianna had come from. She seemed to know a lot about everyone in her mum's life.

"Your mum knows a lot of people."

"She does. She's kept in touch with the people she worked with over the years too, and that's pretty good going since she works in politics."

There was a hint of something in Brianna's eyes as she said this, but I couldn't work out what it was. I followed her eyes to her mum, who was talking animatedly to a bunch of people.

"Anyway, she's having a good birthday, which is what matters."

"You and your brothers make quite the family. She must be enormously proud."

Brianna smiled thinly. There had to be more to her relationship with her mum than she was letting on. But now probably wasn't the time to probe further on that. "I meant to ask, how have you been getting on with," I air-quoted, "'being more human' with the team?"

"Not great. I'm still shit at small talk. I think that's the main problem."

"Then don't talk small. Find out what interests them. What they're passionate about."

"What they did at the weekend?"

"Okay then, try to be more vulnerable with them. Admit when you made a mistake or didn't have it all figured out. I think they might relax a little if superwoman also gets it wrong sometimes."

"So to get people to open up around me I need to show weakness?"

"Vulnerability, Brianna. It's not a weakness. It's okay to have flaws. Look, I can coach you on this. It's fixable."

She scanned the room, distracted. "If you say so." Brianna checked her watch. "Actually, the speeches are starting soon. I need to go do a few things. Are you okay to wait here for a few minutes? I'll get some drinks, too."

"Yep, I'll be fine."

She left the table, apologetically. I smiled warmly at her and then took a large sip of champagne, feeling warm and fuzzy inside. I knew I could thaw Brianna some more. Brianna had let me in, and I was seeing who she really was, and I really liked what I was seeing. She was charming, thoughtful and kind. She didn't have to pretend to be so tough all the time.

Brianna came back with fresh drinks and sat down just as her brother Ollie took the stage. We smiled at each other and she held my hand and gave it a quick squeeze.

"Can I have your attention please?" The party had descended on this main room. Someone must have herded them all in. Brianna, probably. "I would like to say a few words about my mum. First of all, thank you for coming."

Brianna's mum stood just next to Ollie, positively lapping up the attention.

Brianna's brother gave a lovely heart-warming speech about their mum, and then introduced Esther. She regaled the party with tales of their youth, and what Brianna's mum was like as a teenager. Brianna seemed slightly sad while listening, which I found odd.

A work colleague got up, a man in his late sixties, and reeled off achievement after achievement of Brianna's mum. Her chin probably couldn't get much higher as she stood beside it all, looking on. He finished his speech with a touching nod to their time working together and it being the best thing he'd ever done in his working life. It brought a tear to my eye, which Brianna saw.

"I'm sorry, these things make me emotional."

When eldest grandchild, five-year-old Isla, got up, the party took back its familiar light-hearted vibe. She read out from her bit of paper, and we all listened intently. She did well, saying how 'Granny' was the best grandmother anyone could ask for, especially when she lets her have sweeties. When she was done, she ran to her gran who picked her up and swirled her around. Brianna's mum took the stage and the microphone next. "Thank you all for those generous words, I don't deserve them. I've had the privilege of knowing you all, and that has made me the better for it. Except my husband, we all know he's definitely the better for knowing me." She laughed, but not particularly kindly. There was a slight chuckle from the audience, but not from Brianna. "Thank you to my eldest son, Ollie, and his wife, Joanna, for putting this on tonight. I will never forget it. I love you, son."

What the hell? Why didn't she acknowledge Brianna, or her other son? Hadn't Brianna done most of the work?

She made her way off the stage to a lovely clap and cheers from her family and friends, but with a hint of confusion on some of their faces. Brianna looked emotional, and embarrassed, and other things I couldn't work out.

"Are you okay?"

"No." She clenched her jaw, making her cheek muscles visible. "I'm going to talk to her. Will you come with me?"

"Of course."

The band started up again and people were back on the dance floor. Thankfully, the mood hadn't suffered from the bitter comment about the marriage and the weird lack of acknowledgement of her other two children. We found her mum talking to a bunch of women about her own age.

"Mum, can I talk to you?"

"Not now, darling, I'm a little bit busy. I'll be with you in a second."

The other women looked a bit uncomfortable that she was ignoring her daughter. Why couldn't she just fucking acknowledge her?

"Mum." Brianna clenched her jaw again. "It's important."

Her mum looked at Brianna, then glanced at me. I wanted the ground to swallow me up, but also to be there for Brianna like she'd asked.

"Just a second ladies, I'll be right back." She glided towards us, glass of wine in hand, and led Brianna off to one side like she was about to give her a telling off for disturbing her with her friends.

"What was that up there?"

"I beg your pardon?"

"You just dissed our family in front of everyone. And after everything we've done to put this on for you. What the fuck?"

Her mum looked around at her friends and smiled. She seemed highly uneasy about Brianna confronting her like this. She lowered her voice. "Your father hasn't lifted a finger and we both know it. James hasn't a clue. And you are always at work. This is a family affair and Ollie and Joanna have clearly stepped up."

"Mum, we all met up to put this on for you. We worked on it together. But it was me who did most of the organising. Not Ollie and Joanna. Joanna has no time to put on your fucking sixtieth. You would be in a hall above a pub if it weren't for me. You shouldn't have assumed it was them. And you shouldn't have only thanked him in front of everyone and not the rest of us. It was completely thoughtless."

Her mum looked at me. "Please excuse Brianna, she can get a little hot headed like this."

"Mum, what the fuck are you doing?"

Brianna swearing at her mum shocked me a little. I had not expected that.

Her mum deflected the comment just with her energy alone. She wasn't taking it on. You could see it. Her voice turned even colder. Harsh. "Stop making a scene because you didn't get a thank-you. Thank you. There, I've said it now."

They shared a look, but I couldn't work out everything that was going on between them. I didn't really know much about her family dynamics.

Brianna's mum seemed satisfied she'd dealt with this. Brianna's shoulders had slumped forward, and her eyes took on that distant look they sometimes got.

"Nice to meet you, Skye."

At that, Brianna's mum re-joined her friends. Brianna looked dejected.

I wanted to hug her but also not to draw any more attention to this either. I held her hand instead.

"I don't want to be here any more. Do you mind if we leave?" she said.

"Of course not." I squeezed her hand. "Let's go."

***

The Uber home was subdued. We got back to Brianna's flat in less than half an hour. She gave me a muted smile once the door was closed.

"Would you like some pyjamas or something?"

"Sure. Thanks."

We went into her bedroom and got changed mostly in silence. Was it bad that I still found her hot even in this situation?

We sat together on the couch, Brianna leaning slightly away from me. She'd given me a long-sleeved top and bottoms covered in superhero figures. It was a far cry from my earlier outfit but much more comfortable.

"Do you want to talk about it?"

She ran her finger along the arm of the couch as if inspecting it. She'd hardly said anything since leaving the party. "Not really."

I was very aware she didn't seem that comfortable talking about her emotions. Treading lightly seemed like the best way to support her. "No problem."

"I feel like no matter what I do, it's never enough for her. I'm never enough for her," Brianna said quickly then paused.

I didn't say anything.

"She's selfish, and so is my dad. I can't tell you how many birthdays they've forgotten. She sets high standards for everyone, but she doesn't always follow them herself. Take the drinking, for example." There was a long pause. "She's more interested in my achievements rather than me. She just uses me to look good to other people. They should never have had children given they don't give a fuck about us. My dad is distant and it's eating away at my mum. He's completely checked out." She stroked her chin. "I think my mum is an alcoholic and my parents are about to get a divorce."

I pulled her in closer. "I'm so sorry to hear that." I kissed the side of her head. "That must be so hard." I squeezed her shoulder and brushed her hair with my fingers, smoothing it down and away from her face.

Each time I stroked her, she softened, and her shell cracked open a bit further. She nuzzled into me, keeping her head tilted away and her eyes down. I put my arm around her, and just held her.

"I do get that they have their limits and that they did their best. In their own way."

"It doesn't make it any easier though. You're so strong. You're literally the most kick-ass woman I've ever met." I found her eyes. "But you don't need to be like that with me. I see you."

She held my eyes for a beat then looked away, as her chin started to quiver. Her breathing became uneven, and I could tell she was trying not to cry, then she turned towards me and buried her face in my chest. I realised she was crying when a tear seeped through my top and touched my skin. Her cry was quiet. Private. And spoke of a deep sadness. I just held her and stroked her head as her tears came, grateful she trusted me enough to open up, and sad that she carried this.

Some time passed with us just holding each other. I focused on her breathing. I let my eyes close for a few moments.

Brianna stirred and cleared her throat. "Sorry. I think I cried on you a bit." She placed a hand on my pyjama top. Her pyjama top. "You're all wet. And not in a good way." She attempted a smile but couldn't. Her face was red, blotchy, and her eyes were bloodshot.

"It's all right, I'm a superhero, aren't I?"

She looked at me, fondly. "Thanks, Skye."

I kissed her cheek. "You don't have to thank me. It's what girlfriends are for, right?"

"Yeah," Brianna said, shyly.

Her eye make-up was smudged. She seemed tired. I just wanted to wrap her up and make her feel better. "Do you want to go to bed? We could talk more in there?"

"Yeah," she smiled. "That would be good."

We decamped to her bedroom and for the first time weren't ripping each other's clothes off as we lay down. We faced each other on our sides, with our heads on our pillows. Brianna's face relaxed. Some colour had returned to her cheeks. I stroked the soft skin along her jawline.

"You said your parents were divorced?"

"Yep. They separated a few years ago. It still feels recent. I know what it's like to be in the firing line when everything's falling apart. It's important to get support through it. I did."

"It probably helps to be the sort of person who can accept support. And that ain't me." Brianna joked, half-heartedly.

"I'm here for you, Brianna. Whatever you need."

She was quiet for a while. "Tell me about your family. The whole story."

"Um, okay. It's not the happiest of stories."

"I still want to hear it if you're okay to share it."

"I don't know where to begin."

"Tell me everything. Right from the start."

~ 25 ~
Skye

I woke to see Brianna sleeping peacefully beside me. I'd slept well. I checked my phone for the time. We'd slept late.

She stirred. "Good morning. What time is it?"

"Morning." I planted a kiss on her cheek. She looked more rested. "It's nearly ten. Did you sleep well?"

She smiled, sleepily. "Yeah, really well."

"You fell asleep cuddling into me. When you were falling off to sleep you ran a bit. You nearly punched me in the face."

"Oh, sorry!"

"Don't be. It was adorable."

She pulled me in close. I relaxed into her, as she stroked my hair. We looked deeply into each other's eyes. Being in her arms like this just felt so right. We'd shared a lot last night.

"How do you feel today?" I asked.

She kissed my lips, softly. "I feel like a weight has been lifted from my shoulders. I haven't talked much about my family to anyone before."

After a short time just holding each other in bed, we got up, and Brianna made breakfast. The smell of hot croissants and pains au chocolat filled the room. We took seats at her breakfast bar with a pot of coffee in front of us. I took a bite of delicious buttery croissant. We ate in a comfortable silence for a while. Brianna's expression turned more serious as time went on, however. I could feel that something was bothering her.

"Are you okay? What are you thinking?"

Brianna looked up at me precisely as she was about to take a bite out of her croissant. She put it down and shifted in her seat. "I was thinking about the interviews on Thursday. And about what we said to each other last night, before we went into the party."

"Oh."

"Have you been thinking about any of that?"

I hadn't. I'd been living in the moment with her, loving our secret romance. I was thrilled we were seeing each other and so happy to call her my girlfriend. But what it all meant long term ... I hadn't allowed myself to go there. There was a long and heavy silence that got heavier as it went on. It felt like our Sunday morning bliss was disappearing. Perhaps I'd been burying my head in the sand. Was it so bad I wanted to enjoy our time together and not let the complication of our job get in the way? It had been this constant worry in the back of my mind. So I'd pushed it away.

"Not really, no."

Brianna turned towards me. "Can we discuss the fact that we're seeing each other and what it means for Thursday?"

I inhaled, knowing this couldn't be avoided any longer. "Yeah. We can."

"How do you feel about Thursday?"

I shifted in my seat. While I hated interviews, I was confident I'd get this job. It was my job, after all. I hoped Brianna would be okay with me being her boss, and that Helen would accept us being a couple with no adverse effects. I couldn't share this with Brianna though.

"Well. I hate interviews. I don't like having to say what I'm good at, you know. I worry I'll go blank and clam up."

"I wouldn't have guessed that about you. You're such a good talker."

"It's probably why I've stayed at Your View so long. Get promoted internally rather than having to interview with people I've never met."

"Interview skills are something you can learn. You're more than capable."

"How do you feel about interviews?"

"They're a means to an end." Brianna got up and left the room. She came back with a notebook. "Here. I took some notes of our working together. I was using it to help with interview preparation. If you need help preparing and you want my take on your strengths and weaknesses, it's all in there. I kept going until a few weeks ago. I always think that if you're nervous you should over-prepare and let that see you through. You can also focus on your breathing and think positively. Those usually help too."

Brianna handed me her moleskin notebook. I opened it to see pages and pages of detailed notes about our job – and me. My eyes rested on a page with a list of things that Brianna thought I wasn't very good at. The word, 'indecisive' burned my eyes. I couldn't believe she thought that about me. I wasn't indecisive.

"Brianna, what the fuck? Why would you do this?"

She shifted her weight onto her other foot. "It wasn't anything malicious. They were just my notes on how it was going at work and my observations about you at the start. It's mostly good stuff. It sounded like you needed a reminder of how awesome you are. You've got to go into an interview feeling super pumped up about yourself."

I couldn't help but feel uneasy about this. I searched the notes. She did write some positives. However, the weaknesses were all I could focus on. 'Indecisive', 'can't say no', and 'lacks authority' simply pissed me off. Had she been collecting evidence to use against me this whole time? I pushed that thought aside, knowing it not to be true. But something nagged at me.

"Yes, but why did you write that stuff about me?"

"I was just sniffing out the competition. You know how it is."

I shifted in my seat. "The competition?"

"Well, we are, of sorts, for this job. It's not personal."

"It's not personal?"

"It's just a job."

"It's not just a job for me. It's everything I have ever wanted in my career."

"It's my career too."

"I don't particularly like that you think of me as a rival."

"I don't. Well, not any more."

"But you did."

"Yes. I didn't know you like I do now. I was just doing what anyone would do."

I frowned, despite trying not to.

Brianna grimaced. "I'm sorry. I've offended you."

Something had got under my skin. Was she trying to put me off my game? To distract me? Take me down? I knew that was just paranoia and didn't want to communicate from this wounded place. Our connection was too important to me.

"You haven't offended me."

"You do seem quite offended. I feel like we've both been avoiding the conversation about the job. And now it's getting blown way out of proportion. We should have talked about this before."

I looked away, knowing that she meant before things started getting serious. This was too much. "You kept notes about me."

"Not about *you*. About the job." Brianna paused, looking more worried by the second. "I want to clear this up. We've obviously got a very different way of looking at the situation. Look at the good bits," she pleaded. "See the bit where I sing your praises about how well you dealt with those tough questions at the pitch? And how you won us that contract? There's more, too, if you just look."

"I will." I spent a few minutes reading. She was right, there were a lot more positive things she'd noticed about me. It was kind of sweet, in a way. But every now and then when I came across something that wasn't flattering about me, it angered me. I felt raw and exposed, my faults on full display in her neat and carefully structured handwriting. Plus, she was way ahead of me in terms of preparation by the looks of it. I'd completely lost my focus. Thursday was just a few days away and I hadn't prepared at all. I'd hardly even thought about it, I'd been so obsessed with Brianna. Also, more worryingly, I'd assumed the job was mine. What if the things she'd noticed about me were visible to others as well? What if the job wasn't as guaranteed to be mine as I'd thought? I got off the breakfast bar and sat on the couch, with my back to Brianna. How would I feel if she got my job? Could I handle her being my boss? I needed some time to unpack this and most importantly, to prepare for my interview. Brianna looked distraught. I exhaled, feeling awful.

"I meant it as a confidence boost. I'm so sorry it's upset you. It wasn't my intention."

"I know it wasn't." I half-smiled. Logically I knew I had no reason to be upset, but the conversation had left me subdued and shit-scared I wasn't going to get the job on Thursday.

She took my hand. "It is complicated, but we'll figure it out, right?" Her eyes were hopeful, but also strained. I couldn't bear to see her in any more pain.

I squeezed her hand back. I said what she wanted to hear, not quite sure if it were true, but hoping that it was. "Yes. We'll figure it out. I'll try not to take it personally."

After breakfast, I said I'd get the train home. I'd said yesterday that I'd spend the day with her, and we were going to go to her friend's Halloween party later. I didn't want to any more. Brianna insisted on walking me to the station, after I'd turned down the offer of a lift home. It was nice of her to walk with me. On the platform, we held hands and I was sad that there was something in between us just having a lovely time together. Her hand was warm in mine. But she was a little quieter than usual too.

My train arrived. We faced each other as people moved past us to board. I was unsure of what to say, because I didn't quite know how I felt. Her eyes were concerned, but their warmth and goodness still shone through as they searched mine.

"Do you still want to go to Lucy's Halloween party tonight?"

"Um, if it's okay I think I just want a quiet evening at home tonight." Brianna's shoulders slumped. I hated putting a boundary up like this, but I didn't know what else to do. Reality was weighing down on me like a dark cloud I couldn't escape.

"Will you text me when you get home, at least?"

"I will." I kissed her softly on the lips. "I'll talk to you later."

We said our goodbyes and I stepped on the train and looked out the window where she was still standing. She waved as I took my seat and the train pulled away.

***

After a short stop at home, I drove to my mum's for Sunday lunch. It'd been too long, and now she was the only person I wanted to speak to. Arlo wagged his tail lots when I arrived. We sat at the kitchen table and he lay at my feet. My mum attended to her cooking. There really wasn't a much better smell than her Sunday dinners.

"I've got news, by the way." My mum said this with her back to me, facing the cooker.

"What news?"

"I've got a job."

"A job? Where?"

She turned around. "At the garden centre."

"That's wonderful, how many hours?"

"It's only part-time, but it will be a big help, financially."

"I don't mind helping you out, you know that."

"Yes, but I'll be able to cover all my expenses now. I don't want my daughter having to support me."

"I can afford it."

"No, you can't. And you have your life to lead. It's not right."

"Okay, Mum." We talked about her new job some more and she was so excited telling me about it. I was happy for her but struggled to be my usual enthusiastic self. Arlo wandered over to her looking for food. She gave him something from the counter and then he lay back down at my feet. I patted his side, then rested my face on my palm, my elbow on the table.

My mum joined me at the table and regarded me closely. "You've got something on your mind. Do you want to talk about it?"

I nodded, reluctantly.

"You know the woman at work who I had to merge departments with?"

"The one you didn't get on with before but now you do. Your rival for the top job."

"Yes, Brianna. Well, we kind of started seeing each other. Romantically. In the past few weeks."

My mum kept a straight face and just listened. I'd come to her with so many problems in the past, so I knew she could handle this one.

"And now things have got strained because of the job and the interviews coming up. She wrote down all this stuff about me when we first started working together. And I'm starting to get seriously concerned I might not get the job on Thursday."

"Oh dear, Skye. I didn't see this coming."

"I don't think it was *that* unlikely. I talked about her constantly, didn't I?"

"Unlikely? Skye you sat there and went through all the things *you* didn't like about her. In minute detail. I felt sorry for the poor girl. And now you're annoyed she did the same thing about you?"

"Well ..." I scratched my ear. "I just can't believe she wrote down all those things about me. My flaws. My weaknesses. It feels so—"

"Close to the bone?"

"And your point is?"

"What she said has obviously rung true for you on some level. She's challenging you. I think that's a good sign, in a way."

"She said she used to think of me as her rival. Can you believe that?"

"You were her rival. Still are, to my mind."

"She should know how much this job means to me."

My mum frowned. "Should she? Isn't this her career too? No one else is responsible for how you feel. That's on you, not her. And she doesn't owe you anything."

"It'd be so much easier if we weren't up against each other for the same job."

"If it's true love, it won't matter who gets the job. Whatever happens, it'll all work out for the best either way."

"I just hate that we're in this position. I hate that anything is coming between us. It'd be perfect if it weren't for this."

I felt terrible for distancing myself from Brianna today, especially after how hard a night she'd had yesterday and how much we'd shared while talking in bed. She'd really opened up to me. I hoped she was okay. I'd texted her briefly when I got home to say that I was home safe. That was all I'd wrote. I still hadn't heard back from her.

"But you met at work. And you are going for the same job. Perhaps you and Brianna need to address this in order to move forward?"

Normally, I wished the best for the people I cared about. But this was my career on the line here.

"It's just suddenly become quite overwhelming."

"Aren't they advertising this externally as well though? Couldn't someone with more experience than you both easily get the job?"

"Helen wants to give the job to one of us. She's as much as promised us that. The external ads are just for show."

"Hmm. But it's still a possibility."

"Yes, technically."

"So, what is it, really, your issue?"

"I feel the job is mine. It should be mine. It would be a step back in the career I've worked so hard for if I didn't get it. I want the next level, the salary, paying off my debt, and … to continue to help you out."

"Honey, I understand all that. And you really don't need to do this for financial reasons, I'm working now." She squeezed my hand. "There's something else to this that I don't think you've quite said. Perhaps even to yourself."

I was quiet for a while. My mum left the table for a few minutes to check on the food. When she came back, I'd realised it.

"I don't know how I'd feel if she were my boss. And, so, I think that means that we're not meant to be together." I felt a dull ache in my heart as I said this.

"Ah."

"It's all just so hard."

My mum's eyes softened. "That's understandable."

I sat back, mired in guilt. Brianna had been nothing but supportive of me in our time together heading up the team.

"Talk to her. Get this out in the open. Tell her how you feel. It sounds like she wants to work this out too. I'm sure a little space from each other today will help you gain some perspective. Then you can broach the topic tomorrow with a fresh head. I don't think you've got anything to worry about."

But I was worried. Our dynamic would change after Thursday. The job had to take priority. It was everything I'd ever worked for over the past ten years. I couldn't have her as my boss. I just couldn't. She might not like it if I were her boss either and in time, our connection would change. Maybe it was for the best to put an end to things now before they went any further.

"I might wait until after the interviews before I address anything. It's all a bit much right now."

"Be sure to let her know that you just need some time to figure this out."

A knot gripped my stomach. I wasn't sure that even time was able to fix this, but I didn't share that with my mum.

"I will."

~ 26 ~
Brianna

I pumped my legs and pedalled harder through the singletrack, jumping over roots and weaving in and out of trees. My tyres spun furiously over the soft mud. The bike moved at pace and I easily manoeuvred it side to side and handled the drops as they came my way. By the time I made it to the clearing I was a little out of breath. Or maybe I'd been holding it. I was first to appear out of the woods. I took my helmet off for a second and waited for the next riders to arrive. I wiped some flecks of mud off my face. The sun was starting to set yet it was only late afternoon. Lucy appeared out of the woods, quickly followed by Nicola. They skidded to a stop beside me, huffing and puffing.

"You made it down quick today," Lucy said. "You got a death wish or something?"

"Yeah, that was fast. Even for you," Nicola said.

"Was it? I dunno."

Lucy regarded me suspiciously. "Are you okay?"

"I'm fine."

"From the look on your face you don't seem fine." Nicola stepped off her bike, rested it on the floor, and started stretching.

"You do seem like there's something on your mind," said Lucy. "If you want to talk about it, we've got about half a minute until everyone else gets here."

We all laughed.

The rest of the crew came out of the woods – a multi-coloured bunch with all the mountain bike gear and enthusiasm of weekend warriors.

"No seriously, let's have a chat when we get to base. We've not caught up in ages."

Sometimes there was a benefit in being this close with your ex. She knew when something was bothering you.

"Yeah, let's do that. It'd be good to catch up. But last one down has to go first."

Nicola picked up her bike, and Lucy looked at me. "You're on." She sped off and I spun my wheels after her.

After an intense descent it was over. Lucy won. I got us some chocolate from the shop, and we sat on the benches next to the car park while our group dismantled their bikes and loaded their cars. I needed my fleece as it had turned a little cold in the fading light.

"So what's up?" Lucy asked me.

I told her about Skye. About everything that had happened over the past couple of months. Lucy listened quietly the whole time.

"And you really want this job?"

"Yeah, of course. I mean, I guess."

"How do you feel about her? If you had to choose between Skye and your career, which one would you choose?"

That was a pointed question. Lucy looked off towards Nicola, her current girlfriend, removing her back wheel from the frame. Me choosing my career and working a lot had been one of the many things that'd eventually ended our relationship a few years ago. It wasn't the only reason, but Lucy had cited it as a factor, and I know that I'd hurt her with it.

I thought about Skye. These past few weeks had been life-changing for me. I'd never felt as alive. Our connection was real and true. Did the job even matter to me as much any more? As much as it mattered to Skye? It wasn't like my parents actually cared. And did they even deserve it? They hadn't checked in with me in ages. They were too busy with their own lives. I finished the last bite of my chocolate bar.

"Honestly. I think I'd choose Skye."

***

Later that night at Lucy and Nicola's Halloween party, I sat in the corner by myself drinking whisky. Music blared from Lucy's new speakers, and people in well put together costumes stood in front of me. Lucy had bought a ninja-turtle costume online, and Nicola was dressed as a giant pizza. I'd come as a ghost, opting for the easiest of costumes and one that fitted my current mood. I'd cut out holes for my arms, mouth and eyes, drawing dark circles around the two eye holes.

It was nearing the end of the night as some people had started to leave. I sighed, feeling heavy. I wished Skye was here. But she wasn't. I replayed our conversation this morning over in my head. I hadn't been able to stop replaying it. Was there something I could have said to make her stay? Had I not seen this coming? Skye was very committed to Your View. I'd only known her a short time whereas her history there went way back. Did I really think she was going to be all chill if I won the promotion? I hadn't been at Your View for very long, how would that make Skye feel if she lost to me? Sadly, I realised, taking a sip, the closer the interviews got, the more the reality of how messy the situation was had kicked in. It was like we'd both been denying the impending change. It was sweet, in a way, but it had certainly blown up in our faces the second we'd tried to talk about it.

"How's misery corner getting on?"

I looked up. Lucy and Nicola stood over me. It was as if I was staring into a life-size cartoon.

"Sorry. I'm bringing the vibe down."

"You're fine. Don't be silly," said Nicola.

"If anything you're adding to the spooky atmosphere taking sips through that mouth hole like that."

I laughed, despite myself. "That bad?"

"Yep. You also look as white as a sheet," said Lucy.

Nicola slapped her upper arm, which was twice the size in her green muscly uniform. "Not as bad as that pun."

"What pun? That was a humble joke." Lucy pleaded. "I thought it was fitting. Like a fitted sheet, you might say."

"Stating the obvious, more like," Nicola said.

I sighed. Seeing them together was both reassuring and making me feel slightly worse. They'd got together not long after Lucy and I had split up, which I'd been fine with, and was probably a reason why we weren't meant to be together. They'd been friends for a while and I think I always knew there was something between them. They worked together in a way that Lucy and I never had. I wanted that with Skye. I thought I had that with Skye. Maybe I didn't know Skye well enough yet? We'd only been in each other's lives since August, and that wasn't long at all.

"Bri, seriously, are you okay?" Lucy said. "You don't seem yourself."

I looked up at them again. Was the floor moving? My head was spinning from all the whisky. I'd been here since seven. I'd been drinking since five, and it was now after twelve.

"You know what. I'd better go. I'm so drunk, and I've got work tomorrow." I got up, but was unsteady on my feet.

"You can stay here," Nicola said, putting her arm out to steady me. "It's late and you're in no state to travel." She spoke to Lucy. "Shall we put her in the guest bedroom?"

"Yeah. I'll go move the jackets," Lucy replied.

"Thank you," I murmured, letting her guide me out of the room and away from the party.

***

The cycle into work the next morning was wet, grey and miserable. I'd had to travel home from Lucy and Nicola's first, get ready and then get to work. My head was pounding, too. I thought some fresh air might wake me up a little, but the cycling wasn't helping. I was soaked by the time I got into work and in no mood to talk to anyone. Not even Lynn. I trudged up to my office. When the door was safely shut behind me, I closed the blinds and took my work clothes out of my pannier bag. I got changed quickly. The last time I'd been half-naked at work was with Skye. That felt like an eternity ago now. Knowing my make-up would be smudged, I headed to the toilets to sort it out, emergency facewipe in hand. As

I pushed open the door someone was coming out. I bashed into Skye and startled myself.

"Hi."

"Sorry," said Skye, at the same time.

We just looked at each other for a moment. I felt emotionally naked. Could she tell that I'd just been thinking of her? That she was always on my mind?

"Good morning. How are you?" I stumbled over my words.

"I'm good, thank you." She scratched her head. "How are you? You look a bit, matted."

She stepped back and we stood inside the bathroom. My instinct was to reach out and hold her, but I hesitated. Suddenly it felt like all we were was work colleagues who'd got involved for a short time, possibly by mistake. The latter part being the energy I was getting from Skye.

"I got soaked on my cycle in. Is my mascara running?"

"A little. Not much."

We looked at each other awkwardly for a beat. Her text yesterday afternoon had been brief, and decidedly cooler. I'd given her space but I thought surely she would have sent a goodnight text or something. I was trying not to freak out about it, but I was.

"Hey, would you like to grab some lunch today? I'd really like to see you. To talk." My heart slammed in my chest. I already felt the no that was coming.

"I can't. I have meetings through lunch. I won't have time," said Skye.

"What about after work. Are you free?"

"Um, tonight I really need to do some more preparation for Thursday."

"Oh sure. Of course." I'd practically forgotten about Thursday.

She held my eye and stepped into my space. She cupped my face and slowly planted one kiss on my lips. The intensity of her kiss made my knees wobbly, but something still felt off.

She stepped back. "I was thinking it might be best if we cool things down for a few days until after the interviews. It's just this week is really busy, and we'll be losing Thursday to the interviews. Could we see each other on Friday and talk then?"

This hit me right in the stomach.

I lowered my voice. "Skye, I can't wait until Friday. I need to talk to you. Like, right now. Can we please go through to my office?"

Her eyes were hesitant, but still kind. "Sure." She spoke quietly. "I'll meet you there in a few minutes, so it doesn't look suspicious."

The door swung closed behind her. Her comment unsettled me. She clearly didn't want to be open about our relationship at work. I quickly cleaned myself up in front of the mirror, observing how unhinged I'd become. I had gone crazy over Skye. She had completely unravelled me, and I could do nothing to stop it.

I stood in the middle of my office, waiting for her. When she finally knocked and came in, I relaxed a little.

"What did you want to talk about?"

"Skye, I just feel like something isn't right between us any more. If it's about the notes I took—"

"It's not that."

It wasn't easy for me to ask her any of this, but I had to. "What is it then? Yesterday we were really happy and now you don't want to see or talk to me until Friday. I'm kind of freaking out over here."

She held both of my hands in hers. "Please don't freak out. We just need to focus on Thursday. I need to focus."

"If that's all it is then why doesn't it feel like it?"

She looked lost for words.

I continued. "Don't you think we should talk about what happens if one of us gets the job? What that might mean? How it might change things?"

"Maybe we should just wait and see what happens, and then talk? All I know is that I've been really distracted lately, and I need to get my head in the game. I have to prepare for Thursday, and I have a shit ton of work on. I'm sorry."

She let go of my hands and looked away. I knew there was more to it than what she was saying. She left me with no indication of what she was really thinking and feeling. I sat at my desk cradling my aching head in my hands. Skye was going to focus on Thursday, which was fair enough. But it felt like she had chosen the job. She wanted the job more than anything.

More than me.

As the day wore on, I sank deeper and deeper. I attended to things, but it was like I was outside of myself, watching myself go about my day. I'd assumed we'd figure this out together, but now I wasn't so sure. When she had kissed me earlier, it had felt slightly different. She was different. Had her feelings towards me changed?

I cancelled my three o'clock meeting, and then my four, hoping no one would notice I'd locked myself in my office. I wrote in my work notebook but this time about personal things. I dumped the contents of my brain onto the paper. It all came spilling out, unfiltered, and messy onto the page. All that was there was Skye and how worried I was about losing her to this work situation. Our coupledom was new and fragile. I knew that the outcome of Thursday had the potential to taint whatever we had. Whichever one of us got the job, it would change the dynamic between us. One of us would become the boss.

Lucy's question had stayed with me. Did I really want this job? Did I want it more than my relationship with Skye? I lay down on my floor with my knees bent and the door locked. Sometimes I thought better when I was horizontal. She mattered to me now. I wanted her to be happy. I knew how much this job meant to her. She was more than capable of doing it and doing it well. She'd worked so hard for it. And if I was being super honest with myself, I knew that she was the best person to lead this company. She inspired people, and over the past two months had got better at keeping the team in line. She was brilliant and a better leader than me. She cared about her staff. She cared about this company. Could I really take that away from her?

And then it came to me.

I could just not do the interview. Not go. Not compete. Turn it down. Stay at this level and accept Skye as my boss. I breathed more fully at the prospect of just dropping it all. Of no longer playing in this stressful rivalry. I sat up and sat cross-legged. Yes. This was the solution. I would take myself out of the running. What did I have to lose? I'd already got a temporary promotion out of the situation, which I hadn't been expecting. I didn't have to force my career up to the next level just yet. I knew I would get there. I was happy where I was, wasn't I? I'd learned a lot and worked with new people.

I'd got to know Skye.

I got to my feet, as clarity about the situation solidified in me. If my mother asked, I'd tell it to her straight. I didn't have to be the best any more. I was done trying to get her attention by achieving things. It was never enough, and I was too old to play that game any more. I checked my watch. Helen might still be in the office if I went now.

I threw open my door and raced upstairs. Helen had her coat on.

"Helen."

She looked up, aghast. "Whatever is the matter?"

"Can we have a quick chat? I can see you were about to leave but this is important."

She studied me for a few seconds. "All right, I have five minutes."

We moved back inside Helen's office and stood by the door. She kept her hand on the handle.

"I wanted to inform you in person that I no longer wish to be considered for the director role. I hope that I've helped see through phase one of the merger in my role as Interim Co-Director. But that's as far as I want to take it right now. I would be more than happy to stay on at my current level, under the new director, when they are appointed. Thanks again for the opportunity.

Helen let go of the handle. "I must say I wasn't expecting that. Can I ask why?"

"It's just not the right step for me at this time."

Helen eyeballed me. I stood my ground. She wasn't getting the real answer.

"Okay then. A word of caution though. Be careful about how many opportunities to break through the glass ceiling you throw away in this life. It didn't come easily to me. I had to fight for everything." She paused. "That being said, I can see you going far in this industry. When you're ready."

"Thanks, Helen. I'm glad you understand."

"I'll let the board know tomorrow." She opened the door and we stepped out into the corridor together. She made to go then turned around, briefcase in hand. "I hope that one day you'll tell me the real reason. Have a good evening, Brianna."

She got on the lift, and it took her away within seconds. I took the stairs back to my office, waiting to see if I felt any regret about my decision. None came.

***

I didn't hear from Skye on Monday night. I kept checking my phone to see if she'd contacted me but she hadn't. I went to sleep feeling like everything that had happened between us was for nothing. While I understood that she needed to focus on Thursday, I couldn't help but feel that she was putting the job first, and that I'd always come second. At least I knew that I was no longer in the running, and she didn't have to behave like this.

But she was.

On Tuesday, we kept our distance. I had lunch alone in my office, trying not to think about how close she was all day. We only saw each other once in a meeting. It was painful. I couldn't believe it had only been Saturday that she said she was my girlfriend.

If she got the job and then tried to start things up again, I didn't know how I would feel. I got that she was just doing what was right for her career, but this hurt. My parents always made me feel like I wasn't a priority, and now Skye was doing it too. What made it worse was that she knew how much pain this had caused me, and yet she was doing the exact same thing.

I buried myself in work. I'd stopped signing off my emails to Skye with my name, choosing to leave only my standard signature. Petty, but I was growing resentful at having to wait like this.

She texted me on Tuesday night around ten thirty. I was already in bed.

I'm sorry, was all it said.

I didn't text back.

I worked from home on Wednesday because I couldn't face seeing her again on these terms. I missed her. Clearly, she didn't feel the same way about me, or she wouldn't be doing this. A slow realisation settled in me that the chances of Skye and me getting together properly were slim. We'd only barely acknowledged to each other that we were dating. If I hadn't invited her to the party, would she have brought it up? I didn't think so. And now she was treating me like I was nothing. I didn't know if I could ever forgive her for this.

It was just a job!

What else would she put before me?

By late on Wednesday afternoon I was flagging. I hadn't eaten lunch because I wasn't hungry then. I had some chocolate, probably too much, and felt a bit sickly afterwards. I yawned, staring at my laptop but not getting any work done. I hadn't slept well last night either. I looked around my living room, suddenly feeling very lonely. As soon as it turned five, I shut down my laptop and went for a lie down. It was all I had the energy for.

~ 27 ~
Skye

The past couple of days had been horrible. I hated what I was doing to Brianna, yet I couldn't see any other way. Her eyes had been so sad yesterday. This was breaking my heart. She hadn't texted me back last night.

Why had it taken me so long to face reality? If it hadn't been for Brianna inviting me to her mother's party, I think I would have stayed in a sexed-up bliss with her, no thought to the future or where this was heading. And no thought about the impending interview situation.

That was so unlike me.

I'd spent every available second of Monday and Tuesday preparing for my interview. I had practised example questions, and I'd thought about my strengths. I'd focused on the things Brianna had highlighted and found ways to put a more positive light on them. Brianna's feedback, while triggering, had been exactly what I'd needed to hear. If they came at me, I'd be ready for them. I mainly worked with positive affirmations, and repeated them to myself constantly.

I laid my outfit out on my bed.

Later, at work, I'd heard in the kitchen that Brianna was working from home today. Even though we weren't speaking, I was sad I wasn't going to get to see her today, even from a distance. I stayed in my office as much as I was able to. I got an email from Brianna and she hadn't signed it off again. Just the basic signature. It was cold. But what did I expect?

When I got home that night, I was grateful for the streetlights in my quiet country neighbourhood. You could see the rain falling sideways if you looked right at them. I'd had to stay longer in the office and sort out a mistake made with focus group recruitment. Double the amount of people had been asked to attend, and the kitten, no, junior researcher, didn't know who to turn away.

Thank God I'd prepared for tomorrow already.

I still felt stressed about the interview, though, which I was annoyed at myself for. It was probably to do with the way I was treating Brianna. I sighed, feeling close to tears. Today had been a hard day. I had nothing left.

I had been in the door less than a minute when I noticed something wasn't right. There was a loud dripping sound echoing down the stairs. I rushed upstairs to find the bathroom ceiling swollen and thick droplets of water streaming down into the centre of the bathtub.

I gasped. I thought the repairs could wait a little longer. The guy I'd had in for a quote gave me six months. I guessed we had had a lot of rain recently. I went out into the back garden. A few tiles were missing. It had been windy. I went back inside. Thank fuck the leak was over the bath at least. The ceiling was holding, but it didn't look like it would hold for much longer.

A panicky feeling rose up as I tried to think about what to do. My first thought was Brianna. She would be calm in a situation like this. A crisis. She'd know what to do. I wanted to call her but realised I couldn't, and that it was all my own fault. That thought alone was like a kick in the stomach. I shook my head. I had to deal with this. Taking a deep breath, I found my phone and searched for emergency roof repairs in my area. It would have to be contained this evening although I expected the job itself would take longer. I was very aware it threatened the entire roof, and this could cost more than the house itself was worth.

I sat down and focused on my breathing.

It wasn't long until a company came out. They pulled up outside my gate quite leisurely. I'd been fretting over the situation for the past half-hour.

I let him in and he surveyed the ceiling. He looked completely unfazed by it. "I can fix this temporarily but you are going to need to get the roof looked at first thing in the morning."

I stared at him. He was a round man with a bald head and a sincerity that I appreciated. I agreed and he squeezed himself and his tools up into the loft, above the leak. I don't know what he did but he managed to stop the dripping.

After he'd gone, I was still quite shaken. I called my mum and she wanted to come straight over but I put a quick stop to that. She reacted too similarly to me in situations like this. I didn't have the strength or patience to manage her right now.

The one person I wanted to talk to about this was Brianna. What on earth was I doing pushing her away? This was real life. Why was I risking our relationship over a job? Would I miss this job if I didn't get it? Would I miss it more than I missed Brianna right now? Was I really going to choose this job over the connection we had and the possible future we could have?

I realised that she meant more to me than any job ever could. The moments we'd shared had been so sweet. Romantic. Tender. We'd been so passionate together, and our sexual connection was off the charts. She was excellent at her job. She was the best person I'd ever met. When she'd been upset at the weekend, it broke my heart. When my house was literally falling down, she was the one I wanted to go to.

I loved her.

I let that sink in.

So what if she were to become my boss? I'd get over it. I did want her to be happy and successful, so I'd get used to it.

I'd be a fucking grown up about it.

My finger hovered over her number. I couldn't call her. Not after what I'd done to her.

I had to see her.

I wanted my girlfriend.

Before I knew it, I was on a train, heading back towards the city. She probably didn't want to speak to me tonight. But I knew how I felt now, and I knew that clearing the air between us before the interviews tomorrow was critical if we were to have a chance.

She buzzed me up straight away. When she opened her door she seemed concerned. "Are you okay?"

"Hey, yes, I'm fine. I needed to see you about something. It's important. Also, my house is falling down but that's not why I'm here."

Her eyes were even more alarmed now. "Sure. Come in. What's wrong with your house?"

"Oh the roof is leaking. I've had it fixed temporarily. It almost certainly won't last another day."

"Skye, that's awful!"

"I'm sorry to turn up here like this, unannounced. I had to see you." I held my breath, not knowing how she was going to respond.

Brianna held my eye for a beat. Her eyes were soft. "Skye, you're my girlfriend, it's okay to show up at my home. A little warning would be good, but it's still okay." She smiled, sadly.

I hated myself for acting like I had over the past few days. Brianna deserved better. I perched on the edge of Brianna's couch. Brianna sat down at the other end. Her place was less tidy than I'd seen it. She also looked like she'd been sleeping. She crossed her arms and waited for me to begin.

"Brianna. I'm so sorry about the way I've been acting recently. You were right, we should have talked about how we want to manage things at work and our relationship, especially if one of us should get the job on Thursday."

She shrugged.

That wasn't a good sign, but I didn't blame her. I was the one who'd caused this.

"Before tomorrow, I want you to know that I don't care what happens about the job any more. I want to be with you, Brianna. The job's not important. The whole thing has been a fucking nightmare. I choose you."

"I thought this job was important to you. Why the sudden change?"

"That's why I'm here. Tonight, when I was stressed out and freaking out, you were the first person I wanted to call. I realised that what we have is very special and I was stupid to risk that. The past few days have been horrible. I put the job first when the only thing that matters is you." I wanted to reach out and hold her close, but I didn't deserve that.

She nodded.

"You deserve this job as much as I do. If you get it and you become my boss, I'll accept it and give you my full support. I'll get on board. I respect you and I want you to be happy too."

She reached over and squeezed my hand. The warmth in her eyes had returned. "You don't care who wins?"

"Well, I am still going for it, and I would like it to be me but no, I'll be okay if it's you. I'll be your underling."

"I'm not going for the job any more."

I shook my head a few times. "You're not going for it?"

"I told Helen on Monday. I'm out."

I closed my eyes for a few seconds as I tried to absorb what Brianna had said. "Why would you do that? And why didn't you say anything?"

"I don't want it as much as you do."

"I can't believe you did that."

"I'm sick of constantly pushing for higher and higher. I've been striving to achieve things my whole life to get my mum and dad to notice me. They don't even care. I realised that I'm happy where I am. I've even been daydreaming about opening up my very own bike repair shop. Leading the team and dealing with everyone is your thing. You're brilliant at it. A natural. People love you. You've worked so hard for this, and I didn't want to potentially get in the way."

"But you have a great chance at making director. Wouldn't that make you happy?"

"I'm happy where I am. I still like the numbers and statistics. That's where I can help the most. I'm still a data scientist at heart."

"I thought you were super committed to getting the top job, advancing your career. Being the best."

"Yeah well, not any more. Things have changed. I've changed. I've pushed myself enough already."

My heart slammed in my chest. "Brianna, I can't let you do this. I want you to call Helen back right now and tell her you've changed your mind."

"I'm not going to do that."

Without thinking, I straddled her on the couch, pinning her down. She seemed shocked. My hair brushed against her face and I tucked it behind my ears. "Brianna, for fuck's sake. You are being crazy. You deserve this opportunity as much as I do. Whatever happens, we'll work it out. We'll be happy for the other. I just needed to get my head around things and face up to it. I'm sorry that I pulled back from you and freaked you out so much you felt the need to throw away everything you've worked for."

She was quiet.

"Call her. Please."

"It's probably too late."

"Here." I got my phone out of my pocket. "I'll call her myself."

"No, don't. Skye, I thought you'd want this."

"I don't want this. I want what's best for you, dumbass. Go for the job, and go for it because you want to go for it. Not for your parents, not for me. I know that you want it. You owe this to yourself. Plus, I want to beat you fair and square."

She suppressed a smile for a bit then let it out fully. I felt that pull, that spark between us again.

"Maybe it was a little reckless," said Brianna.

"You think?" I moved off her. "Call her."

Brianna was quiet for a few moments. I could see she was re-assessing the situation. I couldn't believe she had taken herself out of the running. It dawned on me why she would have done that, and what it suggested her feelings were for me. Now wasn't the time to discuss anything like that but I wasn't going to forget it.

She shifted in her seat. "And it isn't really my style to quit. I do want a shot at this job, deep down. If we're going to be okay no matter what the outcome is, it couldn't hurt to try, right?"

"It's the right thing to do." I picked up her phone from the coffee table and thrust it towards her. "Now get yourself an interview again."

~ 28 ~
Skye

Sitting outside the glass doors to the boardroom, my mind was focused and ready to go. Brianna had me standing like a superhero this morning while looking into the mirror.

"Skye." Jacinda popped her head out of the boardroom. "The panel is ready for you now."

I shook hands with the board, all men, and Helen. Smiles were polite and brief. We all took seats and I said yes to water. Jacinda filled my glass and stepped outside. I filled my lungs and did my best to breathe out as slowly as I could.

This was on.

"Thank you for coming in today, Skye. We are really interested to know more about you and see if you are the right fit for this role. If you would like to begin with your presentation, that would be great," said Angus Robertson, the most high-profile member of the board. As far as I was aware, they knew nothing about me, apart from what Helen would have told them. This was only the second time I'd ever met the board members, despite working there all these years.

I stood up by the screen and spoke with confidence and ease. I was nailing it. The nods of approval helped me too. These people didn't show enthusiasm unless they meant it. After ten minutes, I finished. And sat down.

"Thank you for that. Very illuminating. I'll kick us off with the first question. Skye, why are you the best person for this job?"

I'd practised this answer thoroughly and aced it, making sure I mentioned how I'd increased the bottom line by fifteen percent.

Helen's eyes were full of approval. Hopefully that was a good sign.

"Now, the next question will be from Douglas."

Question after question was fired at me and I batted back with demonstration after demonstration of my experience, successes and abilities. They tumbled out of me one after the other. I was on fire, and completely calm. Interviews no longer fazed me. I crushed a question about my age, saying I'd more than proved my worth already compared to the average director, and made a mental note to complain to Helen afterwards about the question. There would be no discrimination in my company. It felt like my company. The more I talked, the more certain I was that I had a pretty good chance of getting it. The last question came from Helen.

"Skye, what's the biggest lesson you've learned since taking on the role of Interim Co-Director."

I paused, having to think about that one. Fuck. Was she trying to trip me up? I took a deep breath. "I'd say the biggest lesson I've learnt over the past two months is recognising how ready I am to become the director. When I've needed to make the tough decisions, I've made them. When I was required to follow through on a disciplinary matter, I had the guts to do it. I've learned that sometimes you have to take a risk and speak up, even when it's not easy. It hasn't been easy, but I've learned a lot from my colleagues, particularly Brianna

Phillips, who shared the job with me. I think most of all, I've realised that being able to collaborate and having an empathetic approach to leadership is vital. And I offer both of those." I paused and took a deep breath. "In prepping for this interview, I did a lot of self-reflection. Am I the right person? Am I good enough for this role? Well, I believe I am. If I'm fortunate enough to be given the opportunity, I'll do my very best to make this company the success we all want to see."

Helen nodded once. "Thank you for that Skye. That gives us a lot to think about."

I left the room on a high trying hard not to break into a skip. Outside, Brianna sat on a chair waiting to go in. She was the last person to be interviewed. Brianna had left a voicemail with Helen last night and called her first thing this morning. Helen agreed to offer her a slot at the end of the interviewing schedule. Hayley told me the board had already interviewed the three external candidates yesterday and had another two besides Brianna and me earlier today. I was grateful to hear that Peter hadn't been given an interview.

We discreetly gave each other the thumbs up. I mouthed 'good luck'. She had her game face on as she sat there with her legs crossed and hands clasped on her lap. She looked so smart in her fitted black suit.

When I'd seen her across the office earlier, I couldn't take my eyes away. I was perhaps a little too obvious but in the moment I hadn't cared. She was talking to the team, spending time with them, laughing and finally opening up. It was a joy to see and I was proud of her.

Back in my office I finally let myself relax. Or tried to. My pulse still felt high, and I was a bit jittery. Eyes had followed me all the way through the floor to my room, as everyone knew the interviews were today. I sat behind my computer and scribbled down some of the questions I'd been asked before I forgot. I wanted to remember my performance and go over it again and again in my head. I felt I'd done well, and I hoped it would be enough.

How I felt when I saw Brianna waiting to go in was so different to what I thought it would be when Helen had first told us about everything. I no longer saw her as a rival. I wanted her to be happy and if that meant she was deemed the better person for the job, then I would accept it. I had been in awe of how her mind worked once I understood her. Whilst totally different to me, we shared the same commitment to Your View, and the same commitment to being excellent at what we did. I trusted that she would do right by Your View, despite the wobble this week where she had been about to chuck it all in.

She'd been *emotional* in the way she'd acted, and the gravity of that still wasn't lost on me.

Last night, Brianna insisted we drive straight back to my house to check on the leak. I watched her assess the leak for herself and check on the job the emergency contractor had done, and it felt so right. Brianna had consistently shown to me that I could trust her. I felt safe with her. Protected. I loved how taken care of she made me feel.

She'd brought her suit for the interview with her, so we could drive straight to work the next day. This morning, the company arrived at eight. Two white vans and an array of expensive looking equipment was laid out on my front lawn. I'd had no choice but to get them in, and didn't dare think about my bank account.

About an hour and a half later Brianna came into my office. Her cheeks were flushed and her eyes were laser sharp. She was buzzing.

"How did it go?"

"I smashed it." Brianna walked across the office and stood beside me.

I held her hand. "That's excellent."

"And yours?"

"I think it went well."

"Well done." She leant down and planted a soft and slow kiss on my lips. I instantly forgot about the job and just breathed her in.

Jacinda came straight into the office just as Brianna had stood back up. I don't think she would have seen anything, and she didn't give any impression that she had, but it was close. "Skye, Brianna. Would you like to follow me back upstairs? The panel would like to speak with you both."

We looked at each other, confused. Why did they want to speak to us both? Silently, we followed Jacinda back upstairs. She gave nothing away. In the boardroom, they were all still sat in the same seats, as if the interviews hadn't finished. I sat down, very aware of my every move.

Helen addressed us in her usual icy way. The panel was still straight-faced and serious. I had no idea what was going on. Brianna looked impressively composed.

"Thank you both for coming back in. We have interviewed all of the candidates now and we've made some decisions." Helen looked between us. "Based on your performances today, and over the last two months, we would like to offer you both a job as Director of Research." Helen paused. My mouth fell open. I held my breath. "I'll be upfront with you. You two have been brilliant. And brilliant together. You got over your differences and you handled the merger extremely well. You each bring something to the table, and you complement each other well. You are a team. You've shown us that. You've shown us what is possible and how it can be if you work together to integrate your different specialisms. You've won new business already and you've inspired us all. We want more of that at Your View. The offer is director level for both of you, with you continuing to jointly lead the department. You will need to recruit four new heads of department, and finalise the new structure at that grade. The money is there to get what you need. Also, you would continue to report to me, as we have been doing."

I exhaled. A quick glance at Brianna showed she was also still trying to get her head around this.

"This is a new model of leadership, and you two young women are more than capable. You have our full support and every confidence." Helen sat back having said her piece. The panel was now smiling, which in itself was an unusual sight.

I did my best to keep my reaction professional. I was stunned. I'd just got my dream job, and I was going to get to keep working with my new girlfriend, doing what we loved.

"Thank you." I smiled, not knowing what else to say.

Brianna also sounded off-kilter, but happy. "This is wonderful news. We weren't expecting this. Thank you so much."

"I'll have your contracts drawn up straight away. We think you'll be more than happy with them. Do take the night to think about it. We'll be delighted to hear from you in the morning."

Brianna and I mumbled our agreement to this. I was half-worried Helen was going to change her mind and take it back.

Helen stood up. We all copied her. She shook our hands firmly, giving us both a respectful nod, which I appreciated, and then the whole room shook hands again. I knew Brianna would be overjoyed at this. Only once we'd safely floated back to my office, did Brianna and I acknowledge what had just happened.

The door clicked shut and I locked it. Massive smiles broke out on both of our faces. We wrapped our arms around each other and held each other tight.

Brianna looked into my eyes. "I'm so happy for you. You deserve it. Well done."

"Thank you. So do you."

"Shut up. I nearly threw it all away. But I didn't, thanks to you."

"Why choose one when you can have both? It's going to be so great. We're going to rock this."

"Yeah. And now we don't need to worry about which one of us is going to be the boss."

I lowered my voice. "I think we already know who that is."

Brianna pulled me in closer and whispered in my ear. "I hope you mean me."

Our lips brushed and we kissed lightly for a few seconds. A hunger gripped us both and we deepened the kiss, searching each other and forgetting where we were.

I pulled back. "We're going to be the youngest directors this company's ever seen."

"Um, I think that means me. I'm two years younger than you," said Brianna, almost apologetically.

I laughed. "Oh yeah. I'll still take it as a win though."

"For all we knew we were going to get another old white guy in as the boss and both of us could have lost our jobs."

"True. But that's not happening. This company is ours now."

"Is that the power going to your head already, Skye?"

"I'm giddy with it. Hey, I'm just going to call my mum. Do you mind waiting?"

"Of course, not at all, go ahead."

I frowned, feeling sad momentarily that Brianna didn't feel she could call her mum at a time like this.

"Don't worry. This is my normal," she said as if she had read my mind.

I squeezed her hand, still unsure about it. My mum picked up right away. "Mum. I got it. And so did Brianna. They want us to keep sharing the job."

All I heard was indiscriminate cheering and screams of joy. I held the phone away from my ear for a second, which Brianna chuckled at. "I'm so proud of you, darling. So so proud. Well done. Well done to Brianna too. I can't wait to meet her."

I was smiling as I ended the call, and looked up to see Brianna still watching me, with an amused look on her face.

"What?"

"Nothing. Just that you're so cute."

I smiled at her, loving the life that was developing between us. "Let's celebrate! I want to take you out, buy you some champagne."

Brianna pulled me in close again. "I'd love that. But maybe we should go back to your house and check on the builders first?"

"Oh," my shoulders slumped. "I'd almost been able to forget about that."

She caressed my arm. "We'll celebrate once I've taken another look."

My house could be in tatters but in that moment, I didn't care.

***

By four in the afternoon the following day, everyone who was still in the office had been asked to congregate on the third floor in among the desks, as Helen had an announcement to make. It was already dark outside, so the office felt a bit more claustrophobic than normal. In the bright lights, the windows acted like mirrors at this time of day. Bottles of wine had been hauled up from the viewing room, and plastic cups laid out. Brianna had sent Siobhan out for some nice bottles of wine, and had her discreetly put these out instead of the cheap ones. She'd asked me if it was okay if she did so. I was grateful she'd thought to run it past me first, encouraged at how well we were communicating lately.

It was a badly kept secret that the drinks were about the new Director of Research. No one except Hayley knew this was about two people instead of one.

We'd each received an email this morning with our contracts. The salary was significantly higher than I was expecting, and I was still stunned by it. I'd be able to pay for the roof and take care of my mum properly now.

We'd been through the paperwork and given our final acceptances to Helen.

There was one thing still outstanding though. We hadn't disclosed our relationship yet. After the builders left my house last night, we'd shared a bottle of wine to celebrate the job and discussed what we were going to do. We decided we'd sign the contracts first, and then deal with telling Helen.

We'd signed the very un-romantic conflict of interest forms about half an hour ago, but this little drinks party didn't quite feel like the time to open up about it. Was our relationship stable enough yet to risk communicating it to our boss?

Helen picked up the microphone and asked for our attention. The microphone was a new addition. Brianna had come up with it. It looked good and sounded better too.

The office fell silent. Helen told the office about us both being the new Directors of Research, and how it was going to work. I'd wanted to hold Brianna's hand through this but that was out of the question. The office clapped at the news and gave us their congratulations. I saw relief in many people's faces, which I found heartening. Thankfully, Helen didn't invite us to do any speeches this time.

"So please join me in congratulating Skye and Brianna, and do stay on for some drinks if you can and help them celebrate."

I got the sense that the team was genuinely pleased about it. Siobhan was one of the first over, followed by Lynn and then Hayley.

We'd recently promoted Siobhan to senior researcher, and she'd already been performing admirably in her new role. I was happy for her, and certain she'd continue to excel at Your View.

Peter had disappeared, but that was no surprise. Hopefully he'd leave Your View altogether and we could be done with him once and for all.

Hayley hung around me the entire time. She seemed even more upbeat than usual. "How's everything with you?" I asked her. "You seem really good."

Hayley smiled, her eyes dancing. "I am really good, thanks. We've made a breakthrough in therapy. We both feel like we've turned a corner." Her face was all lit up and I couldn't remember a time when I'd seen her as happy as this.

"That's great news, Hayley. So great to hear."

"I think we might just be okay." We clinked glasses, nodding and smiling at each other.

"You know, I've been meaning to tell you something for ages," I said. "Our friendship means a lot to me. Thanks for having my back through all this with the merger and Brianna and me getting together. You're the best."

"Aw, it was nothing. You'd do the same for me. Also, does this mean you're my new boss now?"

I chuckled. "I guess it does."

Hayley laughed. "I'll keep your feet on the ground, don't you worry. How are things with you and Brianna? Did she really take herself out of the running for you?"

"She did. But I didn't let her ruin her career for me, and now look what's happened." I smiled.

"She's a keeper."

"I know. It's wonderful. I'm so happy right now."

"Everything worked out right. You also found your future wife."

I gave her a mock indignant look.

"Yeah, yeah. I've seen you two together. I can hear wedding bells already."

I shook my head. "Bit much, Hayley. Geez."

"Are you going to tell Helen that you and Brianna are dating?"

"Brianna wants to tell her right now at this party."

"How do you feel about that?"

"I don't know. What do you think we should do?"

"It won't be a problem but I think you should disclose it as soon as you can. Helen will want to know as soon as possible, and you'll need to reassure her that you'll keep your personal lives separate. She doesn't like drama and she doesn't like being kept in the dark."

I raised an eyebrow. "Because she lives such a drama free life?"

Hayley shrugged. "She owns the company."

Over our wine last night Brianna and I had talked about the need to have strong boundaries between our relationship and the job. We had been thrust into a new situation again that neither of us expected, and we were going to have to consciously enter into it now, or it might explode in our faces again.

And neither of us wanted that.

People stayed around for a while longer, and so did Helen. I wanted to enjoy the moment more, but the issue of us disclosing our relationship still made me uneasy. Brianna appeared by my side out of nowhere, giving my hand a gentle squeeze discreetly. "I've got the forms."

Despite Hayley's good advice I was still hesitant. "Maybe now's not the best time. Shouldn't we wait?"

Brianna frowned. "There's never going to be a good time, Skye. Do you not want to do this?"

"Of course I do."

"Then let's get it done." We held each other's gaze for a few moments. Brianna's confidence helped calm me down.

"Okay. Let's do it," I said.

We found Helen and glanced nervously at each other as we approached her.

"Helen," Brianna said. "Could we have a quick word please?"

Helen gave us one of her trademark icy looks, then followed us into Brianna's office and I shut the door behind us.

Brianna and I looked at each other. She'd gone pale. I was lost for words.

Helen put her hands on her hips and looked between us. "What did you want to discuss?"

I took a deep breath and cleared my throat.

This one was on me.

"Helen, we wanted to tell you something that you should be aware of." I paused, and forced myself to hold eye contact with her. "Brianna and I are in a relationship. A romantic relationship."

Helen was very still. I couldn't be certain what her expression was, which was unsettling. The silence was unbearable so I filled it, nervously.

"We wanted you to be aware and we wanted to be upfront and honest about it from the start, and it has only just started," my cheeks burned at my careless choice of words. "We won't let it get in the way of the job and we have our signed 'conflict of interest' forms here."

Helen scratched her head. "Right. This is quite the surprise."

Yes, but was she okay or not okay about it? My pulse raced. My palms had gone sweaty.

"Brianna. Is this why you opted out of the role on Monday?"

"It is, yes."

"You know, I had noticed you starting to get on very well."

"Does that mean you're okay with it?" I gave Helen my best negotiation face.

She held my eye. After a few seconds she spoke. "I don't see why it should be a problem."

I sighed in relief. Brianna flushed.

Brianna handed her the signed forms. This was the most awkward and embarrassing thing I'd ever been through. Helen gave them a quick scan.

"I'm glad you saw the need to be upfront about it and disclose your personal relationship. I value your honesty, ladies. I expect you will keep things professional and not let either the job or your relationship jeopardise the other. Please let me know if there's anything that begins to affect the work, and I'll see if I can help."

Wow. I could not believe how well she was taking this. How supportive she was being. I had to say something. Anything. "Helen, thank you for being so understanding."

"Yes, thank you," Brianna said.

"Don't thank me. Just show me that it'll work, and I won't mind."

"Will the board be as okay with it?" Brianna asked.

"I'll tell the board at the next meeting in a fortnight. Like me, they won't care as long as it doesn't affect anything." She looked between us, with a hint of something in her eye. "Very good then. That's settled."

Helen moved towards the door. "And ladies." She smiled. "I'm happy for you. Just don't fuck up my company if you no longer wish to fuck each other."

We were both stunned. Helen hovered, clearly enjoying having shocked us.

Brianna spoke next. "I thought you said you were wanting to take a step back?"

Thank God she changed the subject.

"Let's just say I'm excited about this company again. The two of you have inspired me. My cruises can wait."

~ 29 ~
Brianna

I found Skye clearing up empty wine bottles and collecting cups. The little drinks reception had ended. It was great people stayed on that extra bit in the office on a Friday night.

Skye looked up and smiled when I approached her.

"Come with me."

I led her up the creaky stairs to the roof, gently holding her hand. My heart slammed in my chest. I wasn't sure if I'd gone over the top.

Skye put her hands over her mouth as we stepped onto the roof. "What's all this?"

I shrugged, feeling the need to downplay the massive effort I'd gone to. "It's not too much, is it?"

"It's beautiful."

She kissed me on the cheek. I held out my hand for her to take. Our fingers entwined as I led her over to the candle-lit table and chairs in the middle of the roof and switched on the little outdoor heater. Thankfully, the air was perfectly still tonight. I had a bottle of champagne on ice next to a box of chocolates. The lengths I was going to for Skye still surprised me.

The sky was dark, except for the glow of the city below and the bursting of sporadic fireworks in the early evening sky.

Skye arched her head back to look up at a lone firework going off. "Oh yeah, Guy Fawkes night! I forgot!"

"Remember, remember, the fifth of November ..."

"The fireworks are going to be incredible from here." She lowered her head then her eyes came to a rest on me. "Unforgettable."

I gestured for her to sit down. I popped open the bottle and Skye gave a little cheer. Standing beside her, I poured us each a drink, all the while Skye kept her eyes on me.

"To us," I said, holding my glass up, and then taking a seat. "Cheers." We tapped our glasses together and sipped never taking our eyes off each other.

"It's so romantic up here," she smiled, shyly. "I'm really touched you went to all this effort. When did you get a chance to do it?"

"I nipped home to get the stuff today. Then I snuck away during the drinks reception to put it all out."

"I love it. I wish I'd thought of it."

"It's all for you, Skye. You make me want to do this sort of stuff."

She moved a candle and leant across the table. I met her halfway. We found each other's lips and kissed gently. We pulled back, as the mood between us deepened. Everything about this felt so right.

A flurry of fireworks went off, making it too loud to hear one another. It was the longest round of the evening yet. I took a deep breath. Being here with Skye was so perfect. Being with her was all I wanted now.

I stood up, somewhat out of nowhere. I held out my hand. "Dance?"

She took it and got to her feet. My heart was still pounding.

I held her close as we slow danced to inaudible music with our foreheads touching. I remembered how we'd slow danced in her living room to her old record, and smiled. There was a new future for us now, based on our mutual support of one another. Our lives had become so intertwined, and this was only the start. She was my girlfriend, but that didn't mean she knew the depth of my feelings towards her. Despite the butterflies in my stomach, I had to say something. There might not be as perfect a moment as this again.

"Skye." Our eyes met. "I love you. I'm in love with you." I held my breath.

She squeezed my waist and pulled me in close. Her chest rose and fell. She was quiet and it felt like an eternity. Was she going to say it back? My palms were now sweaty, and my heart pounded harder.

She slipped her hands under my blazer and rested them on my lower back. Her hands were warm and her eyes were bright, even in the darkness.

She spoke softly. "I've loved every second we've spent together. I think about you all the time, Brianna. I want to talk to you about everything, go on adventures with you, freewheel down mountains with you, and maybe even swim in the sea with you. There's so much I want to do with you. To feel with you." She looked down again then back up at me. "Brianna," she paused. "I love you too."

My heart swelled with uncontainable joy. A smile burst out. Skye's face lit up as she beamed back at me. It was everything.

We allowed the gravity of what we'd just said to each other to sink in. We leant into one another and kissed as another round of fireworks rocketed up and lit up the sky behind us.

***

"Right, everyone move in closer for a picture. James, that means you too," said Ollie.

We were in a restaurant for my birthday. Skye had organised a meal at a Tapas place in the middle of town. She'd arranged the whole thing without my knowledge. Her investigative skills were impressive, finding Lucy and Nicola through my Facebook friend list, and they'd in turn invited the rest of our group. Hayley and Liam were there too. James and his latest girlfriend had arrived late, and were now getting pissed on red wine together. No one seemed to be paying attention to Ollie except Joanna, and now a waiter had arrived, asking if we were ready for another course.

Skye turned to me, her eyes sparkling. "And how is the birthday girl, sorry, woman?"

I couldn't remember a time when I'd been happier. And it was all down to Skye.

Life was good.

"Very happy. Today has been wonderful, Skye. A perfect day. Thank you."

Skye tucked some hair behind my ear, gazing into my eyes. We leant towards each at the same time and brushed our lips together.

Her lips felt like home.

Ollie called over to us. "Enough PDA you two, we get it, you're in the honeymoon phase, yadayadaya."

"Okay, Ollie." I looked up at him and then back at Skye, noticing how flushed in the cheeks she'd gone. "Take the picture already."

Ollie held up his phone, angling it a few different ways for a second before resting on one. Our exchange must have alerted the rest of the group. Everyone at the long table momentarily paused. Once the picture was over everyone immediately went back to their conversations as some spoke to the waiter.

"Did you like being sung happy birthday to?" Skye rested a hand on my thigh, sending a pleasant warmth down low in my body.

"You know, it wasn't as awful as I thought it was going to be. I can't even remember the last time I'd had that, so thank you."

"You're such a sweetheart, at heart."

I laughed. "No. Badass, remember?"

She nodded. "I remember. How did it go on the phone to your mum?"

I'd snuck away half an hour ago to take a call from my mother. It was the first I'd heard from her all day. I'd been so caught up in my feelings for Skye, it didn't sting like it used to.

Skye had taken the pain away.

I shrugged. "We spoke for a few minutes. My dad texted not long after. It's fine. They've always been like this. It's okay. I'm no longer going to expect more from them. They do what they can."

"That's very mature of you."

"Also, I forgot to mention, she emailed me yesterday about the new promotion. Apparently, I just had to make it to director level to get her attention. She's very proud and has told everyone she knows, which is all that matters to her."

Skye squeezed my thigh. "You matter, Brianna. You matter to me."

I gazed into her kind blue eyes and believed her. A deep sense of peace came over me. I smiled, feeling more loved in this moment than I could ever remember having felt before.

"Here," Skye handed me a gift wrapped in shimmery gold paper. It was rectangular in shape like a book. "I got you something else."

"Another one, seriously?" I raised an eyebrow. Skye had been showering me with gifts all day. I ripped the paper off. It was a sky-blue notebook. I smiled.

"For all your ongoing thoughts about me and our job together. I trust you'll continue to keep me on my toes."

I laughed. "You can bet on that. Thank you." I kissed her quickly on the cheek.

"Which was your favourite gift?"

I raised an eyebrow. She wanted me to rank them? "Um, well," our time in bed together this afternoon popped into my mind. I bit down on my lower lip.

She playfully slapped my shoulder. "Hey. Are you thinking about earlier?"

I nodded, holding her gaze. We had planned on going to a museum, and to wander around the old part of the city. But we hadn't been able to leave the bedroom. "Spending all afternoon with you like that really was the best birthday present I could have wished for."

Skye blushed.

I looked around, but no one was listening to us. I put my hand on top of hers on my lap and gazed into her sparkling blue eyes. "I love you."

"I love you, too."

Since we'd said we loved each other last week on the roof watching the fireworks, we'd been saying it to each other all of the time. I would never tire of saying it or of hearing those words from her.

"I've been thinking," I said, putting my arm around the back of Skye's chair.

"Oh, not about the house again." Skye rolled her eyes, presumptuously. "I do love it that you're all into home improvement etcetera, and I am super grateful you're keen to help me fix my crumbling cottage, but I can only take so much talk of loft ventilation and tile materials." Skye grimaced, dramatically.

"No, silly." I chuckled. Had I been talking about it that much? "About a holiday. I think we should take a trip together, somewhere warm. I'm thinking a beach holiday. Maybe Thailand? Would you be up for that?"

Skye nodded, something clicking into place in her eyes. "I love that idea. Sun, sea, sand ... you in a bikini." She beamed. "I'm there."

"Maybe over the Christmas holidays? Between Christmas and New Year? I'm sure Helen will be fine with it; I've heard the whole office pretty much shuts down over Christmas anyway."

"That sounds perfect." She squeezed my hand. "We can swim in the sea together."

"I can protect you from sharks."

Skye tilted her head, assessing my comment, which was meant as a joke but probably came off a lot more earnest. Based on how I felt about her though, I would absolutely protect her.

From anything.

Up Against Her

She leant into me and spoke softly. "You would, wouldn't you?"

"Skye, I'd do anything for you."

"Oh, the power."

I raised an eyebrow. "Yep, *please do* be careful with my heart, now that it's in your hands."

"Ah. All this from Ms Numbers," she said, playfully. "So many feelings this past week. A tidal wave, you might say." Skye shook her head a few times. "What have I *done* to you?"

Her eyes were warm and caring, despite openly teasing me. I looked down at our hands entwined on my lap, embarrassed. I had been pouring my heart out to her, and I was still a little shy about it. Skye had cracked me open. I was no longer this closed, serious person, afraid to let anyone in. I could fall apart around her and still be loved. She had no idea how much she'd done for me, and I'd be forever grateful for that. I suddenly felt quite serious about my feelings and how strong they were. My eyes began to water, but I made sure they didn't progress to tears. I think Skye felt the change in my energy, too, as she became quite still.

When I looked back up, her kind eyes were there waiting for me. She brushed a strand of hair away from my face and squeezed my hand in hers. "I've got you, baby."

~ The End ~

Thank you for reading *Up Against Her*. It means the world to me. If you enjoyed this novel, and you have a moment, please leave a review, as it really helps connect the book with more readers.

ABOUT THE AUTHOR

Lisa Elliot is an independent author of lesbian romance novels. Apart from writing, she works as a researcher for a non-profit organisation promoting active travel. She lives in Edinburgh with her wife and their dog. *Up Against Her* is her third novel.

Find her at: www.lisaelliotauthor.com

Email: lisaelliotauthor@gmail.com

Goodreads: Lisa.Elliot

Instagram: lisa_elliot_author

Facebook: lisaelliotauthor

Twitter: lisa_elliot

Also by Lisa Elliot:

The Light in You

Yoga teacher Angela Forbes has fulfilled her dream of opening her very own studio, Heart Yoga, on the outskirts of Edinburgh, Scotland. Passionate and principled, she believes in yoga and wants to make a difference. Unfortunately, her studio is hanging by a thread after a slow start. She doesn't have time for love, and isn't attachment the root of all suffering anyway?

Life isn't going the way Emily Mackenzie had planned. She's lost her high-powered corporate job and isn't coping well. She's spent her twenties sacrificing her personal life for her career and now she has nothing to show for it. Stressed and struggling, she might just be at her rock bottom. When Emily joins Heart Yoga she finds a lot more than just a good stretch.

An unexpected kiss forces Angela to question everything she holds dear, and as Emily gets back on her feet is it wise for her to risk getting involved with someone who's not looking for love?

Dancing It Out

Kate has moved to London and is embarking on a new life. She has become an independent, high-achieving young lawyer, who still hasn't figured out who she really is yet.

But when she moves into a house-share in north London and meets Lorraine, an enigmatic filmmaker, whose room is next to hers, an intense bond quickly develops. After an epic night-out clubbing, Kate's crush on Lorraine leads Kate to question and discover her true sexuality.

A slow-burn romance about awakening desire and finding the courage to follow your heart.

Printed in Great Britain
by Amazon